PRAISE FOR K!

The Seven Day Switch

"Making a compelling case for moderation in all things, Harms (*The Bright Side of Going Dark*, 2020) paints her heroines as flawed but loving mothers, each managing in the best way she knows how. The most clever and incisive take on the Mommy Wars since Allison Pearson's *I Don't Know How She Does It*, Harms's latest captures the messy, complicated, and often all-consuming mindset of motherhood."

—*Booklist* (starred review)

"*Freaky Friday* for the mom set, this novel by Harms (*The Bright Side of Going Dark*) is full of fun, relatable, and cringe-worthy moments, as each woman experiences life on the other side of the fence."

—*Library Journal*

"*The Seven Day Switch* is a must-read for the summer."

—*Fort Hood Sentinel*

"Ranging in tone from wistful to laugh-out-loud funny, *The Seven Day Switch* is a memorable experience, thoroughly enjoyable from cover to cover."

—Midwest Book Review

"Harms delights in *The Seven Day Switch*. When polar-opposites Celeste and Wendy chug magical sangria and find themselves literally walking in the other's shoes, they'll soon discover that maybe they aren't so different after all. Heartwarming and hilarious, with an incredibly satisfying ending, we guarantee you will love this book!"

—Liz Fenton and Lisa Steinke, authors of *How to Save a Life*

"Kelly Harms has created a funny, zany story of two moms who drink some sangria with imported vodka and suddenly find themselves inhabiting each other's bodies. (Think *Freaky Friday* with two grown women who don't much like each other.) As she takes us on a ride exploring the ever-present 'mommy wars'—starring one way-too-busy productivity-expert mom and a stay-at-home mother who has become the neighborhood carpooler—Harms very quietly brings us to some profound and unexpected truths about love and parenting and what makes a satisfying life. Written with Harms's disarming humor and honesty, *The Seven Day Switch* is fun and funny—and leaves you with a powerful punch."

—Maddie Dawson, bestselling author of *Matchmaking for Beginners*

The Bright Side of Going Dark

"Refreshingly, each character is a true-to-life individual with complicated emotions and unique voices. A surprisingly easy read containing a little romance, a lot of personal growth, and an honest look at weighty topics."

—*Kirkus Reviews*

"Witty, lively, and au courant, *The Bright Side of Going Dark* will make readers think twice about refreshing Instagram for the tenth time today. Tackling thornier questions of mental health and the toll of constant comparison, this will appeal to fans of Meg Wolitzer and Elin Hilderbrand, who'll adore the intertwining lives of Mia, her followers, and those they encounter IRL."

—*Booklist* (starred review)

"*The Bright Side of Going Dark* is about so much more than the moral quandary of screen time. It's about grief and loss and anxiety. It's about mothers and daughters—more anxiety—and about second and third chances. *The Bright Side of Going Dark* is as dark as it is bright, [and] full of humanity: mobile devices, warts, and all."

—BookTrib

"Even casual users know how absurd and unrealistic social media can be—yet keep logging on day after day. Kelly Harms takes this dichotomy to new heights in a clever and unputdownable story of two women whose so-called online lives collide IRL. I laughed, I cried, I came away from the experience with a newfound appreciation for life—which is to say *The Bright Side of Going Dark* is everything I'd hope for in a Kelly Harms novel and more. I loved every page."

—Camille Pagán, bestselling author of *I'm Fine and Neither Are You*

"Kelly Harms has once again knocked it out of the park with this charming, funny, topical novel about an online influencer who undergoes an unexpected transformation. I honestly had to put my whole life on hold while I read it—laughing and sighing through the clever twists and turns of this plot. Who among us hasn't wondered what it takes to be a person who posts photographs fifty times a day? You'll fall in love with @Mia&Mike as well as the whole cast of wonderful characters. A novel that shines with surprise—and will make you want to turn off your phone and go play with your dog."

—Maddie Dawson, *Washington Post* bestselling author of
Matchmaking for Beginners

The Overdue Life of Amy Byler

"Librarians and booklovers will fall for Amy, and Harms writes a great light read full of tears, laughter, and charming, relatable characters."

—*Library Journal* (starred review)

"Amy Byler's life isn't easy—what with an absentee husband suddenly showing up and reclaiming some getting-to-know-you time with their two teenage kids. But what follows is pure wonder. Kelly Harms brings the mom-makeover story to a whole new level, with twists and turns and dialogue that is so funny you have to put down the book and simply allow yourself to laugh. It's well written, it's original, and I fell in love with Amy and all her well-meaning friends on her journey to find out who she really is. So much fun!"

—Maddie Dawson, *Washington Post* and Amazon Charts bestselling author of *Matchmaking for Beginners*

"Amy Byler's husband ditched her and their kids three years ago, so when he shows up, full of regret, we can forgive her for being less than welcoming. Still, she could use a break—and a life. What follows is so engaging I had to clear my calendar. Harms dances on the knife edge between snort-your-coffee humor and bull's-eye insights, often in the same sentence. As a card-carrying curmudgeon, I resist such tactics, but here I never felt played. Instead, I was swept up in Amy's everymom dilemma, her quest for a full life without sinking into the swamp of selfishness. Whip smart and honest to the core, *The Overdue Life of Amy Byler* is a thoughtful, nimble charmer. Did I mention the hot librarian?"

—Sonja Yoerg, #1 Amazon bestselling author of *True Places*

The Good Luck Girls of Shipwreck Lane

"A perfect recipe of clever, quirky, poignant, and fun makes this a delightful debut."

—*Kirkus Reviews*

"Set in small-town Maine, this first novel is a story of rebuilding, recovery, and renewal. Harms has created two incredibly likable heroines, allowing the strengths of one woman to bolster the weaknesses of the other. While the central conflict of the story appears to be resolved fairly early, a succession of plot twists keeps the reader intrigued and invested. In the manner of Mary Kay Andrews and Jennifer Weiner, Harms's novel is emotionally tender, touching, and witty. Great for book clubs."

—*Booklist*

"Spunky leading ladies that you can take to the beach."

—*Fitness Magazine*

"The story is funny and heartbreaking throughout."

—Melissa Amster, Chick Lit Central

"Another perfect summer diversion is *The Good Luck Girls of Shipwreck Lane*. Kelly Harms writes with love about a trio of women desperate for a change and smart enough to recognize it may not be exactly what they planned. Delicious."

—Angela Matano, *Campus Circle*

"The friction between the Janines, along with a few romantic foibles and a lot of delicious meals, results in a sweetly funny and unpredictable story that's ultimately about making a home where you find it."

—*Capital Times*

"Kelly Harms's debut is a delicious concoction of reality and fairy tale—the ideal summer book! You'll feel lucky for having read it. And after meeting her, I guarantee you will want a great-aunt Midge of your very own."

—*New York Times* bestselling author Sarah Addison Allen

"Warmhearted and funny, *The Good Luck Girls of Shipwreck Lane* pulls you in with quirky yet relatable characters, intriguing relationships, and the promise of second chances. Harms's debut is as refreshingly delightful as a bowl of her character Janey's chilled pea soup with mint on a hot summer day."

—Meg Donohue, bestselling author of
How to Eat a Cupcake: A Novel

"Funny, original, and delightfully quirky, Kelly Harms's *The Good Luck Girls of Shipwreck Lane* shows us that sometimes, all we need to make it through one of life's rough patches is a change of scenery and a home-cooked meal."

—Molly Shapiro, author of *Point, Click, Love: A Novel*

"The characters are so well drawn that they practically leap from the page, charming dysfunction and all! A poignant, hilarious debut that's filled with heart, soul, insight, and laugh-out-loud moments. It'll make you rethink the meaning of what makes a family—and if you're anything like me, it'll make you want to pick up and move to 1516 Shipwreck Lane immediately! I'm such a fan of this utterly charming novel."

—Kristin Harmel, author of *Italian for Beginners* and
The Sweetness of Forgetting

"Clever and memorable and original."

—Samantha Wilde, author of *I'll Take What She Has*

"Janey and Nean each have a common name and uncommon hard luck, and when they suddenly have in common a sweepstakes house, their lives begin to change in ways neither of them could have imagined. Their quirky wit will win you over, even as they fumble through their crazy new life. *The Good Luck Girls of Shipwreck Lane* is alive with warmth and wit; I enjoyed it right through to the satisfying end."

—Kristina Riggle, author of *Real Life & Liars*,
The Life You've Imagined, Things We Didn't Say, and *Keepsake*

"Kelly Harms's *The Good Luck Girls of Shipwreck Lane* is a delightful book bursting with good humor, fast action, and delicious food. Aunt Midge is a pure joy, and I loved Harms's surprising, spirited, and generous slant on what it takes to make a family."

—Nancy Thayer, *New York Times* bestselling author of *Summer Breeze*

The Matchmakers of Minnow Bay

"Kelly Harms writes with such tender insight about change, saying goodbye to her beloved yet troubled city life, and hurtling into the delicious unknown. Her characters sparkle; I loved Lily and wished I could have coffee with her in the enchanted town of Minnow Bay."

—Luanne Rice, *New York Times* bestselling author

"The temperature in Minnow Bay, Wisconsin, may be cold, but its people are anything but. Kelly Harms has created a world so real and so inviting that you absolutely will not want to leave. *The Matchmakers of Minnow Bay* proves that a little small-town meddling never hurt anyone and that, sometimes, it takes a village to fall in love. Kelly Harms has done it again!"

—Kristy Woodson Harvey, author of *Dear Carolina* and
Lies and Other Acts of Love

"*The Matchmakers of Minnow Bay* is a glorious read, full of heart and humor. Lily is the kind of character you'll root for to the end, and the delightful residents of Minnow Bay will keep you chuckling with each turn of the page. Kelly Harms is a talented author with a knack for writing a story you'll want to read again and again."

—Darien Gee / Mia King

"In *The Matchmakers of Minnow Bay*, Kelly Harms weaves together a small town and big dreams into a delightful and heartfelt tapestry of friendship, love, and getting what you deserve in the way you least expect. I was hooked from page one, then laughed out loud and teared up while reading—exactly what I want from romantic women's fiction. Kelly Harms is the real deal."

—Amy Nathan

"In *The Matchmakers of Minnow Bay*, Lily Stewart is Shopaholic's Becky Bloomwood meets Capote's Holly Golightly. This charming tale is filled to the brim with eccentric characters, uproarious predicaments, and a charming (if chilly!) setting. Kelly Harms has created the most lovable character in Lily, a starving artist with a penchant for disaster and a completely unbreakable spirit. One for the beach chair!"

—Kate Moretti, *New York Times* bestselling author of *The Vanishing Year*

"Filled with witty dialogue and an unforgettable cast of characters, *The Matchmakers of Minnow Bay* is a complete charmer. I rooted for Lily from the first page and didn't want to leave the magical town of Minnow Bay. Kelly Harms delivers another heartwarming novel that lifts the spirit."

—Anita Hughes

"*The Matchmakers of Minnow Bay* is the perfect feel-good read. An irresistible premise, a charming—though forgetful—heroine, an emotionally involving love story, lovely writing . . . it all adds up to cozy hours in a fictional place you'll wish you could visit. Don't miss this delightful novel!"

—Susan Wiggs

"Sometimes you read a book that hits all the right notes: funny, charismatic, romantic, and empowering. *The Matchmakers of Minnow Bay* is that book. Kelly Harms's enchanting writing lured me into the quiet yet complicated world of Minnow Bay, and I never wanted to leave. I loved it in every way!"

—Amy E. Reichert

"Delightful, and sure to captivate readers and gain new fans for author Kelly Harms. With sparkling dialogue and a winning heroine who finds her big-girl panties amid the disaster zone her life has become and heads in a new direction, finding love along the way, it had me turning the pages into the night."

—Eileen Goudge

"I loved this book! Fresh and devastatingly funny, *The Matchmakers of Minnow Bay* is romantic comedy at its very best. The talented Kelly Harms is one to watch."

—Colleen Oakley, author of *Before I Go*

"*The Matchmakers of Minnow Bay* thoroughly entertains as it explores friendship, flings, and finally finding yourself. Harms tells the story in a funny, fresh voice ideal for this charming coming-into-her-age novel."

—Christie Ridgway, *USA Today* bestselling author of the *Beach House No. 9* and *Cabin Fever* series

OTHER BOOKS BY KELLY HARMS

The Seven Day Switch

The Bright Side of Going Dark

The Overdue Life of Amy Byler

The Matchmakers of Minnow Bay

The Good Luck Girls of Shipwreck Lane

WHEREVER the WIND TAKES US

A Novel

KELLY HARMS

LAKE UNION
PUBLISHING

Published by Lake Union Publishing, Seattle

www.apub.com

Amazon, the Amazon logo, and Lake Union Publishing are trademarks of Amazon.com, Inc., or its affiliates.

ISBN-13: 9781662507427 (hardcover)
ISBN-10: 1662507429 (hardcover)

ISBN-13: 9781542037945 (paperback)
ISBN-10: 1542037948 (paperback)

Cover design by Kimberly Glyder

Printed in the United States of America

First edition

To Christopher Meadow, who teaches me how to sail

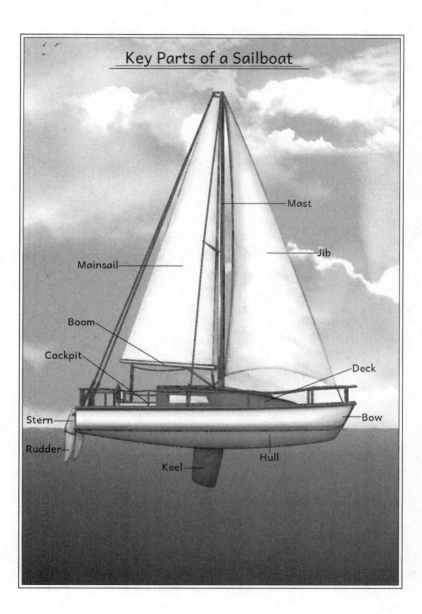

Key Parts of a Sailboat

Mast

Jib

Mainsail

Boom

Cockpit

Deck

Stern

Bow

Rudder

Hull

Keel

1

The day of my divorce is one of the happiest days of my life.

Historically speaking, of course. No one actually wants a divorce. Well, I did, but that's not the point. The point is, you're supposed to be super sad when your divorce is final, and maybe I would be super sad, except it's my daughter's twenty-first birthday. And for some reason, my twenty-one-year-old daughter wants to spend her birthday with me. If that's not the highest compliment a mother can get, I don't know what is.

My daughter is amazing. She's the toughest, strongest, coolest person I've ever met. And of all the people in the world she could ring this big birthday in with, she chose me.

I am trying not to cry about it as I slide my fortysomething butt into the banquette of this twentysomething hot spot.

Liv—it's so hard to remember to call her that instead of Livvie, which we called her since birth—is looking at me with wide, worried eyes. The same wide eyes she's given me since I left her father three months ago. Worried, yet impressed. Or so I tell myself. "Mom. You're here! How *are* you?"

I tsk. "Don't 'how *are* you' me. I'm fabulous! I'm a free woman, and the world is my oyster."

She looks at me skeptically. "I'll buy you a drink."

"Thank you. After all, we're celebrating!" And I'm broke. "Are you having something?" My daughter is a college junior, so of course she's having something. She's probably been drinking with her friends since she lived back at home. But let me believe, for a moment, that she's going to consider the drinks menu carefully and then order the sweetest, schnapps-iest thing she can find, and still make a face when she first tastes it. Do they make banana daiquiris anymore?

"I ordered two gin martinis, dry, one with a twist, one with olives. You can pick which one you want."

I cringe. That is the exact opposite of a banana daiquiri. "It's your birthday, sweetie. You pick."

When the drink comes, she takes the one with the olives and lets a healthy gulp slide down her throat without so much as a shiver. I ask the waitress for extra olives and fish the lemon peel out of my drink with Liv's discarded toothpick. Mother and daughter take their martinis the same way, it seems. My first sip, even without that perfect hint of brine, is lovely.

"Did it go as expected?" she asks.

I came straight here from the courthouse, where we had a largely uncomplicated divorce proceeding. As Liv knows, I blithely signed a prenup twenty-two years ago without batting an eye, knowing I had nothing and Alistair's family had everything, and thinking at the time that it didn't matter anyway—we were so in love. We really were back then, and yet somehow every aspect of this divorce was planned before our daughter was even born, by Larkin family lawyers and bean counters who have been part of my life ever since. The plan held up perfectly. With one exception.

"The judge was . . . feisty," I tell her. "He asked me if I wanted to contest the prenup. Twice."

"Why didn't you say yes?" Liv asks me. Her martini fairly dangles from one hand; her eyes study me intensely. For a moment I'm not sure how to answer. I don't want to tell her her family money is filthy, that the father she loves is a rat. That's between me and her father.

"Because I don't want to contest it, baby," I finally tell her. "Fair's fair. Most of the money was Dad's before we even met, and I didn't set foot in a workplace for the entire time we were married. I signed that prenup without coercion. The settlement is just a natural unfolding of a course we put in motion the day we said *I do*."

"Ugh, Mom, you're such a fatalist. Maybe you didn't have a typical job, but you worked in the home. You're seriously entitled to something. I have a friend in world econ whose dad pays her mom five grand a month. And she was his second wife!"

"First, my darling snowflake, I hate the word *entitled*." Hate it so much, it might be the reason I finally left Alistair. Or, perhaps more truthfully, it's the reason I stayed ten years too long—because I wanted to keep Liv from turning out entitled like everyone else hanging off that diseased family tree. "And second, I have no regrets," I tell her, wondering if that's entirely true. "I stand by my actions. I was able to have a beautiful family and raise you without the slightest bit of financial pressure. My dear daughter is able to go to a Very Fancy school without incurring so much as a penny of debt. I have a wardrobe full of beautiful clothes, shoes, and bags and a very nice car. If that's not a lifetime of privilege, I don't know what is."

"You'll have to sell all of those things—"

"And I have my wits. Which will take me far in this world. I have a college degree in the classics, which Larkin money paid for, lest we forget, and I have life experience." Liv looks unimpressed. "I'm the winner here." It's true, I am the winner, but the real reason? Because I'm out of the marriage. Out of the toxic family around the marriage.

"Then why was the judge so feisty, if you're the winner?"

I straighten my back. "I think he is unused to seeing a divorcing person handle herself with such grace and forbearance."

Livvie—no, Liv—chokes on her martini.

"Oh, let me have this," I tell her. "Anyway, there was one little surprise that perhaps is adding to my sense of grace at the moment."

"Oooh! Spill! Maintenance? The cape house? A secret offshore bank account?"

I consider my daughter. Underneath all the joking, she's worried about me financially, I think. She has zero confidence that I can make ends meet without her dad's Amex. I suppose this reflects how she feels about herself—he hasn't cut her off, after all—and it weighs on my heart. I had a life before Alistair Larkin. I've been broke before. I've been on my own. Something will work out. It always does.

Or it always used to. Maybe the benevolence of the universe is just another name for the immense privilege attached to being Alistair Larkin's wife. Exhibit A:

"The *Becky Ann*," I finally tell her.

"What? Dad's boat? His fiberglass baby? How on earth did he decide to give it to *you* of all people?"

I describe the scene for Liv. A judge who seemed displeased that I wasn't contesting what my lawyer assured me was an airtight pre-nuptial agreement. My husband's mother, Liv's grandmother, in the news again last night for getting a particularly disgusting white-collar scumbag out of jail. And then the judge, reading off the massive list of assets that would go to Alistair at the time of dissolution. The house, of course, which I won't miss cleaning; the vacation home, which was always about appearances; his collectible cars, which were about as real to me as Hot Wheels in their storage hangar; and the assorted detritus of twenty-two years of building a life. A grand piano neither of us could play. Alistair's retirement portfolio. An embarrassment of stocks, bonds, and other investment vehicles protected by inheritance laws. The heirloom three-carat rock from our engagement went back to the Larkin vault, but I kept the half-carat earrings that were my push present. They glint in my ears even now.

4

But then the judge read something that gave him pause. "It says here the boat's name is *Becky Ann*."

Both Alistair and I were distracted, even a bit confused. "Your Honor?" said his lawyer after a silence fell over the court.

"This boat. A forty-foot Black Watch monohull sail-powered pleasure yacht, ten years old, and mainsail, roller-furling jib, weather jib, Garmin satellite navigation, Harken autopilot, and so on. Quite a fine vessel. It's called the *Becky Ann*. Miz Larkin, your middle name is Ann, per the records of the court."

My lawyer nudged me, and I realized it was my turn to speak. "Yes. Your Honor."

"One might presume, then, that this boat is named for you? You are the patroness?"

I supposed I was. Alistair had purchased it brand new years ago after a lucrative win for his family's firm. We'd gone out on it a couple of times with a hired captain and various senior associates and their spouses. My foggy impression of it: big, unwieldy, rather a lot of trouble for what it was. I made cocktails with Mount Gay rum and served . . . I can't remember what. I just remember trying to assemble a presentable meal as I roiled around the bottom of the boat, wedged between a tiny fridge and a tiny stove and a tiny sink using tiny everything. And always, there had been the smell of diesel.

I just called it *the boat*. Never *Becky Ann*. Even then, naming it for me had been weird. A performance, and maybe the smallest of intentional slights. I hated it when he called me Becky, but he said it made him feel like Tom Sawyer. Which was a good thing, apparently?

"Yes, Your Honor."

"It must be quite a blow to part with it, then," he said. Vaguely, I started to sense where this was going. I was about to tell him it wasn't a blow at all, but my lawyer held up a hand to me, and the judge moved on, finished the list of our marital possessions. Out loud, he read all the terms of the prenup: Alistair got almost everything, I got my retirement account and my car, and Liv got a trust—my one irrefutable, unmovable stipulation. And then he added, almost to himself, "And the *Becky Ann* shall stay with her namesake, Rebecca Ann Larkin, for use or sale as she sees fit, with all maintenance and insurance costs moving to her as well."

And then he literally hit his gavel.

Alistair's chin hit the ground.

"I bet it did!" Liv now cries with surprise. "Holy shit, Mom!"

"Language."

"Twenty-one," she says, pointing to herself. "Dad is going to be so livid."

"Well, he can buy another boat, honey. He can buy ten more boats."

"He doesn't want another boat. He loves *Becky Ann*."

Apparently he does not love Becky Ann, I think, a little wistfully. For the last ten years, Becky Ann—the woman, not the boat—had been threatening to leave him as he lost touch with his moral compass, began slinking his way toward the family tradition of defending the worst of the worst clients. All I wanted was for him to realize enough—enough money, possessions, status, power, and bad karma—was enough. But for ten years he ignored my threats. Told me I needed him. And yeah, made me believe it, even. And then he did the thing I couldn't even pretend I could overlook anymore. The thing that finally, finally made me pull the plug. It has not been easy, walking away from that life. Now that I've finally done it, I hardly want a boat left over from that era to bob behind me as a reminder of how long I was led astray.

"I'm selling it," I tell her.

"I don't know if I should tell you this, but Dad will pay double."

"To anyone but Dad," I add.

Liv's face transforms to shock. "Are you serious? You won't give him back the boat?"

I don't know if I'm serious. Wouldn't a little revenge feel great about now? Wouldn't it be sweet to, I don't know, just sink the boat while

Alistair looks on in horror? There is a Becca Ann, a girl from long ago who believed in adventure and rebellion and poetic justice, who would have seriously considered that path. That woman is long gone, replaced by a wife, a mother, a Larkin.

"No," I say at last. "I don't know what I'm going to do with it yet. But I know I shouldn't be discussing this with you. It's important not to make a child of divorce feel like she has to take sides."

"I'm not a child of divorce," she says. "I'm an adult of divorce. And I know you weren't happy together. But Dad adores that boat, and I'd say it to him if he asked: I think he really does owe you some kind of life after this. He used up the best years of your life."

The best years of my life. This isn't the first time I've heard they were over. And yet I still kind of wish I could take away Liv's martini, as though it were bedtime on Christmas Eve and she'd had too many cookies and couldn't be held responsible for what she said.

"The paperwork shows *Becky Ann* still has a six-figure value. No matter who buys it, I can use that money to buy myself a lovely little house with a kitchen window that looks directly into your apartment after graduation."

Liv laughs. "You're joking, right? Cause it just feels like there's some real danger of that."

I smile at her. "I will be the queen of boundaries after this is all over. You will beg me to spend more time with you. I will be so busy in my new career, with my new house and my new . . . um . . . tropical fish tank . . ."

"Fish tank?" Liv asks, eyebrows raised.

"I don't know. I'll have hobbies. Non-Dad-related hobbies." Alistair and his wealthy family were, in a way, a full-time job. So many appearances to keep up. So much ego to stroke. I won't be sad to see that end. "I'll develop passions. Maybe I'll be an architect."

"I love your spirit, Mom, but I'm pretty sure you have to apprentice for years to be an architect."

"A brain surgeon, then."

She laughs, and I beam. I love to make my daughter laugh. With that sound, it was all worth it, twenty-two years of marriage, the divorce, my rags-to-riches-to-rags saga, the reality that until I find a job and sell this boat—this windfall—and pay the taxes on it, I can't even buy my own martini. And yet, still, it was worth it, because I created this cool kid with this bright, clear laugh who will come into a generous trust one day, when the time is right, and have everything she's ever dreamed of, just like I had at her age. Except when it comes to Olivia, she'll have it all without the strings attached.

"Maybe I'll be a sea captain," I tell her. I'm joking, of course, but it makes me think of my long-ago childhood dreams. To work on a cruise ship. To be a flight attendant. To do anything that started you off in one place and ended you up in another. "I'll need sailing lessons. You took sailing at that country club of yours, right?"

"You mean my *college*? Yes. I took two semesters of watercraft. I can sail, kind of. Dad's boat is huge, though. Much bigger than what we use in class. And I don't think 'sea captain' has been a job for a hundred and fifty years."

"I might make it have a comeback."

"I'll just give you my trust," she says. "When I turn thirty and take possession."

"You're drunk," I tell her. "And I'm not taking your money. You were born into it, fair and square."

She laughs about this but shakes her head. "Really, Mom. In nine years I'm going to start getting more allowance than most people make working full time, and you, who ironed Dad's pants for an entire lifetime, get nothing. It's not right."

How do I explain how I feel about that money? About how it came into my life, and how little it appeals to me, without screwing up all her family relationships on her dad's side? The answer: I don't. "Don't worry about me. I'm a survivor, I have a degree, and I know several places

8

hiring for assistants and secretarial positions." In fact, I know of only one, but they have my résumé right now and seemed delighted to get it. "And as for you, when the time comes, you'll be able to achieve amazing things with that trust." A trust that, I'm happy to say, is irrevocable, and as such, will let her, not the Larkin family, make her own decisions. "Start a business. Or a charitable foundation. Travel the world, see every continent, make all your dreams come true, and save some for the next generation, and the next. Your trust is your *legacy*. I want that for you far more than some handout from my kid in nine years."

"What about what I want? It's my twenty-first birthday!" she cries. "You *have* to do what I want." She could be eight years old now. We could be arguing over a Barbie Dreamhouse.

"We'll talk about it when you're older." And then I'll say no again. I would sooner die than touch a penny of my daughter's money. I would sooner be a sea captain.

"How old do I have to be before you stop saying we'll talk about it when I'm older?"

I shrug my shoulders, examine my tipsy baby girl, as tall and curvy as a woman, as accomplished, too, waving her martini around and not spilling a drop, wearing dangling earrings and red lipstick and maybe, somewhere, a tattoo, and yet somehow simultaneously six years old in a tiara and tutu. I feel like I'm twenty-one myself, a newlywed, clutching a tiny little baby who couldn't possibly survive without me. How could I be forty-two, divorced, broke, on my own, after living an entire other life? How could my daughter be a child and a woman at the exact same moment? Did that whole life even really happen? Was it all some weird dream, with nothing to show for it?

Well, nothing but a sailboat.

"Two hundred," I tell her. "When you're two hundred years old, that's when I'll stop knowing best."

2

That night I dream of the sea.

As I sleep, my subconscious plays a game of This Is Your Life. I see Alistair when we met, an ambitious, idealistic young lawyer, heir to the Larkin law fortune, with dreams of opening an environmental law division in his family's offices and changing the world. Me, just a little younger than Liv is now. In my uniform of flip-flops, cutoffs, a tank top with a little shelf bra I barely needed. A child, in other words. I floundered academically in college, not like my daughter, who grabbed her adulthood by the teeth, and I was awed by Alistair's maturity. His apartment, his car, his real life, his big dreams. I had nothing but a maxed-out credit card, an ancient Ford Escort, and a hundred thousand dollars in student loans. But while I was broke, I was brave. I believed in myself in a way I can hardly understand now. When I finally graduated, I knew I'd be up for anything. I'd find a job that promised travel, and I'd live out of a suitcase. I'd meet fascinating people and learn new languages and in every way explore what the world had to offer.

On our first date, Alistair took me to dinner and ordered us a bottle of wine that cost maybe forty or fifty dollars. I was dazzled, not by the money but that he knew how to pronounce the name of the French vineyard, and by the slight intimation that he would love to show me the valley where the very grapes were grown. Maybe it was a tired pickup line, but maybe it was the answer to my future. After all, if travel was fun alone, think how amazing it would be with someone you loved! I'd always imagined myself flying solo through life—after all, my mother's love life had hardly been an advertisement for marital bliss—but what if falling for someone so successful and smart, so worldly and sophisticated, wasn't a step away from my dreams but a step toward them?

With that in mind, I let one date turn into three and five, a romance, a proposal I simply didn't know how to answer. And then there were the repeated ministrokes that came for my mother and the promise from Alistair that if we settled down together, I could take care of her while the entire Larkin family—all their money and privilege, their good doctors and great nurses—took care of me.

I don't know why I got the idea that I was old enough at twenty-one to be married. But marry we did, one summer later, and then we had Olivia, not exactly on purpose, not exactly an oops. I loved introducing her to my mom, and together Alistair and I put her in a baby sling and carried her around Europe on a delayed honeymoon—my first-ever trip outside the country. I finished college when she went to elementary school, not so I could get a job—by then it was clear Alistair's career was the only thing we needed—but so his family would be proud of me. I, too, was proud of myself.

But in my dream I dream about our family's last overseas trip, when I was only twenty-five. A bucket-list-worthy Atlantic crossing on the *Queen Mary 2*. The trip where, three days out, I got word that Mom was failing fast. In real life, there was nothing I could do but wait until we made landfall in Southampton. It was too late, and I came home to a painful emptiness where she had been. After that, grand dreams of travel lost their luster. I was a mother, a wife, and I had things to do at home.

In my dream, though, somehow I try to take a lifeboat back to my mother. The water is stormy, there is lightning in the distance, and I have no idea what to do, but because of dream logic I feel completely confident I will get to my mom in time to say goodbye.

When I awaken, I can't remember right away: Am I twenty-five or forty-two? And when I realize that I have, indeed, mislaid the best years of my life, many of which have been in a profoundly unhappy marriage, I think I'd rather be back on that doomed boat from my dream.

The bed I wake up in is no longer my bed. Alistair has been kind enough to let me stay in the house while I find my feet. He said to take as long as I need, but I need to get out of here as soon as possible. This house—it was once so *mine*, so much my dominion. I never let a housekeeper touch my floors nor had a nanny to cuddle Olivia in my stead. Never wanted an interior decorator when I could pick out a perfectly good sofa myself. I loved selecting the colors, draping everything in plastic, rolling on thick paint alone for hours until everything was perfect. I browsed the stores for decorator fabric and sewed lush window dressings, watched auctions for the perfectly mismatched dining chairs, and knitted my own bulky throws to toss on the sofas. We put up framed photos we'd taken from our happier years. We had beautiful portraits of Livvie as a baby, child, and teen, framed and matted and lit up like they were Lebowitzes. Alistair liked bulky masculine furniture; fine, no problem, but to counteract this I leaned, in my thirties, toward chandeliers. There are chandeliers everywhere in this house. On this front, I have no regrets.

But despite the love I've put into it, the house isn't mine anymore. Not even a little. Leaving it is part of how I will leave this whole chapter behind. I am going to find an apartment with two little bedrooms, one for me, one for Liv to come and stay whenever she likes. I am going to put the girliest floral linens on the bed, the laciest throw pillows, the gauziest curtains, stop just short of Disney Princess, let myself be the mistress of my domain. Isn't this what divorce is meant to be about, after all? No more compromise. No more clutter, either—I am starting fresh.

With a largesse that I've come to realize stems from entitlement, Alistair waved at the house a few weeks before our hearing was set and said, "Take whatever you want or need. It's only stuff." And yet when I was left alone in the house, I couldn't help but notice that his collection of Supreme Court justice autographs was missing and the combination of the safe had been changed. I had already liquidated my real jewelry—it just covered legal fees, as I had never had a taste for sparkles. Now I'm posting pictures online of each handbag I own and becoming rather an expert reseller. I mean to take him at his word and sell everything I can find that fits in an eBay box. I don't want these bad memories, and I couldn't afford them even if I did.

I could have sunk into despair. Instead, I try to consider myself lucky. How many empty nesters do I know who had to go through decades of belongings, touch everything, ask themselves if it sparks joy? Just to get the kind of fresh start I'm getting. Whereas all I have to do is call a taxi. Anything that doesn't go with me when I leave, I never have to think about again. I never have to take trunks full of too-small clothing to the Goodwill and face the fact that my body has become a stranger to me. And the five totes of marital keepsakes and mementos I so carefully sorted and stored long ago are now as relevant to me as the marriage certificate itself. I already packed up Livvie's baptism gown wrapped in tissue and her stuffed Eeyore, tattered but still frowning, and a stack of her various T-shirts from camps and activities and school. Those I will take with me wherever I go, forever. Maybe in my retirement I'll make one of those T-shirt quilts. *Maybe,* I think with a start, *I'm kind of retired now.* I know I am broke, but it doesn't feel any more real than the idea that I'm divorced and alone. I'm in the same bed I always slept in. I'm as alone as I've ever been since Liv left for college. Alistair is off somewhere with someone else, just like he was when we were married.

You want it to feel real? asks a bitter part inside me. *Go try to buy groceries.*

That part is right. I'm living off of handbags. And not unlimited handbags either.

I've got to sell that boat.

I dreamed I was on a boat, alone, adrift. My subconscious is hardly Proustian in her metaphors. The dream feels all too real. I can't sail in the best of cases and certainly not single-handedly steer and run the sails. I can't use the naval charts required to go anywhere outside the little bay it's tied up in, and if I just want to motor around, I don't exactly know how to start the engine, come to think of it. I'll have to sell it without knowing if I'm being ripped off, probably use the boat traders that work right out of the marina it's in now, as I can't even move her from one dock slip to another. And the price that it was appraised at could be completely out of touch—you insure something, after all, for much more than you expect to resell it for, don't you? For replacement cost. I know that was the case with the engagement ring. Like diamonds, sailboats don't appreciate, so I probably need to dump it fast. And despite my carefree demeanor around my daughter, I am very afraid about money. I haven't paid my own bills since I was twenty. I haven't worried about having enough since I was thirty. Now, in my forties, I've only just opened a credit card in my own name. They set my limit at five hundred dollars.

If the world is an ocean and I must navigate it alone for the first time, this far along in my life's journey, then yes, I am afraid. Frozen at my kitchen island, waves-of-nausea-and-tears-level afraid.

I send Liv's best friend's mother, my best friend at first by default and now by choice, a picture of the *Becky Ann* and a link to the original sales page. This is mine now, I type. Do you guys want to buy it?

Her husband is a lawyer too. He's living proof that you can do well and do good, or at least not do as much harm as the Larkins have done. And Natasha is a tenured researcher, a very celebrated one. They can certainly buy a boat off of me twice over, if they want to.

I would rather chew off my own foot than be trapped in a boat. It's my living nightmare. I get seasick in the bathtub, writes back Natasha. *Do you need money?*

No, I lie. *I'm fine. I don't want a boat either, though. How does one sell a boat?*

I'll research it. Natasha believes, perhaps rightly, that all life's answers are in LexisNexis, JSTOR, EBSCO, or PubMed.

Oh good! In that case I'll make muffins.

Natasha and Rich live near campus, and Natasha gets paid most of her salary by grants, not by the school, so she views office appearances as something of a favor she does for the university. If she's working from home on something really good, she'll go in or not, and her students—she only has grad students—can run the show without her. But she will never miss a chance to eat any baked good I make for her, no matter what she's up to. Her favorite muffins are ridiculously simple, but she thinks they're the second coming. Liv likes them, too, so I will make a double batch. Come to think of it, I don't have to look good for anyone's reputation anymore, so I will make a triple batch. Ah, I remind myself. Another thing in the pro-divorce column: no more watchful eyes on my waistline from my mother-in-law. She can keep her body dysmorphia to herself from here on out.

I have the muffin batter and three variations of filling ready to bake when Natasha lets herself in to my ex-husband's house. I glimpse the clock and wager it'll take her the twelve minutes of baking time these muffins need just to take off her coat.

"I left while I still had a student on Zoom," she tells me. "I had her on mute and then forgot her, and my phone buzzed while I was pulling out of the driveway, and sure enough, it was her trying to get back into my virtual room after I disconnected her. Oh, Rebecca. She is the saddest kid I have ever met. Everything is a tragedy, and it's all happening specifically to her. I've got her doing comps that don't really need doing that badly right now, and when she effs it up, she behaves as though the data are out to get her. Never mind that the pretense is that she's *assisting* me in my research and I'm waiting with bated breath for her to get this stuff back to me. She's the one who is really suffering. If I were actually waiting on her, I'd be a fool. What a twit. I might as well have hired a *boy* for all the good she's doing me."

"You're not supposed to say those things out loud," I remind her. Natasha is always voicing her reverse-sexism stream of consciousness, and then I am always reminding her not to be such a lady supremacist, and then she is saying how if men could do the work of women, she'd be the first to hire them. I always feel a little bad for her poor husband.

"Ok, you're right. I might as well have hired a *man*."

I try not to openly laugh.

"I am in trouble, though. The college says I can't run my lab with so many students unless I can give them all adequate hours. They don't understand—I need extra students as spares when I'm trying to figure out which ones are dum-dums, and there are so many dum-dums."

Natasha knows I think she's not a great manager. The one time I thought our friendship was in trouble was when we tried to plan our kids' senior prom together. The only way we made it through was when I took away her authority and put her on chaperone duty. So I say nothing.

"Remember when they were up my tail because I didn't take on enough students? I was 'too picky.' Now I have too many, and this poor girl is calling me on Zoom in my driveway after I forgot her existence and saying virtual meeting programs never work right for her, and I don't know if I should tell her that Zoom works fine if you're not annoying."

"Actually, you know that you should not," I clarify.

"I didn't. I said that she was one tiny piece of a mighty cognitive machine and that machine was my department and that any hope of a postdoc was resting in the hands of the data that was so vigorously out to get her."

"Natasha," I say.

"I said it nicely."

"I'm sure you didn't. I'm not giving you any muffins."

"What kind aren't you giving me?"

"Sweet potato chocolate chip, raspberry mascarpone, and elder-flower orange."

She moans. "She did cry, and I am awful. Can you even imagine being so incompetent at twenty-three, though?"

I stop spooning batter and turn around to look her in the eye. "Because you were the picture of precociousness."

Natasha laughs. Our girls have been best friends since they were seven, so I know Natasha's life story almost as well as I know my own. In fact, she had the life I thought I wanted back then. In her twenties she was backpacking Oceania, chain-smoking, and falling in love with a series of unsuitable European tourists and one sheep farmer who made Crocodile Dundee look like James Bond. Her daughter, Minerva, was a "geriatric pregnancy," so she had plenty of time to get her ya-yas out before settling down, but at fifty-seven, she is my coolest, smartest friend, and I trust her to my core even if she is basically the only true reverse sexist in the entire world.

"I may have had a youthful foible or two. But I was never self-pitying. I despise that trait in people. Especially people who have it all."

I make a face. "You might want to take your muffins to go, then. I am very self-pitying today."

"You don't have it all," she says. "You don't have even most of it, not anymore."

"No no, don't worry about my feelings," I tell her.

"More to the point, you don't seem that self-pitying right now. And if *you* don't feel sorry for yourself, then jeez, who *should?*"

"It's fine. I can take it," I say, now mostly to myself.

"You're broke; you're living in your ex-husband's house, presumably on his credit; and you haven't held a job outside the home in . . . how long?"

"Never," I say. "I'm already fixing that, though. I am now an official certified eBay reseller."

She laughs and then coughs it away. "I'm giving you money."

"Keep your money. But do take off your coat and sit awhile. We can have tea."

"You have time for me to stay? You're not too busy?"

Every single time she comes over, she asks me this. "Natasha, I am never too busy for you. And besides, you're supposed to sort out this boat business for me—remember? I called you in a panic? Because I am divorced and alone and broke?"

"Never alone," she says. It's sweet, and I love her for saying it, but I am more alone than I've felt since . . . well, since I lost my mom. The Larkins have long been my only family.

In an attempt to keep things light—I feel one step from tears as it is—I add, "And I want to be there when you call the grad student back and give her some real feedback on how to behave professionally in a situation where she's stuck."

Natasha launches into another soliloquy about work, her students, and how Minerva and Liv could outsmart all of them with their prefrontal cortices tied behind their backs. Then she tells me how Rich, her second husband after the dalliance with the Aussie went bad, is doing as he starts to downshift for early retirement, and how Minerva is taking an extra full hour of classes at MIT and had to get special dispensation from the dean, and how the bigwigs at Apple are circling her but she wants to travel after graduation, and just as I am reminding Natasha that Minerva is only a sophomore and has a lot of living to do before she makes any big decisions, the timer dings.

"Muffins!" Natasha cries, and she sounds for all the world like her daughter did when she was eleven and here for a sleepover. I miss those sleepovers acutely and tell her so.

"Minerva says Liv is worried about you."

I shrug. "She's a worrier."

"She feels Alistair owes you a settlement."

"Who can say?" I respond. Maybe he does, but then, why fight for dirty family money I don't even want?

"The judge, apparently. This boat . . . the *Becky Ann*. I completely forgot about it."

"Just now or completely?" I ask her. Natasha's mind is a wandering labyrinth of surprises and delights.

"Since you guys bought it. I feel like you were kind of excited at one point."

When Alistair surprised our family with the boat, it was with the promise of all kinds of family adventures together. It was a Hail Mary. And it worked, for a while. "It was ten years ago. I still liked that guy."

"Fool."

"Don't I know it. Anyway, a boat seemed like a romantic idea. Cozy and yet adventurous. It has a kind of kitchen, so I imagined I'd make tasty things and he'd take the helm and we'd all be tan and lithe by the end of the summer. He told me we could sail to Bermuda in five days! In fact, I remember him saying he picked this particular boat because it was so easy for just one experienced sailor to traverse great distances. Something about the winches? I didn't even need to know what side was port, that's what he told me." I think back on that. Why didn't I *want* to know what side port was on? Why didn't I try to learn to sail on that boat? Twentysomething Becca Ann would have been all over it. Thirtysomething Becca Ann hadn't thought she could.

"You didn't ever sail to Bermuda."

"We did not. We went out in the bay as a family a few times, and then we entertained his junior partners there before big votes now and then. It was all right. I got a little queasy, and there's not much you can make in a kitchen that's two feet square. My takeaway: sailing is something really expensive you do so you can drink gin before eleven a.m."

"Ah. The golf of the seas, then."

"Exactly. I can't wait to be rid of the thing."

"Well, pull up a chair, because my most pitiful student is about to call with everything she knows about the Black Watch 4100. Including, most important, the resale value."

"You didn't."

"I called her back before I was even out of my neighborhood," Natasha tells me. "I told her straight up—she's doing fine but needs hours and perspective, and I was creating busywork to get her those things. More important: if the data and her aren't friends, and she really wants to be in our line of work, she needs a second stats class to bring her up to speed. I said I would help her find the scholarship money to pay for one. If she can go deep for some fortitude, I'll help her get over this speed bump. And that means I will need to whore myself out somewhere new to fund what she needs to get back on track."

"You're a hooker with a heart of gold," I tell her.

"A heart of gold and a dossier on sailboat values."

"Lay it on me," I tell her, and then prepare myself for my future with two muffins, milky tea, and a deep, hopeful breath—provisions for what is about to become a very stormy passage.

3

The marina where Alistair keeps *Becky Ann* is less like a boatyard and more like a country club. I pull into the parking lot, and someone tries to wave me toward the valet. I am not a person who enjoys a valet at the best of times (the interior of my car reflects the interior of my mind), so I ignore him and head to self-parking, where I can use the lanyard I found in my ten-year-old boat bag to open the gates. I am now the rightful owner of this vessel, and I probably also own the lease on the boat slip, forty feet of wood planks that stretch out from long corrugated metal fingers replete with heavy-duty plastic dock boxes, welcome mats, and six-figure vessel after six-figure vessel. To my left in the harbor are the larger boats, massive superyachts with hot tubs and seventy-two-inch indoor/outdoor TVs. To my right bob the smaller boats, which still seem big to me, especially the sailboats, whose towering masts pierce the sky.

Closer to land, it gets down to smaller and smaller crafts—daysailers, deck boats, and ski boats—and then the rocky shore and the clubhouse and pool. Livvie had a fun time at this marina in her tweens—we always let her bring a friend or a cadre of them, and she had charging privileges at the snack bar and ice cream window. *Charging privileges.* Looking back on my marriage, that's what I had, too—not wealth, but charging privileges at the clubhouse. That was the Larkin family lifestyle. And starting this summer, I think with a twinge, I'm out of the club.

This isn't to assert I'm somehow badly off. The website for this marina advertises that a membership here is more than three thousand dollars. *Becky Ann*'s berth is paid through the end of the summer. Having that covered is a coup in and of itself. But after that, this boat must become someone else's problem. Boats aren't exactly liquid assets, no matter how good the pun might be, so I go to the harbormaster's office before I so much as peer at my new possession. The office is whirring with a window-unit air conditioner, and when I open the half-glass door, the burst of cool washes over me. I didn't realize I was getting hot until just now, when some part of me inhales the AC in relief. I'm in almost-white jeans today—I'm not sure why I wore jeans to the marina, except that I'm never sure what else to wear anymore. Sometime between when I had Olivia and when she moved out for school, pants fashion changed so much that I feel constantly lost from the waist down. Liv left this soft, faded ankle-length pair at the house sometime last winter, and I slid into them happily, thinking that if she had purchased them at some point, wearing them had to be at least within five years of the latest style. On top, I'm wearing the strappy tank of a tomato-red cotton twinset. Yes, a twinset. I'm not quite sure how to dress now that I'm not Alistair Larkin's wife. But he always hated this color on me—said it argued with my russet curls. So this is my new favorite shirt.

All told, it's a fairly appropriate outfit for late May by the water, but when I see the man in the marina office for the first time, my first thought is that I wish I were naked.

That's the kind of good looking he is. I find most handsome men very intimidating and tend to want to get away from them as fast as possible when I meet them in real life. In fake life, I'm happy to stare at all the various Avengers in turn, but I need that screen between them and me. Somehow, though, this man doesn't make me squirm; he just makes me think of sex. Sex—the very idea of which hasn't crossed my mind for five years. The man in front of me is a walking dose of lady Viagra. I don't say hello when I realize he's there in the little office with me. I say, "Oh!"

"Hey," he breathes. He has rich dark hair with sun streaks, a six-day beard, and a tan. Green eyes. Really green. I stare into them for a second.

"Ricki isn't here today," he tells me. Or maybe he says Ricky? Those eyes. I'm weirdly salivating. My mind is working really fast between dirty thoughts I thought I didn't have anymore and reminders of why I'm there. *Sell boat. Take off pants. No! Sell boat.* "Is Ricky who I should talk to about putting my boat up for sale?" I ask this guy.

"You're selling a boat?" The guy licks his lips. I mean, really. The thought of a boat for sale makes him lick his lips. I wish it was over me. Still, I enjoy it all the same.

I nod.

His brow furrows. "But why are you selling?" he asks.

Oh, Lord, what a question. Why am I selling? Because it's not really my boat, and I want to liquidate it before my ex-husband somehow appeals the judge's decision. I want to buy a little bungalow near my daughter where I will start a second, much older, much quieter life, hopefully in a job with benefits, and nice coworkers, and not too much stress.

"I'm not a sailor," I tell him vaguely. "The whole scene's not for me."

His face falls. "Forget the scene," he says. "If you're worried about the scene, you can hardly enjoy the water."

"I get seasick," I tell him.

"I can give you some suggestions for that," he says. I think I detect the slightest accent. In case he wasn't sexy enough already.

"I need cash," I blurt to put an end to the negotiations.

"Ah. I feel that," he says. "What are you selling?" Yes, it's an English accent. No, Irish. Oh *swoon*.

I take the papers out of my bag because I can't quite remember at the moment what my name is, much less the model of boat I own. "It's a Black Watch 4100," I read.

"The one out on dock C?" he asks. "The 2012 sloop?"

I nod. "And I'm also selling the main and two headsails," I continue. "A one hundred and fifty percent genoa and a ninety percent jib. Full galley and two berths."

"Oh yeah. I know the boat well. I'm the guy who was working on her," he says.

"Working? What kind of work?"

"Getting her ready for haul-out," he says. "And she'd only just splashed."

"Haul-out? Splashed?" I ask. Boat talk is cooling my loins rapidly.

"Work order says she was coming out and getting ready for a long transit over land. Didn't you just buy her cradle from us?"

I absentmindedly comb through my hair. I'm not sure what a cradle is or why Alistair was getting ready to take the boat out of the water. Maybe he intended to sell her too. I wonder how I feel about that. I guess it takes a tiny bit of pleasure out of the idea of my dumping her on the first buyer I can find. But I remind myself: revenge is a dish best not served at all.

"I'll sell the cradle too," I tell him, because whatever, I don't actually want a sailing education, even from Mr. Sex here. I want to sell *Becky Ann*, yesterday.

"Well, yeah," he says, as though that goes without saying. "If you'll hold on a moment, I can get one of our sales guys up here to talk price. Though . . ."

I look him in his green, green eyes. He looks back.

"You might be better selling her yourself, by owner. The dealers here . . . they take a huge percentage. And *Becky Ann* is pretty much perfect."

This makes me smile, as if he's actually talking about me. And then I think about sex some more. It's a really pleasant thought, actually.

"Perfect." I let the word roll over my mouth. "But do you really think I could sell it—her—myself?" I ask him. "In the next few months? Without knowing much about boats?"

"Oh yeah. No trouble there. I'd buy her from you myself if I could. She's the perfect boat to teach on. And I'm—well, that's what I'm supposed to do here. I'm Grant Murphy. Sailing coach." *Grant Murphy,* my brain tries to memorize, so I don't have to ask him ten more times. *Grant Murphy. I would like to be* Grant*ed permission to come aboard,* my libido thinks. *Jesus.*

"Becca Larkin," I tell him.

"Becca Ann Larkin?" he asks. "As in *Becky Ann?*"

"The very same. Though I prefer not to be called Becky."

He looks me over for a long moment, movie-star-about-to-kiss-the-leading-lady long, and for a second I think maybe we're actually going to have sex in this little cold office, and I get kind of excited about it. Then he says, "She resembles you, you know. It fits."

"She?"

"Your sailboat."

Oh. I look like a boat. Ok. So we're not going to have sex in this office. Fair. I take some leveling breaths. "Thank you?"

"No trouble," he says. "Let's go take a look at what I've been up to. She hardly needed anything, but I did take her out to the bay to scrape the hull. Some fresh antifouling wouldn't go amiss if you take her out next winter, but if you sell her in the water, that can be the next guy's problem. I buffed the gelcoat on the port rise and the fore—did you bring her in hard to the pontoon at some point?"

I blink.

"Or maybe that was your husband? He was the captain?"

I nod.

"Well, you'd never know it now. You didn't sail it much, I take it. Engine's got less than forty hours on her."

"Only a few times, years ago."

This time it's Grant who looks mystified. "Pity. Great wee boat," he says.

Wee? "It's forty feet," I say.

"Forty-one, really," he replies.

"Not that wee," I say.

"Well," is all he says. I'd be offended, but I'm trying to remember if the berths are big enough for energetic sex with a sailing instructor.

And that thought alone is startling. This is not something I would necessarily share with, say, my divorce lawyer or my daughter or even maybe my best friend, but the part of me that thinks about kissing, touching, and all manners of intercourse is not normal anymore. It's . . . well, Westley in *The Princess Bride*. Mostly dead. I remember having a sex drive—it was there at the beginning of my young adulthood, and it was kind of a menace for a while, leading me into all manner of situations, getting confused for love, that sort of thing. Then after Livvie was born, it crawled up inside me and went dormant like one of those Antarctic toads. I loved Alistair, but motherhood took it out of me. Every Wednesday evening after Livvie was long asleep, Alistair pushed the correct buttons to create a physiological response in me, and we had a nice time and went right to sleep after, but every Thursday morning I woke up relieved that *that* was over for a while.

Then, as things began to unwind, we stopped entirely. I talked to my doctor about it when I turned thirty-eight. I told her that I was expecting some kind of big sexy ramp-up in my late thirties. She suggested marriage counseling.

Looking at Grant Murphy today, I realize she should have suggested a divorce lawyer. As I follow the man down the docks, our steps clanking on the metal, it seems like the joints in my hips and waist are unhinging. There's a spot just behind my palate, in the middle of my head, where I feel a kind of blood flow, or maybe it's some old dusty neurons lighting up. The sexual energy rushes down the center of me and then back up again. It's not weird or alarming or worrisome—it's lush and feels great. In fact, it feels oddly . . . safe?

And I suppose it is. Like the guys on the screen in superhero costumes, Grant is no danger to me. He must be ten years younger, and he's definitely not interested, and I just let him believe I'm married, so no one could accuse me of flirting. He's like a sexy film that I'm an extra in, but only for the next half hour or so. It's really lovely.

"Lovely," he agrees. I start and then realize he's talking about *Becky Ann*. It's—she's a nice enough boat, I suppose. When she was new and we had those grand dreams about her, I thought she was the most beautiful sight. Most of the other sailboats on this dock are white fiberglass on the sides and deck, but *Becky Ann* is painted a rich navy on her hull up from the waterline to the toe rails, and her deck is a rich faded teak. Her name is lettered in perfect loopy white script, the *B* ornate, the *A* almost a wave in itself. I've yet to see the private yacht with anything less than a cheesy name, but at least Alistair avoided the "knotical" puns that amuse themselves from every direction around us.

The boat opposite us on our slip is a younger, sexier model. She has a bigger, cleaner sunshade—bimini, I think Alistair called it when we were shopping—and fancy long windows into the, uh . . . saloon. And the cockpit has a lot more going on, too—computers or something, and plush cushions, and . . . is that a wine fridge?

Grant catches me staring. "Yours is the better boat," he tells me. "Especially for you to learn on. Twin wheels, one on each side of the craft—a lifesaver when you're getting your legs. Self-tailing winches. You'll love those when single-handing. Roller furling. That can be a pain for racers, sure, but for cruising in mixed weather, you'll love it. And she's not slow. If you wanted to learn race tactics on her, you'd find her capable enough. She's a bit big on the bottom for racing, but that makes her comfortable."

Tell me about it, I think, smoothing Liv's denim over my hips.

"I'm selling her," I remind him.

He inclines his head at me. "Then this is all for the online ad, I suppose."

I study him for a moment. "Grant, I'm wondering . . . would you sell it for me? I mean, for money? Are you allowed to have a side hustle like that?"

He makes a face. "Probably not *allowed*, per se. But even so, I can help you, sure. Or . . . I could teach you to sail her."

"I really don't want to sail her."

"She's just such a great boat," he says. "You're a fool to sell her without even taking her out once."

Ugh, goodbye sexy thoughts. Hello another man who doesn't listen to my wishes. I scowl.

"We'll sell 'er, then," he adds when he sees my face turn tight.

I nod. Brusquely.

"Any idea how you want to price this boat?" he asks me, now back in line.

I look at *Becky Ann*. We still haven't climbed aboard. I wish I never had to go aboard the damn thing at all. In our one marriage counseling appointment, the therapist suggested I try to spend time recalling happy places from our relationship, and yes, I thought of sailing as a family. I pulled up memories of my kitchen island, where I'd serve coddled eggs and perfectly done bacon to a very appreciative audience of two. I went back to our honeymoon and the twin hammocks tied from the rafters of our ocean-view cabana in the Bahamas. They were all wonderful memories. But the exercise didn't work. The images felt a thousand years old, almost as if they belonged to someone else. The therapist said we needed to create some new images of peaceful togetherness. But I couldn't tell that to Alistair in marriage counseling. He didn't come.

My brain goes back to something Natasha told me over muffins yesterday. About the boat's displacement—how much water it pushes out of the way. Its keel weighs 6,500 pounds, and it moves almost ten tons of water weight when afloat, yet it can be rooted into a single spot by use of a relatively tiny anchor. That is my fear—a fraction of myself that drags so heavy that for ten long years, I could not seem to move off my spot. Now, even with the divorce, still that fear is hooked on the bottom of the sea, making sure nothing I do or say can bring me far from where I've started.

So instead of answering Grant about the price I actually want, I dig in my tote bag and pull out a printed listing of a very similar boat that sold six months ago. I hand it to Grant, anxiously. "What do you think about that listing?" The asking price was mammoth. Not just a down payment on a bungalow. The whole house.

He looks it over for a moment, then nods. "Yeah. Yeah, you can get this. Maybe more. I mean, it'll take a moment. There's not a huge number of people with this kind of money standing by. On the other hand, a boat in this condition is rarer still. People usually only sell younger boats like this if they have some kind of baggage, and *Becky Ann* is as clean as they come."

My heart, momentarily, feels loosened from the seafloor. "That is wonderful news," I tell him. "Amazing news. Thank you." I can already see my pretty window boxes, my gauzy curtains. My brightly painted door. Liv will help me pick out new furniture; IKEA is fine. I imagine myself building a Brijøérk on the floor of the bedroom as an audiobook streams through the fading light. It's not the stuff of my childhood dreams, but it sounds . . . safe.

"Not necessarily gonna sell as fast up here, you know," he adds.

"What do you mean?"

"You might get more for her after you offshore. This kind of price range, people like to do these deals in the Bahamas, Cayman Islands. Maybe you could broker in Florida. Tax implications are different everywhere."

"This boat has tax implications," I repeat. "Right. This boat is worth more than a house. Of course it does." *Used* IKEA furniture is fine, I tell myself. "I appreciate your advice," I tell him.

"It's probably too much information. Look, I'll just suggest that when you list, you tick the box that says you'll transport. You'll get way more page views, and someone who knows someone who needs this exact boat will see it, Bob's your uncle and Fanny's your aunt."

I love how sailing talk makes a thirtysomething sound like a geezer. "I'll tick the box," I agree. I am not sure what offshoring is, but if I need to do it to sell, fine. I make some uneven steps sideways. Eager to get away from this boat, to get on to the next part of my life. Wondering what I'll wish I would have asked this knowledgeable geezer-in-a-sex-god's body when I'm gone.

Will I wish I'd asked for his number? *No. Absolutely not.*

"Uh . . . ," he says. "Hey look, you want to, um . . ."

I look away from *Becky Ann* to Grant. His eyes are darting around the marina. Like he's afraid of something or distracted, maybe. "I'm thinking we could . . ." His voice trails off again, and there's more looking around. I take a peek behind me. An angry boss maybe?

We both see there's no one. He clears his throat and leans in toward me just enough to send my senses tingling again.

"Becca Ann, if you want me to write the listing, I know the boat. I don't mind. I—it would be my pleasure."

"How much would it cost?" I ask him.

He puts up a hand. "No. Just, to help. You don't . . . seem to . . ."

"Know anything about the boat, or any boats, or sailing?" I finish. He cough-laughs in relief.

"I don't, Grant. I really don't. And in most situations, I'd probably take the time to learn. But in this one . . ." How to even explain my predicament? "How about a thousand dollars as a retainer? You do the listing, respond to all comers, show the boat. I'm sure they'll have a lot of questions I can't answer. And coach me if there's a negotiation so I don't get robbed. I know the sales guys would be looking for a lot more."

He nods slowly. Now his eyes are on mine. Not distracted at all. Money. It will do that—I know well from a life with Alistair. Now this guy has a thousand reasons to give me his attention. After a moment he says, "Yeah. You pay me only after she's sold." He cocks his head. "A grand, really?"

"Win-win for both of us," I tell him. I nod to the paper he's holding to indicate the selling price. "That's a lot of money."

"Some people would think it's a bargain for this boat."

I laugh. "Find me one of those people, please."

He runs his hand over his stubble. "I will. Maybe I'll find a couple."

"Great," I say.

"It'll be easy."

"Hope you're right."

"Just watch me." He brushes his shoulder off like he's about to execute some Herculean feat of strength.

And to my great horror, I say out loud as I think it, as though I'm with Natasha in front of my oven and not at this marina in front of this sex sailor, "I really wish I could."

4

A week after the trip to the marina, I sell my Chanel bag for a cool eight thousand dollars. Yes, you read that right. When I was growing up, I remember someone told me he bought a car for eight thousand dollars, and for about ten years after that, it became my example of the most expensive purchase a person could make without a mortgage. Today, I sold something that doesn't even fit a graphic novel inside it for eight-freaking-thousand dollars. Used. Alistair gave it to me one Christmas, and now I get why I was supposed to be so grateful. I wasn't, and that's that, and now I have a nest egg and some other fool owns an overpriced sack.

Maybe I shouldn't accept the money, I think for a second. *Or give the cash to Alistair.*

No. He's the one who bought me a gazillion-dollar purse. That's not on me. And Alistair's firm was on the news today because of a very sketchy retrial, and Liv sent me the video clip with just the word *mortified* underneath it. I will take this eight thousand dollars and get myself a short-term rental to live in and get out of this house. I text my daughter back and ask her about her plans for the day. She responds: Let's go shopping with Dad's credit card!

I ignore that and write back, Let's go apartment hunting with my eBay money!

I'm telling you, she drives over here so quick. Thank goodness, because my car won't start. I don't think it wants to be my car anymore because I'm too embarrassing without my handbags. Well, fine. I don't want *it* to be *my* car anymore, I tell it when it doesn't turn over. It's an unreliable luxury brand, and repairs will likely cost more than I care to pay. And I don't want to call Alistair's AAA account either. When I first told him I wanted to leave him, almost ten years ago, he told me I couldn't survive without him and his family money. And like an idiot I believed him and stayed! For ten years!

Well, now I can survive.

Because my college daughter is giving me a lift.

In the car Alistair bought for her.

God dammit.

"I think we should look near campus," she tells me. "As in my apartment."

"No," I say firmly. "I'm not moving in with my daughter. I'm forty-mumble-damn-years old."

"Mumble-damn is not an age," she says.

"It is now. Where should a woman of my stature, which is to say very little stature, live in the sunset of my life?" I ask her.

Liv puts her head way back on the headrest and gazes up in exasperation long enough that I wonder if I should grab the wheel.

"I know Dad robbed you of your prime," she says, and there's that phrase again. "And believe me, he knows exactly how I feel about that. But you still have your second act ahead of you, Mom."

"A second act? That sounds exhausting," I admit. My first act was all about trying to squeeze myself into an ever-shrinking box labeled "Married to the Larkin heir." Can't I just pry myself out of the box and sort of, I don't know, spend some time stretching my legs?

"Some women haven't even had their first child by the time they're forty-mumble-damn-years old. You could fall in love and have a whole new family."

"Oh my stars, don't even say that. I am ready to be a grandmother, not a mom again!"

Liv pales.

"I mean, a grandmother later. When the time is right. I can wait. I can wait for years. Ten years. You can have your kids whenever."

"Or never."

I say nothing. If she's saying this to pick a fight with me, not today, Satan. If she thinks she means it, what the heck does she know? I start counting backward silently from ten and only get to six when she says, "What do you think about a converted loft? That new building halfway between campus and downtown maybe?"

"What does that mean, a converted loft? I mean, I can imagine it in a big-city context, but here?"

"Same idea. Exposed ductwork, brick maybe. Open floor plan. Big windows."

"But it must be fake converted. That's a brand-new building."

Liv shrugs. "Our house is fake Tudor. It's not like Anne of Cleves is coming by anytime soon."

I smile at her. "Anne of Cleves. Of all the wives to reference."

"See? My school is more than a country club," she says, referencing my dig from her birthday. I meant it as a joke, but now I wonder if that hurt her feelings. We share a lot of what's on our minds, but right now she's probably dealing with thoughts and emotions she's not sharing. I have taken enormous care to protect Liv from knowing what I think about her dad's behaviors, about the family wealth. To let her decide for herself how she feels about her dad now that we're not a unit anymore. And about me.

"Definitely," I agree. "It's a great school." It is, though hardly an inclusive one, with its high price tag and history of legacy admittances. If it were my decision to make, I would have talked her into a state school, where she could spend some time with kids more like . . . well, more like me. "I'm proud of you every day. But I would be no matter where you were right now."

"Prison?"

"Still proud," I tell her. I deeply believe this is true.

"Mom," she says when we pull into the parking lot of the new fake-converted-loft building.

I unbuckle and turn to her. "Yes?"

"It is weird. You and Dad being broken up."

I try to stay quiet. The hardest thing about being a mother is not saying what you want to say in the moment you want to say it.

"I feel weird about Dad and his money. You're broke, you have nothing, you're going to go live in a studio and take an entry-level job. But from his end, nothing at all seems to have changed. We had our Thursday-night dinner like clockwork at the Tornado Room. He ordered the same thing he always does, and we mostly talked about work and school. He wouldn't say one word about you."

"But that's ok," I tell her. "Actually, that's really good. Dad and I do one thing together really well: raise a kid. Him keeping his thoughts about me to himself is part of that."

"It doesn't feel good. It feels fake."

"Like a converted loft in a new construction?"

"Like your second act," she says.

Oof. "Yeah," I agree. "I know exactly what you mean."

"He doesn't even live in that house anymore," she whines. "I told him, it's stupid to make you move. And you know what he told me?"

Hm.

"He said he told you to stay as long as you want. Years if you want. Dad said he's never moving back in. He likes his new place in Boston. It's to his own taste, he says. He has a housekeeper who makes all his meals."

Hoo boy. I try not to think too hard about how easily I was replaced. Like an employee. I try to ignore the pang of hurt that invokes in me.

Liv frowns. "But you told me you have to move out so Dad can have the house. Which is true? Are you trying to make Dad look like the bad guy?"

Here we go. At this moment, my double standard about the family money—good enough for my daughter, too dirty for me—locks me into a situation that requires, if not a lie, some kind of fancy spin. I clear my throat and decide to focus on the simplest facts. "The house can never be truly mine because when we bought it, we got the down payment as a gift from your grandparents. And it will make me happy to have a home that belongs to only me."

Liv's voice rises. "That's stupid. You have a home. Our home. If you leave it, and Dad doesn't want it, it'll just sit empty."

"He'll probably sell it, Liv. And maybe some of that money will go into your trust. And that's a good thing."

To my shock, my daughter starts to cry.

"Mom!" she wails through her tears. "You're being ridiculous about this! How can you say selling our house is a good thing? It's my house too! Why can't you even think about that? I've lived there my *entire life*!" Even in that rush of panic I still get whenever my baby cries, I feel that prickle up the back of my neck. The one that I get when Liv is being . . . well, a Larkin.

"You want me to live in it forever?" I ask her, hoping she'll see for herself how selfish that is.

"Of course! It's a good house, it's where I grew up, it's where we were all together." The kitchen-island memory rushes up again. The toddler baths. Teaching Liv to ride her bike in the driveway, movie nights in the theater, our annual New Year's Eve parties that always spilled out to the back patio, no matter how cold the night. It hasn't been good between Alistair and me for a while, but before . . . there was once so much joy.

All of it coming from our love for our family.

Liv shudders an exhale. "That house has my bedroom, all my stuff. It's where I feel like everything is normal. I *thought* it's where I would spend summer breaks and Christmas for the rest of my life."

Though there are days I swear I can still feel her baby body in my arms, there are other moments I forget she is only twenty-one. Still young not just in body but in mind. She imagines when she is thirty, forty, fifty, she'll be spending lazy childlike summers at our—at Alistair's—house? Where I'll still be living on his largesse?

In the place where we built our life together? Fell out of love? Walked away from each other?

That's . . . unappealing.

My phone buzzes in my purse. Long buzzes.

"Who's calling you?" she asks through her tears, and she sounds a little suspicious. Because I'm her mother, and she's here right now, so who else could it possibly be?

But then, that's a fair question, the way my life is going. Who *could* it be?

"Natasha," I guess aloud. "Or spam, maybe?"

"You should look."

I fish my phone out of my eighty-dollar-and-still-really-nice purse. Oh! It's Grant Murphy. I get a jolt of excitement. We haven't talked since I met him last week. Maybe it's a lead on the boat?

"It's the marina," I tell her, not wanting to sound like I have the hots for a boat guy. "I'm trying to sell the boat, you know. Maybe it's news."

"Oooh! Answer it!" The tears over the house seem to have evaporated.

I open the phone. "Hello?"

Grant's voice is rich and lilting. "Hi, is this Becca Ann? It's Grant from Water's Point Marina—you might remember me."

Oh, I remember. "Of course, yes. What's up?"

"I've got an offer on the boat," he lilts. "Over our asking price. Not what I'm used to hearing."

"Oh! That's great news!"

"Five thousand over," he says. The word *thousand* in his accent sounds like "tao-sent." The entire sentence is just pure music to my ears.

"Amazing!" I cry. "Why, you've earned your own commission and then some!"

"Hm," he says. "Well, maybe, maybe not. Gonna need to crane her onto a flatbed, get a hauling company to get her down there, or maybe you hire delivery sailors, though that puts hours on the engine, miles on the sails. Either way, the five thousand is gone in a flash."

"Wait, what? Delivery?" I ask.

"Remember, I said we'd need to look to sell her outside the area? The buyer takes delivery in Miami."

"Oh . . . I see!" Miami. Florida. Thousands of nautical miles away.

"It's expensive. But could be worse—they asked me for Saint Kitts first. I think Miami is better, because you can still overland."

I'm not sure what to say, so I just say, "Oh . . ." again. The logistics of this feel somehow insurmountable. Why, I wonder, does anyone want to own a sailboat?

"We can wait around for a local buyer," Grant says, detecting my concern. "You want to know what I think, though—you should go forward with this deal," he tells me. "Full-price cash offer, plus costs, 'tis pretty unusual. It's in writing, and I've got a statement here showing proof of funds."

I decide to take his well-qualified word for it. "Yes. You're right. Tell them I agree. We can . . . deliver the boat as soon as possible. I . . . this is wonderful news." I am a perfectly capable woman, I remind myself. I can figure out how to move a multiton watercraft from one marina to another.

"Right then," he says. "Though, not necessarily great for me; I would have liked her nearby a bit longer. But certainly it's a good thing for what you wanted."

Poor lovelorn boat guy. He was really into my boat. "Don't forget, Grant, now you'll get paid."

"Well," is all he says back. How does he make that into a complete thought? And what the hell does the complete thought mean?

Sensing that's all he's going to say, I add, "I mean to say thank you."

"Cheers, then. I'll tell him to set up the paperwork for you. I'll look it over too."

"Really, thank you so much."

"My pleasure," he says, "Rebecca." And with that, he disconnects.

I drop my phone and squeal in delight.

"You sold the boat?" Liv asks, and now any last vestiges of sorrow have completely vanished from her eyes.

"I did! It's still ok with you, right?" After that house drama, I am hesitant to take anything for granted.

"Of course it's ok! Better than ok! It's perfect! You can make Dad an offer on our house now! Surely the boat is worth more than whatever Gran put in all those years ago."

My mouth opens, goes dry. That couldn't be further from what I want to do. "I . . . ," I stammer. "You want me to buy the house from Dad?" The one I have cared for throughout my entire marriage, the one I shared with my ex-husband, the one that witnessed our happiest family moments and our most heartbreaking ones as well?

"Of course I do. Then it would really be yours, like you want. And nothing has to change. Promise you will!"

I think of Grant. Of how he uses the word *well* as a complete sentence. Handy, that. "Well," I try.

"Well, nothing. This is so awesome. Screw some stupid fake loft." Liv starts the car. "Let's go get coffee and cake and talk about how you're going to remodel Dad's office into a . . . what? A yoga studio?"

I sigh. Her heart is in the right place, even if her reasoning—and financial understanding of real estate—is highly faulty. She wants her mom to be happy. But at twenty-one, with no kids of her own, how could she ever know what would make me happy? I barely know myself. "It's an office, honey."

"It could be any kind of office, though," she says. "It could be anything you want. It could be a sex dungeon."

I gasp and then laugh, and she laughs, too, and I'm just so damn glad she's not crying anymore that I'm not sure why I ask her what I ask her next. Except I *do* know why I ask. I ask because I'm her mother, and mothers know when their babies are hurt. And when the hurt is not totally about a house. "Honey, who did you think the call would be from? Just now. You wanted me to check my phone. Did you think it would be Dad?"

She is looking for an opening to pull out of her parking spot, but she stops trying and puts her car back into park instead. "Mom. I know it's wrong to want that. I don't know what's the matter with me. I want you to be happy, I really do. But as a kid, I just felt like we all belonged together, and now everything is so weird. You're Mom. He's Dad. Mom, Dad, and me. It's always been that way." Tears fill up her throat. "A few months from now, he'll regret letting you go so much. But then it will be too late . . ."

I don't try to explain to her how many years he's spent without regret. I just put my hand on her back. For the last few months, the divorce has been happening to me. And now, when there's no going back, it's finally happening to my daughter.

It hurts a thousand times worse this way.

I'm not going to cry, too, or if I do, I'm not going to let myself do it now. "It's a hard time," is all I can manage. When she falls over into me and starts to sob again, I repeat myself. "This is a hard time, honey." And in that moment I would give anything to have had my life go a different way.

It is only after five minutes of crying that she finally says what we both believe to be true, deep down inside. What I have held on to all this time. Our family motto, no matter if it's a family of one, two, or three. Heard around our dining table whether we were talking about grieving my mother, surviving a tough case at work, or learning to live with second place in a debate competition at school.

"We can do hard things, right?" she asks me, her voice choked with tears.

"We can do hard things. I promise. We can do anything."

5

I don't know who the big idea hits first: me, Olivia, or Natasha. But of course it is Natasha who takes credit, who calls me at 6:30 a.m. to tell me what I must do, even though the thought, the sparkling little thought, like pixie dust, has already lit all over my mind.

"You've got to sail the boat to Miami yourself!" is what Natasha says when I answer the phone, bleary and confused from sleep.

Since I got the offer yesterday, a thousand thoughts have rushed through my head, and this has been the main one. "I know," I tell her.

"You know?" she says, horrified. "I was prepared for a litany of arguments! You can't sail, you get seasick, you hate baking in the little kitchenette thing—"

"The galley—"

"Right. You hate the galley. You would probably crash into a pirate freighter and be fed to the sharks. It takes too long, you don't have enough money, you're busy not doing anything already, something about window boxes—you keep talking about window boxes."

"Well," I announce, "the window boxes will have to wait a couple of weeks."

"I'm transformed into a human question mark right now," says Natasha.

"I'm going to pack up my stuff—my own stuff—and move out of this depressing house," I tell her. "For now, at least. And then I'm going to ask Olivia to sail to Miami with me. There's a motor on the boat, and she took two semesters of sailing lessons besides. So it'll be fine. I read an entire six-year blog about it last night at two a.m."

As I speak, I realize that I mean what I am saying, and I find myself as shocked as Natasha. Holy cow. I'm going to sail to Miami. Twenty-year-old me would be so proud.

"Whoa," we both say, almost in tandem. She adds, "Are you sure about this?" and I say, "I'm very, very unsure. I only decided while I was talking just now."

Natasha laughs, but it's skittish. "That's quite unlike you."

"Natasha, I am suddenly divorced after twenty-two years of marriage, with a grown child and no job. I feel very unlike me. And yet. Yesterday, I realized that Livvie thinks I'm going to live out the rest of my days as though Alistair and I are still married. Still in this house, still on his payroll. She can't see me doing anything else. I've got to change that."

"It's a nice cushy house," she says. "I haven't read any sailing blogs, but I hear boats are not cushy."

"This boat is pretty cushy. It's a good boat. It's not sink-y, or crash-y, and it has all kinds of conveniences. And consider this: the harbor is full of tipsy yahoos sailing away happily. If they can sail, I'm perfectly able to learn to sail too." As I talk, I feel the excitement building. "I'm going to sail this boat to Miami and save myself thousands of dollars on transporting the damn thing, and then sell it for a life-changing amount of money. And in so doing, I will spend a couple weeks with my beautiful kid, and hold her tight if she cries about the divorce, and make all her favorite foods and sing along to our favorite songs. And just bond the damn hell out of ourselves. We'll get through this transition together, and when we get to Miami, she'll see me in a whole new light—Mom, the sailor, the survivor, the woman who isn't afraid of anything—and be ready to get back into her own big dreams. And also find her own Mr. Right and get to work on three or four grandbabies."

Natasha pauses conspicuously. Finally she says, "That's *some* boat ride. What are you going to do for money?"

"What do you mean for money? Sailing is free! Wind power is the cleanest kind there is!"

Natasha snorts into the phone. "I suspect you may be mistaken. There will be costs. Rich told me that *BOAT* stands for 'break out another thousand.'"

"That's silly. The boat is sitting there in pristine condition with a full tank of diesel, with everything I need except wine already on board. It's got two bedrooms, like a floating hotel, and it has plenty of special toilet paper, and a barely used mainsail ready to go. It even has a roller-furling jib!"

"What is a roller-furling jib?"

"I have no idea. But it's good!"

"Won't you need more fuel? And food? And a place to tie up the boat at night? And money to fly home when you end up in Nova Scotia?"

"I thought you were on team 'sail to Florida'!"

"I was, until you thought it was a good idea. Now I'm taken aback."

I laugh, too excited by this idea to let her get to me. "Natasha, you could be the devil's own devil's advocate. Look. I sold that little black bag with the white stitching on it for a small fortune. It's worth at least three months' worth of rent, groceries, and gas. Or three months of marina fees, tiny cooking implements, and diesel fuel. You'll never believe who bought the purse—an ethics teacher in Pennsylvania. Who's a former nun!"

"A nun bought your Chanel purse? That is weird. I thought handbags like that were for heiresses and traders."

"She asked me for authenticity codes. She knew her stuff. Anyway, it's my ticket outa this joint. Gonna call Liv next so there's no takebacks."

"Wait, really?" Natasha hyperventilates into the phone. "I thought this was such a good idea when I called you. Now I'm worried for you and also realizing the seriousness of my coming muffin drought. When you get back, where will you live and make my muffins?"

"Your basement?" I joke. "No, after we get to Miami, I'll have enough to buy a small house and get started in a nice job." Or enough to ask Alistair to sell me this place at some kind of pity discount to keep Olivia happy, though the very idea makes my heart feel like a brick. "I can start applying while we're sailing, and if I am lucky, I'll have some interviews scheduled the minute we get home. And then, best of all, I'll just be a regular non-Alistair-Larkin's-wife person." I think for a second. "Maybe I'll get a Roomba!"

Natasha laughs. "The Roomba represents regular-person life to you, eh?"

"Beats a regular vacuum, I guess?"

"They're expensive. Just take the vacuum you have."

"It's Alistair's."

"The *vacuum cleaner*?" she asks.

"Yep."

There's a pause on the line. "Becca, has he ever touched it in his life? If we had it examined forensically, would we find so much as a partial print?"

The idea of Alistair vacuuming is comical to even think about. "Everything is his, Natasha. Everything. I was just . . ." I try to think how to explain my glorified housekeeper status over the last several years. "Like, a squatter here. I served at the pleasure of the Larkin family."

"But you know that's not true, right?"

The part of me that knows that's not true is a scary part. An angry seed that, if I water it, could grow into a lifetime of bitterness and pain. So I ignore her. "The fancy Dyson's too big for the boat anyway. The whole point of a boat is no vacuuming, right? And hopefully my next house will be little too. Except for the—"

"Window boxes. Great big sprawling window boxes."

I smile to myself every time I think of them. "It'll be so pretty. Maybe I'll have a porch. For the grandkids."

"The imaginary children of your career-minded twenty-one-year-old unmarried daughter?"

I breathe in the thought. "The last decade of my life has been a long, agonizing slog of 'should I leave Alistair or shouldn't I.' I did, and now I think the next decade will go by in a flash. I think odds are pretty good I'm going to get that admin job at the school district—I know all the players after all those years of volunteering, and with the difficult personalities over there, no one else wants that job. That means I'll be working full time by September. This trip is my last chance to be there for my daughter before I start the rest of my life. Get on board, lady."

Natasha's smile is audible. "Ok. You're doing it!" Another long silence. "I'm going to buy you a life jacket."

"The boat has ten life jackets in the big storage thingy under the seats."

"Arm floaties, then. For you to wear twenty-four seven. Even in your sleep."

"I'm going to have the weirdest tan lines," I joke.

"I hope you're a back sleeper. Oh, Becca, I'll miss you so much. And worry. I'll just worry nonstop till you are back on dry land."

"When I get back I'll bake makeup muffins till you're drowning in simple carbohydrates."

"I'll start job hunting and stalking real estate. You're welcome, by the way, for the great idea."

"Thank you for telling me my own idea so I would see how great it is. Love you."

"Love you back. You're very brave. I can't wait to hear what Liv says about this."

Oh. Liv. Wow. Is there a chance this brilliant plan of mine won't appeal to my daughter? No. She's my friend to the end. My partner in crime—though most of our crimes revolve around ice cream and gab sessions. But still. She said she likes sailing. She said she didn't know what to do with herself this summer if I wasn't in the house. She's the right age for an adventure. "She'll say yes, right?" I ask my friend.

It's quiet long enough that I start to brace myself for a too-honest answer. At last, Natasha says, "She'll say yes. She might even be happy about it. Either way, she'll say yes."

Not what I was hoping to hear. But then, at this point, I'll take what I can get.

6

Never in her life has Natasha been so incredibly wrong about anything as she is wrong about my daughter's interest in sailing *Becky Ann* to Florida. In fact, when I broach the idea, she simply cries, "I WAS HOPING YOU WERE GOING TO ASK!!!" and then says something excited to her roommate and then sort of shouts down the phone, "THE LARKIN GIRLS TAKE TO THE SEA!!!"

So it's official. I download a PDF called "sailing cruiser's must-have list" and proceed to Amazon. After that's done and I'm back to mostly broke again, I get out all the boxes and suitcases I can find. It's now time for the most elemental downsizing of my life—if it doesn't fit in Liv's storage unit or within the lockers of *Becky Ann*, it goes. Hours go by where I do very little packing and quite a bit of abandoning. Goodbye, maternity parka. Why exactly did I keep you? Goodbye, four billion kindergarten artworks that amount to a splotch of paint on scrap paper. Why did they send you home in the first place? And to you, wedding photos, I say . . .

The album falls open. My heart falls open too. Alistair is so handsome. I am really kind of beautiful, compared to what I see in the mirror now. I look like a teenager—and then it hits me that I practically was one. I was younger than Olivia is now. Alistair wears a dark-gray suit and he's dashing and I remember how I adored him, looked up to him, saw the world in his eyes. I'm in a plain silk dress, no veil, but with flowers loosely laced into my hair. Compared to now, our younger selves both look rather casual and earthy. And though I remember feeling a little anxious about our future, in the photos I look very relaxed. Assured even.

Oof. *Close that ish up, Rebecca,* I order myself and push the book away. It's obvious the album should go in the dumpster, but I can't bear to do it. Instead I put it back in its protective case and then place the album carefully on the shelf where it's always been. In its place I pick up my favorite decanter and start a new box. I label it *Mom—bar,* because in my new life, with the window boxes, I intend to drink a very good cocktail from time to time, and the married version of me was someone who could afford to buy quality gin in bulk. I add three unopened bottles of fine spirits, some vermouth, a lot of wadded-up paper, and my favorite glassware. I seal up the box, wondering as I do what its odds of surviving a stint in a college storage unit are.

To which a tiny part of me says, *At least Alistair doesn't get it.*

That part of me is trouble.

That part of me pours a glass of wine around four p.m. that day, with that picture of the young happy couple we once were still fresh in my mind, and chases it by writing *stuff to sell* on a large moving box and stripping the house of things that aren't exactly mine, but not exactly *not* mine either. These are things that weren't named in the settlement, whose individual values aren't more than a couple hundred here or there. But this is a big house, and the box is a big box. I have no trouble finding things to stuff into it. A set of Miyabi Kaizen knives and their block. An impractical Le Creuset crock shaped like a giant artichoke. Taking all the silver seems tacky, but would Alistair ever notice I skimmed the sauce ladle, the hard cheese slicer, the fish server, the iced-tea spoons?

Oh how I love those sterling iced-tea spoons. I move them into the "FOR THE BOAT" box.

The bitter, small part of me drinks another glass of wine and packs up yet more resale-friendly trinkets. A reproduction Tiffany clock from the living room. I'm the only one who ever wound it. Oh, here's a gem: a hideous enamel frog holding an umbrella. Two inches tall, the entire thing, and easily worth a hundred bucks thanks to its collectible pedigree. Thanks, random person who gave it to us for a hostess gift umpteen years ago. I wrap up the frog and glance into the "stuff to sell" box. There's a grand in here easy now, and it's not half-full.

My revenge fire burns a little brighter. What else shall I pack up today?

Alistair is a fine-timepiece guy. He keeps a watch briefcase open in his closet, or he used to—that went with him to his new place. Only the watches that have fallen out of favor remain, forgotten, in a cedar drawer, in our walk-in closet. I steal two of them.

And then three silk ties. A never-opened box with a Canali pocket square inside. I am reaching, tentatively, for an Hermès belt when my phone starts ringing.

It's Alistair.

"Hello?" I answer, guiltily. Tipsily too.

"Do you need money?" he asks me.

"What? No. Why would you think that? I'm just fine." It's not a lie, exactly, as I will be fine once I sell *Becky Ann*.

"Nanny cam in the walk-in," he says.

"What?" In this fog of wine, I cannot make heads or tails of that sentence.

"Put down the Hermès, Rebecca."

My hazy brain clicks and whirrs. I look up, see a little Wi-Fi-enabled camera like the sort that faces out in every direction from under our eaves outside. The belt drops from my hands. Well, this is really embarrassing.

"I was just . . . ," I fumble. My face becomes the heat of the sun, and I cannot think of an excuse, not while I'm simultaneously dying of shame.

"Packing up for your vacation?" he asks. "Liv called and said she was going on a sailing trip. I thought she was trying to piss me off at first, but no, she says you two idiots are really going to sail my boat to Miami."

"My boat," I correct. Slowly I wave my hand and watch the camera eye buzz and move. "How long have you been spying on me?"

"It's on motion-detection setting. So only since . . . ten minutes ago?"

"Are there others? Have you been watching me in bed?" Horrified, I think of the other night. When I came home from the marina and broke out my, ah, personal massager for the first time in a long time.

"No!" he says, outraged at the very accusation. "That would violate your privacy. This is the only one in the house."

"But then . . ." Who bugs his own walk-in closet? "Why?"

"Because I own a lot of nice things, and I thought you might decide to steal them. And it looks like I was correct."

"I wasn't exactly stealing . . ." There's really no good answer for what was happening here. "You told me I could help myself to anything I needed."

"You need a Canali pocket square?" he asks.

I fish around, stammer more, finally land on honesty. "Ok, fine. You caught me. I was fundraising."

"For your sailing trip on my boat."

"No," I tell him honestly. "This is money I'll need to recover from twenty years married to you."

"Ah. I knew the claws would eventually come out. Should have used them during the divorce. Classic move, Becky. Bake a cake, settle for the crumbs, then wonder why you're so hungry."

Deep down, I don't even want crumbs, not if they've come from this marriage. But when the smaller, pettier part of my personality drives the bus (and the bus, to be clear, is fueled by red wine), all I can see is how unfair it all is that Alistair is set for life and I'm starting over after a lifetime in his service. That he owns the house I ran, the ties I took to the cleaner, the ugly frog enamel thing I dusted. And he still owns my daughter's heart, and this one-hundred-and-fifty-dollar pocket square that I am now putting back into his cedar closet delicately, and so much more. A house, apartment, vacation cottage the size of a regional airport. That all I got out of him is a stupid, idiotic boat.

"I can count my regrets while I sail *Becky Ann*," I end up telling him, still looking at the nanny cam.

"You don't know how to sail."

"Guess we'll sink it, then."

"Your plan is to revenge-sink a boat that cost me half a million dollars?"

"Cost *us*," I clarify. "Alistair, I know the money's yours now. I know it was always your family's to start with. But while we were married, I was a Larkin too. I was an equal partner."

"If you really feel that way," he asks me, "why didn't you contest the prenup?"

There is a sadness in the way he says that, almost like he's disappointed in me. Maybe, I realize, he is. Alistair was always conflicted—between the spoils of his family's infamous law practice and his own sense of justice, between the responsibilities to his family of origin and his family of choice. For years, I tried never to put him in a position where he'd have to choose sides. But then, eventually, he chose of his own volition. And he didn't choose me.

"Why did you enforce it?" I volley back. Into the silence that follows, I supply, "To please your parents."

"When you told me you were leaving me, you said you didn't want our dirty money."

Cornered, I hear myself tell him my deepest truth. "What I didn't want was for your money to have gotten so dirty in the first place. Now that it's too late, I'm going to start fresh. With my head held high."

"Starting with some light larceny. Keep that head high, Becky."

Oh, the way he can cut me where it hurts. "Go to hell, Alistair."

"Get out of my closet, Rebecca."

"Maybe I will," I say, reaching for the camera and facing it toward the wall. "Maybe I won't."

"I'll do an inventory, file a motion. You want to pay legal fees over that old ugly belt?"

"Are you sure you ever even owned such an ugly belt?" I ask him. "I don't remember it. It certainly doesn't seem like your style. Did you keep the receipt? Wear it in a photo?"

The thing about being part of a family of top trial lawyers for twenty years: you learn a few things. Things you kind of wish weren't in your emotional vocabulary.

Alistair makes a disgusted sort of grunt. "Oh, ok. Fine. Enjoy your belt, then. Way to hold on to your dignity. Remember that dignity after you've sold off all the nice things I brought into your life—you'll find out just how much those principles cost you. Oh, and Becky?"

"What?" I ask him.

"When I say goodbye this time, I mean it in a whole new way." He clicks off the phone.

I look at the wall, confused for a moment. Does he mean he'll never talk to me again? I didn't really expect to hear from him much anyway, until our daughter's graduation at least. Does he mean I need to get out of his house? Well, fine. That is exactly what I am packing for. After I leave tomorrow, I won't walk through these doors again, no matter how much Liv begs. I won't speak to him again. I won't even acknowledge that he or his money or his overpriced haberdashery pocket square ever so much as existed. Let him "goodbye" me. I will show him goodbye. The wine still driving the bus, I grab my phone to text him exactly that.

But into this head of steam a new text alert comes through. Not Alistair—it's AT&T.

They're so polite. They're helpfully letting me know my phone number and data account have been disconnected as of now at the request of the account holder and it is within my rights to port my number to any new service I desire. With a new two-year contract, I can even reinstate this phone for the low initial fee of three hundred dollars.

Oh crap. That IS a different kind of goodbye. Because of course, though I only realized it just now, even the phone line we just fought on, like everything else I have ever had, actually belongs to Alistair.

7

Life without a husband is pleasant. Life without a cell connection is less so. Thank goodness Alistair leaves on the Wi-Fi—but then, I suppose it powers the nanny cam. Liv ends up coming over twice the next day and three times the day after that, just in case, she says, even though we can text each other any time I'm home, which is always. Each time we load up the back of her car with a little more stuff—not just my things and the sort-of-stolen objects of the home, but the new purchases I've made for the trip—rapid-deploying CO_2 life jackets that are supposed to be comfortable to wear all day long, four grocery sacks of the non-perishables recommended by my new favorite sailing blog, a new first aid kit, two UV-blocking sun shirts, bungie cords, a flashlight on a rope (I shudder to think why I need this), and special bags that keep things dry no matter what. The most expensive thing I buy is a satellite phone converter, which I try not to use on land. Also, a lot of dryer sheets, because mice apparently hate dryer sheets but love boats. I will not mention this to my squeamish daughter, who takes after her squeamish mother. If she asks why our entire boat is wallpapered in Downy, I will make up a lie about static.

There's more, but all of it is small and relatively affordable. The boat itself—its radar system, autopilot, and the "heavy weather" sails that so excited Sexy Sailing Dude—those are the spendy bits. Grateful for what

I have and careful with what I need, I sidestep anything that has the word *marine* in it. Bungie cords, for example, are bungie cords whether you buy them online with free shipping or at the special boat-stuff shop where they cost ten times more. The last thing I pack is something called an "abandon ship" bag. Like the dryer sheets, I keep it to myself. No sense in worrying my daughter, or myself, when all we're doing is bobbing down the coastline. These bags are recommended by people who have traversed the Atlantic or darted through treacherous straits. I never plan to be out of sight of land or out of reach of the coast guard. If clouds so much as form, we'll go back to shore and wait it out. After all, we have three weeks from Saturday to make a trip that—according to the internet, at least—takes only ten days.

When Liv picks me up for the last time at the house, I feel nothing but happy anticipation for what's next. In fact, I feel more like myself than I have in years. That girl who wanted to travel for a living and live out of a suitcase? Well, she's getting her wish at long last. I tuck a postcard I sent myself thirty years ago into my purse for luck and fairly bound into my daughter's car, only to see she has tears in her eyes. I remind her that Alistair told her he won't sell the house until Liv's truly ready, and she shakes her head. "I'm ready, I think. Or I'm not ready, but I see now it's not totally about the house."

So I hug her tightly. "Rarely is heartache ever about real estate," I affirm. "But Dad won't make any moves till you're back on dry land and have a chance to be sure. As for sure . . . are you still up for this trip?"

She nods. "I'm so glad we can do this. Three weeks, no work, no school, no roommates, in the sunshine, just you and me. We're about to become the Gilmore Girls of the high seas." My heart gives a squeeze. That show depicts the pinnacle of mother-daughter friendship. If my little girl thinks of me as half as cool as Lorelei Gilmore, an extra ten years in a bad marriage has all been worth it.

"The food won't be as good," I warn her.

"As Luke's?" she says, referring to the diner in the TV show that the lead characters practically live at.

"As what I usually serve. I don't really do two-foot-square kitchens."

"Oh!" she says and then rummages in a tote bag behind my seat. "That reminds me. My friend Cori, from work-study at the pool, gave me this."

"Concentrate on the road," I say, then wince. Would Lorelei Gilmore say that?

She keeps rummaging. "Have you ever heard of Laurie Colwin?"

I shake my head, and she plops a book in my hand as she drives. "*Home Cooking*," I read aloud.

"Advice on small kitchens," she tells me. "I mean, you don't have to make anything special, but you always love to cook, and I love your food."

"I love to bake," I correct. "I cook so we can eat what I bake afterward."

"Ok, well, you'll have to be cooking on the boat, because you can't sail."

"And you can't cook," I add.

"We'll make a perfect team. How much tonic did you pack?"

"What do you mean, tonic?"

"For gin and tonic. How much? We need a lot. I don't mean to worry you, but I am legal now and have no intention of missing out on the whole point of sailing."

"The whole point of sailing is gin and tonics?"

"Or rum and Cokes."

"I see. I packed neither Coke nor rum."

"I'll go back to that liquor store, then." She immediately moves into the left lane and begins signaling for a U-ey. I grip the door handle and think of the box of small-batch booze that is already stored away in her apartment complex for my someday martinis.

"Ah . . . about the liquor store . . ."

She waves me off. "Come to think of it, are we the sort of people who also drink mojitos on a boat?" she asks me. "Because I already packed everything I need to make those."

"Oh! Yes, we are!" I say, but this line of conversation has begun to worry me. "Hey . . . Liv . . ."

"What?"

"I really, really don't know how to sail, you know that, right? I don't know how to even turn the boat on. I watched some YouTube videos, but it was . . . a lot to take in. I don't know how much mojito time you'll have with such a useless crew member."

She laughs. "Oh Mom. You've had a boat for ten years! You'll be fine."

I panic. It's just now occurring to me how much of the weight of the sailing itself I've mentally entrusted to my mercurial twenty-one-year-old daughter. "Do you know how to start the engine?" I ask her. "Did the boats you used at school have engines?"

Liv rolls her eyes with vigor. "Mom, please. It'll be fine."

My panic only increases. "I think maybe we should make sure we can start the boat before we get into this."

"We're already into this," she tells me.

"Well, we could always delay a week. I'm sure the buyer would understand. I could spend the time taking sailing lessons." Oooh, with Grant Murphy. Why didn't I think of this sooner? "This is actually a great idea. Sailing lessons for me, one more week of summer for you, and then we go. It means more taking turns at the, ah, *helm*, and more time for you to muddle mint leaves. Or sunbathe. Or I don't know. The satellite hookup comes with unlimited Twitter. Do you want to spend a week on Twitter?"

"Mom, I can't take an extra week."

"Why not?"

A long, pregnant pause and then she says, "I gave up my room in the apartment."

I stare at her, shocked. "What? Why? When?"

"Chill, Mom."

I force myself to stop staring. "Chilling . . . but my questions stand."

She sighs like I've asked for state secrets. "I decided last weekend, when you asked me about going on this trip. Katie let me pack my stuff up and put it in her giant closet, and we're renting my room out furnished until school starts again."

"What? Why would you do that?"

"To save money, duh. You're the one who always says I have to remember the true value of money."

"But now you have no place to go!"

"I have the boat. Everything I need is gonna be on the boat."

"We're selling the boat in ten days!"

"Well, you told the buyer three weeks, right? To be on the safe side? So I'm just going to stay in Miami for the extra time. And then I'll come back and couch surf until the semester starts again. Or stay with you, wherever you are. Or . . . I'll stay with Dad."

"Baby. This is really weird. All that trouble to save two months' rent?"

She sort of shakes her head. It's a nonanswer.

"Are you doing this out of worry for me?"

"Kind of?" she says. But not in a "you've got the whole story" kind of way. I wait to see what else is there, and for a moment I have to sit through an uncomfortable silence when what I really want to do is hammer her with questions. Finally she inhales to speak again. "Also, I'm having some roommate problems."

"With Katie and Nicole?" I ask, surprised.

"They are my roommates, yes. And they are kind of ganging up on me."

This takes me utterly by surprise. "Really? Why?"

She shrugs. "I think it's about the Weinoff guy," she says, referring to that odious client Alistair's mother just sprang. "And . . . well, your lawyer gave this interview, I guess. It made things weird."

"What?" Why would a legal interview relate to Olivia? Unless my attorney talked about my case? "I need to see that interview. Right now."

"*Boston Review of Law*," she tells me. "Mom, it might upset you."

"I'm googling . . ."

The headline is enough. It reads, "Larkin Ex-Wife Says She'd 'Rather Be Penniless Than Spend Another Day in Family of Ruthless Defense Lawyers.'"

I scan the rest. It's an inside baseball justification from my lawyer about why she got me nothing in my divorce, strictly a way for her to cover her own ass around other divorce lawyers. The only people who would normally read this would be on the bar, and Alistair knew there'd be something like this in the press. In fact, my lawyer actually tried to threaten him with these stories. Utterly pointless. If this kind of shaming bugged the Larkin family, they wouldn't be representing Larry Weinoff, who sexually assaulted several Olympic figure skaters over the course of twenty years. Or the other rich dirtbag untouchables they now specialize in.

"Katie and Nicole care about this?" I ask Liv, surprised. "How'd they even see it?"

"I dunno. TikTok?" She looks at me. "Did you really say that about Dad and Grandma?"

"I think I did, honey. I thought it was privileged, but now that I think about it, it was in a deposition. I lost my temper. I'm very sorry."

"The girls think I should stop taking money from Dad. They won't . . ." She pauses, clears her throat. "They won't accept my rent payments anymore. They say my money is rapey."

"Ohhhh," I say. That does make sense. I can certainly see their point. At the same time, my heart goes out to Liv. I will never forget having my check returned a few years ago when I decided to channel some of our family's annual giving to a prestigious center for women's advocacy. The center was polite but told me it was simply too dangerous for their image to be attached to us at the present time. I was gutted. "Oh crap. So you didn't move out, exactly. You got evicted."

"They say they'll try to keep the room open for me in September, if I can find another way to make rent."

"That seems really harsh," I say. I try to recall how Nicole and Katie came by their rent checks.

"They say you're an example of living your truth. They think I should do what you did."

"Divorce your father? How exactly does a daughter do that?"

"Well, cut him off. They say that if I continue to be in his life and take his money, I'm basically for sale."

I gasp in anger. "That's not true at all," I say.

"And they think I should stop having Thursday dinners with him so he sees the consequences of his bigotry and woman hating."

"What? Your dad doesn't hate women! Half his colleagues are women, and he has an impeccable reputation with the League of Women Voters and the ACLU. And anyway, why on earth do they think his client choices reflect on you?"

She shrugs. "I'm his daughter."

I sigh. All this time, I've been trying to protect Liv's relationship with her father. To keep her from seeing what I saw in him as he began to change. I've been trying to walk a tightrope between keeping my daughter grounded and preserving all the privilege and status she's so used to. All while I tried to escape the whole mess for myself.

"Have you talked to your father about any of this?"

"No. No way. I have already heard all the 'Foundation of America' lectures on the importance of a good defense attorney to the workings of our court system. Remember when Dad said he was a great patriot? Remember when he shouted 'Whatever happened to "innocent until proven guilty?"' at the Benihana at high school graduation?"

That little scene would be hard to forget. "Gotcha," I say. "Listen, I don't love Larkin and Larkin clients, don't get me wrong, but I think your roommates are being extreme. There's a little bit of mob mentality happening here. Your grandmother may represent Weinoff, but she did not do the terrible things Weinoff is accused of."

"Accused of, my butt. I saw the documentary. It was horrifying."

I inhale sharply. "Ok, yes. It is horrifying."

"He really should rot in jail."

"Maybe so, but that's not how the rules work."

"It would be, if we weren't standing by to get him off. Nicole says Dad should be working in her neighborhood to get people out of jail who have been stuck there for intent to distribute, possession, stuff like that. She says in the time it takes the firm to make sure Weinoff can hurt as many more girls as he wants, they could empty half of Framingham of unjust convictions."

I sigh. This is not a quandary I can answer for Nicole or Katie. And honestly, the hell with Nicole and Katie. They don't know what Liv's life is like. They've never been asked to make these choices. "If they don't want to be your roommates anymore, screw them. I mean, it sucks, it really does, to be held responsible for things you have no control over. But in a few weeks we're going to come back from this trip all tan and happy and ready to start fresh. And maybe you're getting a fresh start, too, babe. Maybe it's time for a new apartment, or even a studio off campus, and some space from people who think they know how you should live your life."

"Outside of Minerva, who lives hours away, they're my best friends."

"They don't seem to be acting like best friends."

"Are they right, though? Should I stop taking Dad's money?"

"Was it ok when it was from both me and Dad?" I ask her.

"Of course it was, then. You were both my parents. That was before you publicly chose destitution over living with Dad."

I want to put my head in my hands. I can tell her, again, I'm not destitute. That there's a huge difference between broke and poor. I can tell her I didn't mean for that comment to be public. I can tell her that being married to someone is different from being born to them. But yes, deep down, I think the money is gross. If it wasn't my daughter here, the girl I've given up so much to take care of, I think I would tell her to walk away from just a tiny bit of the privilege she's born into, and see just how much she can accomplish on her own.

But it's way too late for that. Everything I've done all these years was designed to make sure my daughter had everything she needed in this world to be happy. Even the timing of the divorce was supposed to be about protecting her—we intentionally waited to finalize until after her exams. And now she wants to give away all those advantages because of Nicole and Katie? It's a kick in the teeth.

The anger that has built in me over the years, anger at Alistair and then at myself, is now bleeding over onto my daughter. And it's not a one-way flow. I can feel her stewing at me as well. If I had gone with the status quo, stayed married, stayed quiet, she wouldn't be forced to look at the world in this new way. This uncomfortable way.

I try to take deep breaths. Silence fills up the car. Finally, as we enter the marina lot, I get my head back together and say, "Well, I guess we're sailing tomorrow, then."

"Guess so. And I checked PredictWind. Our weather window is great, so we can try for the crossing, if we want to."

"Oh no. Absolutely not." There are two good ways to get from Maine to Cape Cod, and one of them is to slowly motorsail down the coastline, stopping around Cape Ann for the night and then heading on to Provincetown. The other is to cross straight across the bay, sailing overnight, in the middle of the freaking ocean, and hit Provincetown first thing the next morning. "Abso-freaking-lutely not," I reiterate. "However, I am very glad you're in charge of weather. I easily spent four hours yesterday trying to understand a single forecast."

She laughs. "You're gonna learn so much on this trip, Mom." It sounds like a warning, not a promise.

We park and start loading ourselves up with the last set of essentials for our trip. Maybe I will learn how to understand wind patterns, but it's totally fine with me if I come away with nothing but a big check in my pocket and some quality time with my daughter. I sincerely doubt I'll need to ever get on a sailboat again for the rest of my life.

"Oh, weird!" she gasps as we walk closer to *Becky Ann.* "Oh my god, Mom. That guy. What is he doing on our boat?"

She's out in front of me, laden with bags, her arms too heavy to point. I'm pulling a duffel with rollers that's full of all the fresh groceries for the week it's supposed to take us to get from Maine to Norfolk, Virginia, where a long string of rivers, canals, and inlets form the Intracoastal Waterway—a pathway loaded with cruising amenities every few miles. I peek from behind her and see, to my surprise and maybe a little delight, Grant Murphy, standing on *Becky Ann,* literally swabbing the deck with a long scrub brush.

"Oh I know, Liv. He's crazy hot, isn't he? Like if Thor and Loki had a third brother who was truly related to both."

She turns around and gives me a look that is more outraged than anything I've ever seen on her face before. "Ugh, Mom, you're disgusting."

I blanch. "Sorry? I'm sure he's a very smart person too. He's been a huge help with selling the boat. And, uh, keeping it shipshape," I add, unable to stop myself in time.

"Mom, that guy is not a boat salesman," she tells me. "And you should not be lusting after him. He's from my college. And also, PS, his name is Grant Murphy, and he's my ex-boyfriend."

8

"Grant?" calls Liv.

"Grant?" I echo, stunned. He isn't facing me head-on, so for a second I think, *That can't be him,* though which *him* I mean, I'm not sure. The sexy boat guy to whom I owe a grand? The ex-boyfriend of my twenty-one-year-old daughter? Instantly, I prefer he would be neither.

He turns. He doesn't *look* twenty-one. But . . . he can't be as old as I thought, or Liv wouldn't touch him with a ten-foot pole. "Ach, Olivia?" he asks. I notice she doesn't chide him to call her Liv. "What are you doing here?" Oh, that musical lilting accent. *He's an infant,* I remind myself. Still. I have eyes.

"What am *I* doing here?" she replies, and she sounds sharp, colder than I've ever heard her before, but her embarrassment tell, the red that rises over her collarbones, is blazing. "What are *you* doing here? You said you were teaching this summer. That's what you told the entire class."

He colors too now. It's clear there are no two humans less psyched about running into each other than these two. "I'm . . . ah . . . I haven't had as many sailing students as I hoped." He looks down. "I've been helping in the yard when I'm not teachin'. Odd jobs, here and there."

Olivia is frozen still on the dock at the end of the boat, her loads of bags sliding off her shoulders. I have to stop short to keep from ramming my luggage into her legs. "You *said* you'd be unreachable all summer."

"Well," he says. And I know in an instant: the unspoken part of the sentence, in this case, is that he hoped he would be unreachable, wishes he were unreachable even now. Especially now. An awkward silence falls, and I think, in the romantic comedy that is my daughter's life, this is the time when a mother either utterly mortifies her child or saves the day. The problem is, I don't know how to do the second thing. I'm too busy reconciling the man I found so attractive with the boy who dated my daughter and apparently blew her off. My mental GPS is stuck recalibrating.

Luckily an idea hits before too much more time. I just have to do what Alistair would do. For all his faults, he has always been an amazingly loyal father. I take a deep breath and say, "Liv! You didn't tell me the guy before . . ." My brain goes hunting for the name of someone way hotter and taller than even this guy and retrieves, inexplicably, Manuel. "Manuel was a boat hand. And us with such a big boat to take care of. What a funny coincidence."

"I'm a sailing coach," Grant says to me, looking injured. "I'm an adjunct at the college."

He's my daughter's teacher?! I start to really fume, but I'm determined to hide it. "That's right. Very different," I try to add casually, as though the last time we met hasn't been written in detail on my brain with copious stars and exclamation points. I can feel Liv nodding at me, so I continue. "I never put it together. Probably because she never mentioned you by name." I fake an embarrassed look. "But we are so grateful to you for helping us sell this boat. Manuel doesn't know the first thing about boats, does he, Liv? He's so into his Cessnas. Well, it makes sense, of course. He basically grew up in private jets."

Liv smirks at me. I give her the tiniest, most imperceptible wink and think with pride, *Take that, Lorelei Gilmore.*

I roll the duffel right to the edge of the dock and put my hands up in an exaggerated shrug. "And yet Manuel's so down to earth."

Liv rolls her eyes and smiles contritely at Grant. Already her color is returning to normal. "Mom is the queen of dad jokes, sorry. It's nice to see you, though, ah, Grant," she says, as though sometime between spotting him on the boat and remembering wealthy, handsome Manuel, she forgot his name.

He takes us both in, along with our bags and the groceries, and tilts his head. "Are you taking *Becky Ann* out, then? In all this wind?"

I shake my head and try to remember what the name of Liv's weather app is. "Not today, but Garmin ActiveCaptain says we have a clear weather window tomorrow to head south."

"PredictWind, you mean?" Grant says with a raised brow.

"Right. Still learning," I say, with a modest head shake.

"I thought you didn't want to learn how to sail." If anything, this news seems to cut him deeper than learning of "Manuel."

"That was before my daughter offered to teach me," I say, smiling.

"Are you still selling 'er to that buyer in Florida?" he asks me.

"Oh yes. Definitely. We just . . . decided to do the delivery trip ourselves," I tell him, chin up.

"From here?" he asks.

"Yes."

"To Miami."

I try not to look openly freaked out, although his response is just one more worrisome element of a plan that's looking less brilliant with every passing minute. "Well, it's just the ICW most of the way down," I say casually, like I knew what the Intracoastal Waterway even was before a week ago.

"And Olivia's helming?"

My daughter tries on a casual laugh. "Oh, don't look like that, Grant. You're the one who signed me off for heavy weather." This is news to me, but the pieces are all falling into place. My daughter in the middle of her parents' divorce, a hot teaching assistant at her college, a forbidden fling, an uncomfortable parting, some baggage. It all makes sense now. I don't love it, but I get it.

"Not single-handing, though," he says. He casually canters off the boat, as though there isn't a massive leap between bow and pontoon, as if there isn't a ring of lifelines—stanchions with nylon cording—he has to hop over first. He comes right up to Liv and hauls up the bags she's dropped like he's a bell captain at the Four Seasons. "And never on a boat like this."

"I've been on *Becky Ann* with my dad like, a dozen times in the last couple years," she says. *What? Is that true?*

I pretend that news doesn't cut like a knife. "And we're not offshoring," I say to Grant, to clarify. "We're going to hop down the coast to the cape."

"Or we'll offshore to P-Town," says Liv, and I now get to wonder if I'll be risking my life in the open ocean tomorrow to prove my daughter is over a boat-obsessed crush. "We'll watch the weather."

"Any waves over five feet, you can forget it," he says. "I won't letcha go. I'm going to check your radar. When was the last time you went through your ditch bags?"

Without waiting for an answer, Grant starts hauling our gear over the side of the lifelines and into the cockpit of *Becky Ann*. "I mean, she's ready," he mumbles to himself. "I've seen to that myself. I thought you'd have 'er delivered, though," he carries on. "By professionals. It's a long trip."

I'm not sure if he's talking to himself or us, so I just let him put things on the boat for us. I've clambered up on it each day we've been here, loading it with the canned goods and extra propane and diesel, checking for flares and tools, stocking the chart table and setting up the sat phone. But this is the first time I've seen Grant—presumably he's been off teaching or fixing or whatever. And maybe he hasn't been down below and seen the stack of feminine throw pillows we added to the fore and aft berths, the odor-absorbing gel pearls I liberally placed all over the head and by the inboard engine, or the six open boxes of Downy dryer sheets that have hopefully been scaring off any rodents like, well, rats off a ship.

Hey. Liv is right. I do lean toward dad jokes.

Now Grant is up in the big locker under one of the port side benches—starboard? No, definitely port, because four letters in *left* and *port*—fishing around for something. He pulls it out. "The Lifesling is supposed to be on an aft stanchion at all times," he lectures me. I have the word *Lifesling?* scrawled on my checklist for tonight, so I thank him for handing it to me and get to work affixing it with huge built-in Velcro straps to the back of the boat. He takes it from me. "You need to make sure it's loaded, ready. If there's a man overboard, you won't want to pull it out and find a frayed line."

Oh. That's what a Lifesling is for. Good lord. This sailing business is such a sketchy hobby.

"Don't go overboard, Liv," I call to her as she launches herself onto the boat and starts skittering over the top of the cabin merrily.

"I'll try not to!" she calls back. Grant looks green at our casual joking. I duly unfold the Lifesling and read the instructions inside. It, like everything so far I've learned about on the sailboat, is an ingeniously simple piece of equipment that would cost a fortune to replace. This is just a floating cushion that you throw at a person who has, ah, lost hold of the ship. Then a big yellow line flies out behind the sling, and there's some dye that stains the water so it's easy to spot the lost person.

Grant eyes me firmly when I finish the inspection and restrap the white vinyl pouch to the metal post. "You can use the winches," he says. "If the victim is unconscious. To haul them back into the boat."

"Why would someone be unconscious when they fall off the boat?" I ask. "What kind of trip are we talking about here?" I mean, there's mojitos in the plans, not roofies.

Grant only pats the boom, the long horizontal bar that holds the base of the mainsail over the cockpit and swings from side to side, and says, "Things happen when you're sailing." Except it sounds like "tings." I am extremely grateful that his accent is so thick that I can focus on the way he makes such ominous declarations rather than the meaning behind them.

"Grant, you're freaking out my mom," scolds Liv.

I force a smile. "I'm ok. Tons of people do this trip every year, in both directions, and they're fine. I even watched a couple on YouTube who bought their boat without actually being aboard one before. They made it south while holding cameras the entire time! And we're not going anywhere far from help or outside the reach of my sat phone." Then I turn to Grant. "And remember, you said the Black Watch was the perfect boat to learn on, because of the twin helms." I still don't understand entirely what this means, but he nods curtly and seems to settle down a bit.

"I think if you have everything you need, and the lifeboat and the ditch bag are set, and the radar is working, and you don't run aground too many times in the ICW, you'll be ok."

"Run aground?" I ask him.

"When you do, just call TowBoatUS. Number's on all the ICW charts. They sell bulk packages. Draft like this, it's pretty much a sure thing you'll be needing them more than once."

Liv pops up from the companionway. "Aren't we supposed to hoist the main and use the wind pressure on the sail to tip the boat on her side if we run aground?" she asks Grant. "That's what was on the test."

"Call for a tow," he says, with finality. I must be the one turning green now, because he adds, "And I'm sure it'll be fine; maybe the tides will cooperate. You can call me anytime, Rebecca. Keep your phones charged."

I feel so nervous now I can't stop myself from acting cheesy. "Aye-aye," I say, and Liv rolls her eyes again. Grant disembarks—another easy leap, like a water-faring version of a mountain goat—and gives us an awkward wave.

"I'll be leaving you to it, then," he says.

I smile at him and give him a little wave back, but I can't wait for him to be gone. There is so much to do to be ready to make this trip tomorrow, and now, thanks to Grant's cautions, I feel pretty sure that no matter what, we'll never be truly ready at all.

9

Sailors are obsessed with weather. And the moment we finish motoring out of the marina the next morning, Liv deftly piloting, me doing a job we'll just call "jumping around with many ropes" for now, and try to hoist our mainsail, that's the moment I join the obsession.

Hoisting's not easy. It takes me kind of throwing my body weight toward the boat while I yank a thick red-and-white rope and crank the winch handle, then yank some more, to try to get the mainsail to rise up the mast. It catches in places, probably from disuse, and the rope—the line, or sheet, maybe, I've got to start with the lingo now—almost seems to stretch the nearer the sail comes to the top of the mast. Already my hands hurt and I feel queasy. At last, Liv calls from the helm that I've got it, so I wind the extra line around a cleat and then a different cleat to be extra sure.

Then she starts showing me the things I need to know to helm, because hoisting up the reefed jib, the front sail, which we'll eventually unfurl and position on either side of the boat, depending on the direction of the wind, is for pros, apparently. Both sails are giant triangles, just like in a child's drawing of a sailboat, but the mainsail is connected both to the mast and the boom, with only one free edge that fills with wind very quickly when Liv does something in the cockpit to adjust the position of the boom. The jib, on the other hand, runs up a stay in the front of the boat and is otherwise attached by lines only, one running through a loop at the top of the triangle, and one on the far corner that runs back to the cockpit through a series of doohickeys attached to the roof of the living area below. It's a lot to take in, but it all runs consistent to the ten hours of "sailing for dummies" videos I watched last week.

Once I am at the helm and confident with pointing the boat head to wind, using any number of different instruments, then Liv clambers to the front of the boat and clips and unclips things and runs lines and sheets and whatnot, and the next thing I know we're cohoisting the jib. I forget to steer, and the jib starts flapping madly in the breeze, and Liv shouts, "MOM, HEAD TO WIND," and I point the boat in the right direction again, and then, holy cow, the jib fills up sideways, like a flag in the wind. Liv starts yanking on a rope—sheet, line, I don't know, it just looks like a rope to me—and boom, we are underway. Sailing. In a straight line. On wind power. Amazing.

In a few moments, when Liv feels it's set just right, she wraps the jib sheet around a beautiful shiny winch and then tails it off on that special cleat Grant said was a big plus, and joins me again at the helm, arms open for a massive hug. "Great job, Mom!" she cries. "You did it!"

I take my first deep breath in maybe half an hour. Just the time it takes me to breathe causes us to go off course. "Ok, keep steering," she reminds me, gently.

"This is so hard," I admit. I'm trying not to scream from the anxiety building up inside me. There are so many needles and readings on the screens in front of me. And the wind doesn't seem to hold still. Every time I think, ok, we're going in a straight line now, Liv points out the sails backing—losing their air or even getting air fill from the wrong direction. I have to keep adjusting our direction constantly. I have to cope with these little gusts and try not to fall over sideways as the boat heels more and more to one side. I have to not throw up from nerves or the strange sensation under my feet, both a rock and a twist on every wave. An hour passes like five minutes, and I still can't tell what to do when the wind shifts even slightly. Every muscle in my body, including and especially my jaw, is set tight.

"Isn't it great?" says Liv excitedly into my distress. She opens her arms wide. "The wind in our sails, the quiet majesty, nothing but sea and sun and surf. I'm going to go make us coffee. With some Baileys maybe."

My stomach lurches. "None for me, thanks."

"Your loss. While I'm gone, keep pointing toward that headland," she tells me, gesturing at a lump of land that looks the same as all the other land over to my right. I try to burn its particular shape into my brain and keep checking back on it to be sure it's in the same spot as I left it. The rest of the time I glue my eyes to the dials that tell me we are going four and a half knots, just slightly faster than we could motor in the crowded marina—a speed that, if I understand nautical miles correctly, will have us arriving into Miami shortly before Christmas.

Liv disappears down the companionway into the galley. I'm proud of how quickly I outfitted it to have all the necessities and how many downright edible-sounding meals I have planned. I was tempted to buy one of those survivalist buckets at Costco and just rehydrate all our food for the next two weeks, but when I looked into it, I realized that lovely meals of oats and dried fruits, mixed salads with jarred artichokes, bread topped with Italian tuna, and plates of sausage and hard cheese would do us much better and be about as easy. There's a little oven on board, and the temperature and humidity in the galley are just right for no-knead bread, so Liv should be enjoying the sweet yeasty smell of rising dough even now. We have what should be an eight-hour sail ahead of us, and then we'll be dining on a bread board, fresh pickles, and a special cheese assortment I picked out just for our embarkation day.

Eight hours, I reassure myself. That's all I have to do today. Survive eight hours.

Eight hours bobbing on the ocean with a death grip on the helm, a queasy feeling, and . . . is it going to rain?

"Liv!" I call when I feel like she's been down below for three hours. "Are you drunk already?"

"Coming up!"

With relief I see my clear-headed, pink-cheeked daughter bound up the stairs effortlessly, though they are heeling with the rest of the boat and me. "Thank god you're back. I don't think the boat's moving fast enough. And is that rope supposed to be there?" I gesture to a string of line that seems to have appeared out of nowhere attached to the boom, and, as far as I can tell, nothing else.

"Mom, keep steering!" Liv says. I look ahead, and panic, and right the wheel jerkily. Liv sighs and shakes her head. "You're doing good, Mom, but don't stop steering until we get the autopilot set up."

"The autopilot!" I cheer. "Oh thank goodness. Eight more hours of this would kill me."

"Try ten," she says.

"What? We've been sailing forEVER," I say.

"It's nine in the morning, Mom," says Liv, delighted. "We've only been gone for an hour and a half. And there's not much wind, which is why we're so flat and sailing is so easy."

"So easy," I say, shaking my head in disbelief. "So, so easy." I pinch my jaw together tight to stave off impending stress tears.

"Mom, are you ok?"

"I think?" I admit when it's safe for me to speak. "This is really hard. What if I have to pee, or eat?"

"Or tack," she adds, ominously. Tacking, I vaguely remember, is the way you change directions on a sailboat, or what you do if the wind changes directions on you. It looked like a cinch in the videos, but then, so did sailing in a straight line, and here I am. "No," Liv reassures me. "It will get easier. It's like driving. It'll start to feel more natural. And we'll take turns."

"Will I stop feeling barfy?" I ask her.

"You feel barfy already?" she asks me. "And you're watching the headland?"

"I guess? I am also watching the four thousand things going on these screens," I say, gesturing to the equipment. "Depth, radar, the hawk, the compass, boat speed, and wind speed, and I don't know what that one is."

Liv peers at it and says, "Yeah, me neither, so don't worry about it."

My body floods with worry.

"Mostly look out of the boat. Look at the telltales." She gestures at little snippets of yarn coming off parts of the sails that I'm supposed to use to read the wind. They're useless.

"These supposed 'telltales' aren't telling me anything at all. Except maybe, 'Rebecca, don't barf. Don't barf, Rebecca.'"

Liv grimaces. "Maybe you should take those seasickness meds you got. Just get in front of it now. And maybe we should reconsider our crossing plans. If you feel like we're going slowly, there's a fix for that."

"We are going slowly. It's not a feeling. It's a fact."

"Bad news, Mom. Sailing is going nowhere, slowly, and at great expense," she says to me blithely.

I blink at her. "You're telling me this now?"

She shrugs. "I saw it on a tote bag in the ship store. I thought you'd get a kick out of it."

"Hilarious," I say flatly.

"Look, I did the charting for both routes. We can keep to the coast, like we planned, and sail another ten hours at this speed. Or we can run farther offshore, find the wind, and shoot straight down to Provincetown tonight, skip an entire day of this."

I look at her.

"And," she says, "once we get offshore, we can get the autopilot going."

"Ok, yes," I say instantly. "Fine. Let's do that. Show me the charts."

10

Spoiler alert: we don't die that night. We just think we're going to.
Twice.

First, when night begins to fall, and we realize what it means to
sail in the dark. Though there is not much of anything on the weather
radar, the sky is just overcast enough that sixteen hours away from our
launch spot in beautiful coastal Maine, we can see nothing in any single
direction. No stars, no moon, no other boats. Just the tiny lights on
our mast and bow and the backlit screens on the instruments, plus the
pale white of our sails. It's romantic for about half an hour, and then I
spend too long gazing out on that interminable ocean and it becomes
horrifying. What's in there? The water is deepest dark, but not dark as
night. It's dark as squeezed-tight eyelids. Dark like tar burbling, like evil
brewing. It's the color of the inside of a nightmare.

"Are there dementors in there?" I ask my daughter. "Or maybe the
kraken? How much warning do you get before a kraken comes out of
the water and eats your ship?"

Liv laughs at me. "Any warning at all is more than you need. It's
not like you win against the kraken. Better it just comes up and devours
you before you know what is even happening."

"Unless King Kong is around. Or Godzilla. They would save us."

"We are miles from the nearest friendly megamonster outpost, if I understand their land habits correctly," says Liv.

I shake my head warily. "The thing is, whatever's in that primordial soup, it's worse than a kraken," I tell her. "Krakens are one-bite eaters. Sharks take off your limbs one by one. A giant squid could suck out your brains while you're still alive."

"God, Mom, stop watching the Discovery Channel," says Liv. "No one is sucking out your brains tonight. Should we watch a nice rom-com and get your head out of the twilight zone?"

"I downloaded *Moana*," I tell her. "I thought it would be cute. But sailing at night is NOT like it is in a Disney movie."

"No, it's better!" she says. "Look around! There's nothing! It's just you and me and the wind. Like," she raises her hands out wide and searches for the right words.

"Like the *Titanic*?"

She throws her seat cushion at me.

"How much farther do we have to go?" I ask her.

Liv examines the autopilot and GPS system. Then she makes a face. "Not that much longer," she tells me.

"More than four hours?" I ask her.

"More than twelve," she slowly admits.

"OH MY GOD," I say. "I thought we were taking a shortcut!"

"Sailing can be unpredictable," Liv says, as though that's not obvious by now.

Several times I have been assured by both internet influencers and my own flesh-and-blood daughter that sailing would become as automatic as driving a car. And while I have no complaints about all the bells and whistles on this expensive vessel of mine, I am hardly about to swing by a drive-through for coffee and egg bites while dazzling myself with my *Hamilton* solos and flossing at the same time.

And yes, I can do all those things in a car.

Over the hours, Liv has mostly been taking charge of trimming the sails to keep our speed reasonable, and we tacked twice when wind changes made it necessary, but the original agreement—she sails, I cook—is already a distant memory. It's simply not practical for me to act like rail fluff. When Liv went down below for a nap midday and I was supposed to be doing the sailing, I actually may have turned the motor on once I knew she was asleep so we kept making good time. And then later, when she was awake again, every time I had to go to the bathroom—the head, I guess we call it now—I would come up feeling queasy and disoriented and need a handful of strong ginger candy before I could look away from the horizon. Oh, and here's a fun surprise if you're not a sailor yet. The boat is always crooked. Always. There is not a time when you are sailing and the deck underneath you is flat. It's either all leaning to the left, or all leaning to the right, and you must become a mountain goat, scrabbling around trying to get to the thing you need, be it a winch handle (for some reason you can't just leave these in the winches; you have to take them and stow them every single damn time you're done) or a mojito. When dinner arrives, the elaborate bread board and salade Niçoise I planned quickly becomes cold Italian tuna out of a can with olives and some crackers.

Also, though Liv seems to think nothing of it, this boat seems in constant danger of sustaining damage. We had to kick one of the cleat levers with our shoes to get it to open and then stomp on it from the top to shut it again. There's a spot where a line of some kind—I just learned the word *halyard*, so let's call it a halyard—goes *inside* the sixty-three-foot mast and disappears to who knows where, and we almost lost the whole rope—why can't we just call it a rope?—in what amounts to a huge metal sleeve forever.

When I ask her what we would have done if we hadn't caught that line in time, Liv says, "Remember that time when you rethreaded my orange string bikini bottom with a safety pin and a free hour? It'd have to be kind of like that, I guess?" There's a very big difference between the inches of fabric on that stupid swimsuit and sixty-three feet of aluminum mast towering into the sky above an ocean as vast and unknowable as the dark web. Liv has to know that, right? No one else is coming behind us to fix our problems. We are utterly on our own.

But despite—or maybe because of—her lack of understanding what we're up against, Liv keeps her wits. She makes one close save after another. She keeps a keen eye on the instruments and finds their readings satisfactory, and hooks up the autopilot and keeps us on course. When she catches me yawning—sea air, nausea, panic, and being crooked all the time is an exhausting combination—she gives herself first watch and tells me she'll wake me in four hours. "Don't worry, Mom," she tells me. "I have hours of amazing true-crime podcasts I want to listen to."

As the mom here, I feel I should protest a lot more, or at least suggest a milder subject matter, but I'm just too grateful to get a break. I go down below to my berth, which, while charming in the marina, is now, you guessed it, crooked. I lie down and roll into the corner where the bed meets the vinyl wall. Cozy. I close my eyes for a second, only to find I've slept straight through my break, waking for a few seconds when I feel my body sliding to the other corner of the bed, where I remain wedged until my phone alarm goes off.

Two in the morning. The last time I got out of bed at two in the morning, it was to change diapers.

I come up the companionway yawning, eyes still mostly closed. "It's me," I say. "I sail the boat now."

Part of me hopes Livvie will send me back down to the bed again or declare me unfit to do this alone. I *am* unfit to do this alone, and I don't know if I would have even taken this trip on if I knew I would have to try. But she just yawns back at me and says, "Thank goodness. I'm wrecked." She goes down below without giving me any kind of instructions, and I go right from half-asleep to panicked. What am I doing? What happened to puttering down the coastline and sleeping at a deluxe marina every night? What happened to the mother-daughter vacation and nights watching our favorite movies in the galley while sipping wine and sampling the selection of fine cheeses I brought along? Did I seriously bring a pedicure set on this trip?

A memory pops into my head. That first overseas trip I took with Alistair. How I packed for two weeks in an underseat carry-on and learned to drive a stick shift because it was all the car rental place had, and strapped little baby Olivia into a baby carrier so I could hike her up into the Alpine cloudscape and show her just how limitless the world could be. That was me. The intrepid traveler. And I'm an intrepid sailor now. A single middle-aged woman, sure. A single middle-aged woman, divorced, penniless, with a grown child, who is a sailor. That is me.

My panic is unconvinced.

But autopilot is set, and all I have to do is look out for things, right?

I stand at the helm and try to see whatever it is I'm on the lookout for in the thick slurry of nighttime all around me. I give myself some gentle affirmations, then some firmer ones as my worry grows. My mind fills with disasters that could happen, real and imaginary. Capsizing the boat. A perfect storm. Angering a giant white whale. I don't even know what to do if the sails backfill while we're on autopilot and I'm alone. Do I override the GPS and steer a different direction to get more wind? Or pull on one of the sheets to move the boom? Earlier today, the jib got caught flapping on one of the lifelines, and I nearly had a stroke until Liv went to the front of the boat and skirted it. If I had to climb up to the front of the boat, which is currently at about sixty degrees off level, and wrestle with a giant flapping sail with hundreds of pounds of wind pressure, I am quite sure I would end up in the briny depths. And Liv would be sleeping. I would just die then. In the water. With no one for miles.

Just as I think I might maybe start crying from stress, I hear my daughter coming back up to the cockpit.

"Olivia?" I ask her, trying to fake competence. "You're supposed to be asleep." If I have to stand out here in the pure darkness all alone, without Maui played by the Rock, or George Clooney, or even Gregory Peck for company, she sure as shit had better be sleeping while I do it. I am about to tell her this when she reveals her duvet cover, an extra pillow, and a thermal mug.

"Coffee for you," she says. "Bedding for me. I'm sleeping up here."

I do earnestly start to cry then, just from relief.

Liv rolls her eyes. "Mom. Settle down. You're ok."

"I'm not ok," I admit to her. "I'm really scared. This was a bad idea."

"You're doing awesome, Mom. You've only been sailing for one day, you're tired, and you don't know what you're capable of yet," she tells me. She sounds like my mother. No—my mom, who worked her whole life as a hairdresser at an assisted living center, would never have tried anything like this. She wouldn't take left turns when driving if she could avoid it. If there had been, by some miracle, a chance to hike me up into the clouds, she would have told me firmly that my place was two feet on the ground. Liv sounds, actually, just like *me*. My heart swells.

"Livvie," I say, and thankfully she doesn't correct me when I use her old nickname. "This is a lot we took on."

"Nah, Mom," she says. "We just have eight more hours to go. Eight hours of sailing. That's all we have to do now, and then we'll be on the cape. Eight hours is a long time, but we can do hard things. Remember?"

I nod, choked up. "Oh sweetheart. You're going to be an incredible mother," I tell her.

"Maybe later, Mom," she says as she yawns again and stretches out as best she can on the low side bench of the cockpit, then rolls into the inside edge to get some sleep.

The minutes pass. Liv's features relax into sleep, and her hair forms a pretty strawberry-gold halo around her. She looks like a warrior goddess painted by an old master. I think of the pure displeasure I saw on her face when she first noticed Grant, and shake my head. He may be gorgeous, but he's a moron for passing up this girl, this brilliant, capable girl. A girl who would sail a yacht through the open sea after just two semesters of lessons. Who can toast her own parents' divorce with a shrug and a smile. Or consider walking away from every privilege she's been born into. How many trust fund babies out there would be contemplating giving it all up, starting from scratch, couch surfing even, to show what she can do?

How did I even make this fearless creature?

I think of the ten years I spent toughing out my marriage. Watching Alistair fall into the trap laid by his family legacy . . . and doing everything I could to keep Liv away from all that. It was a sacrifice. But a sacrifice born not just of selflessness but also of fear. In my shoes, Olivia would have shown a husband like Alistair out the door with the first transgression, not the hundredth. She's just so incredibly different from me. So daring, so fearless. I want to be that fearless, somehow. I want . . .

What do I want?

I think of what comes next for me, now that I'm not a Larkin anymore.

Who am I now? At this moment, I'm a frightened middle-aged woman trapped on a boat. But in a couple of weeks I'll be untethered. Loose. My mother is gone, my old friends largely social media connections. The only vestige of my old life will be Olivia. Without her, I'd be utterly alone and utterly without purpose. The thought is terrifying.

But I don't have to be without her, I remind myself. It'll be a little like this long dark night, where though I am piloting alone, she's wrapped up in a duvet just within earshot. Or it will be, as long as I don't screw it up. And I won't. I won't push too hard, or pry about why she dated her sailing teacher, or try to tell her what to do about her roommates, or mention grandchildren.

It's time for me to let her be whomever she is going to be.

I reach over to pull her duvet up over her shoulders in the chilly night. If she wakes up, she'll be weirded out, but sleeping, I am at liberty to stare at her and ruminate about the future. After all, I have nothing else I need to be—

I hear a beeping. What does the beeping mean? I try to remember. Oh no. Oh no no no.

In the distance, but not the far-enough distance, I see something. Something so enormous, my first thought is literally *ICEBERG*. Then my second thought is that we are all going to die. Me, Liv, and everyone on what must be a fifteen-story cruise ship that is now sounding the world's most enormous horn in what can only be described as the universal signal for:

GET OUT OF THE WAY BEFORE I CRUSH YOU, YOU MORON.

11

I curse. Very loudly. Liv sits up on her bench, shakes the sleep away, and curses too. "Mom! Mom you're about to—"

"I KNOW!" I shout. And then:

"WHAT DO I DO?"

"OH MY GOD I'M SO SORRY!"

"ARE WE GOING TO DIE?"

Liv is up in an instant and pushes me away from the helm firmly. "Get ready to tack," she says. "Get over on the high side, no, over there, yes. Grab the winch handle. Get ready to let the jib sheet off. When I say go. Are you ready? Ok, let it off!" I pull the sheet loose, and it yanks through my hands violently, burning the skin as it runs. The jib begins to flap madly in the wind, basically a sail version of what I would be doing if I wasn't trying to follow Liv's instructions to the letter.

"Ok, now get on the low side," she says, and I realize she is somehow holding the starboard-side jib sheet with one hand while she steers and is handing that rope to me, and after I clumsily struggle to the other winch, I wrap it twice, three times around the winch on that side of the boat. And then she shouts again, "JUST CRANK IT, MOM," and I put the handle in the winch and go to town around and around what feels like a hundred times until she says stop. "That's it!" Liv cries. And then I hear the motor start up and we are slicing sideways out of the way of the cruise ship, just from the front of their bow to the left, which is east, which is open ocean, and the sun is beginning to peek up over the edge of it now, and we are out of the way but still so freaking close, and now the boat is rocking madly from the massive wake, which we must take on best we can under the circumstances. The boat churns, my stomach churns, and I stare in horror at what almost just happened.

A gust of wind comes up, flaps the sails, and grabs hold of all of Liv's bedding from the cockpit, now the high side, and carries it into the water.

Oh crap.

When the danger has passed, Liv puts her head into her hands. My entire body starts shaking uncontrollably. I feel like I can actually see all forty feet of *Becky Ann* churned under the cruise ship, splintered to pieces, and it's on replay over and over again in the low dawn light. If Liv told me we were dead right now, I think I would believe her. I gingerly lift up my vibrating body and grab hold of a metal grab bar so I can wrap my arms around her. We're alive, I tell myself.

She hugs back for dear life, and when she finally pulls back, I see how shaken she is too.

"Did you almost steer us into a cruise ship?" she asks me.

I stare at her in horror, my eyes the only thing on my body I can seem to keep still. "Yes. Well, the autopilot did. And the radar was beeping too. I just didn't know what it meant. Oh god."

There is a long quiet.

"You are very bad at keeping watch."

I force myself to breathe. "I was so distracted!" *How did I get so distracted?* "I was thinking about how cool you are," I tell her, honestly. "About how well you rolled with that whole awkward Grant Murphy situation, and then about your hair and the future and whether I packed enough protein and if you were warm enough, and next thing I know . . ."

"Massive cruise ship directly in front of you?"

"I didn't see it!"

"It's a floating Vegas hotel!"

"It was dark! And . . . I wasn't looking," I admit. "I'm sorry. It's so late, and I am so new at this." Don't cry again, I command myself. You are the adult here. "And your hair is very shiny," I joke lamely.

"You can borrow my conditioner. You can have anything you want of mine, just don't run into any more boats, ok? Deal?"

"Are we ready to laugh about this already?" I ask her, unable to tell if Liv is furious or teasing. Physiologically, I'm still having a nervous breakdown, but Liv is very resilient.

It's resilience, not obliviousness, right?

"We might as well." She shrugs. "I mean, we're ok. We scared the crap out of a cruise ship pilot, probably, and gave him a lot to say in his logbook. But we're ok. Didn't even damage anything."

The integrity of *Becky Ann* hasn't even occurred to me in this crisis. Not once. "Who cares about damage?"

"Mom, the whole point of this trip is to get her to Miami without a scratch."

"Olivia, I don't actually give a shit, pardon my language, about *Becky Ann* or her scratches." I sit down heavily in the cockpit, adrenaline draining away and leaving me empty. "The boat is just a thing, the money just money. The whole point of this trip is to spend some time with you. And then I almost got us both killed."

My daughter tilts her head at me, still at the helm. She opens her mouth to speak and then seems to chew her words back into her brain. I know what to do now. Wait.

"We've got to get back on course," she says. "Don't talk to me while I try to figure out the chart plotter."

I wasn't talking anyway. I look out over the dawn sea.

When Livvie was twelve and finally allowed to be in the front seat of my car, we were bulleting down I-95 around Newburyport, chatting away, when I realized I'd almost missed our exit. I can't even remember where we were going that day. For some reason I'll never understand, I tried to make it from the right lane to the exit lane after the dotted line had gone solid, only to realize there was a semi already where I needed to be, and the lane I was in was about to end, replaced by a barrier on an overpass and loose gravel on the shoulder. There were orange barrels that kept me from merging properly back onto the freeway. We were doing seventy-five, aiming at the bridge, and my life started to actually scroll past my eyes. But at the same time, my foot was on the brake, I was steering into the skid, I was doing everything right after I had done something very wrong. We slid to a stop ten feet before the barrier that would have crumpled my car, maybe flipped us over the edge of the overpass. The whole accident was so smooth and almost, I don't know, slow, I guess, that Livvie didn't actually notice anything was wrong for a beat. My evasive driving was so automatic that somehow we didn't even trigger the airbags, and there were two feet on both sides of the car for the traffic to barrel past us as I sat there, wide eyed, panting. Somehow, I have no idea how, I had turned on my hazards, deployed the emergency brake, done everything with the same brain that was also planning for my own death. And I remain convinced: that capacity was entirely from having my kid in the car. I could have done anything, *anything*, to save her.

I remember waiting a long time, finding an opening in the traffic, and merging, hazards left on until the next exit. Then, again I know not how, driving us to our destination. A tennis tournament, maybe? Yes, because once I got there, I went into the clubhouse and dry heaved for thirty minutes. And Minerva found me there, and she got her mom, and Natasha held me while I cried in the ladies' bathroom, and it was only much later that Liv even asked me if something was wrong.

I remember asking a sixteen-year-old junior coach to drive my car back home that night, and Liv and I riding in the back of Natasha's Audi, and how I couldn't eat for a couple of days after that, and I lay awake, imagining Liv having to live without me, or worse. The opposite.

And then, waking up near dawn on day three after the near miss, exhausted and having given in to the urge to sleep on Livvie's floor, one hand on her body while she slept oblivious, and thinking, as my body awoke, *Ok. We're still alive. Let's get on with it. Maybe a bowl of cereal.*

Now, the sky is about the same color as it was that day long ago. It's a pink tinged with gray-blue, the sun a pinprick through the clouds just on the horizon. The ocean is still opaque and tarlike, but here and there, there are strips of light bouncing off the waves, reflecting into my eyes almost too brightly. Olivia is wedged between the port-side wheel and the equipment tower on the high side, poking at the screen to get our chart amended. I am on the fiberglass bench in front of her, on the low side, letting gravity pull me and my heart rate down and down. And I want, more than anything, a bowl of cereal.

"I'm going down to get us breakfast," I tell her after a long quiet. "And I'm moving my duvet and pillow to your berth so you can get some more rest."

"Mom," says Liv, before I even move. "I don't think I can eat. Or sleep."

I nod, understanding completely. "Then I won't either," I tell her.

Her eyes are watery, and I give her my bravest half smile. She's going to talk now. I can feel it.

"I love you, Mom. Even though you almost killed us just now."

"I love you, too, honey."

"But . . . that thing you said, about us spending time together . . . after this trip, I will always try to be there for you, but I can't be your whole life anymore."

Now the tears threaten again, and I swallow hard. Am I choked up because of what my daughter just told me or because she felt she had to? "There are two sides of me, Livvie," I tell her, forgetting not to call her that. "A mother side and a woman side. Sometimes transitioning back and forth between them is"—I fish around for the right word—"clunky. But you'll see, soon enough, that I can handle myself just fine. Think of what it took for me to leave my marriage. Or how I just did a successful tack for the first time in my life, while in the middle of a crisis."

Liv shakes her head at me. "You came out of that marriage with nothing. You survived the tack because I was shouting orders. You've had three months to figure out what you're going to do with yourself next, and you're still at square one."

I try not to let her words burn me, even though they sound eerily similar to something Alistair would say. "I have a plan," I tell her as calmly as I can.

"A house next to my apartment?"

"Or a few doors down," I lamely joke, desperate to lighten the mood.

"That's not a plan, Mom. Your whole life you've had everything you want or need taken care of. Dad's been paying all your bills like a . . . like a child."

I inhale sharply. At first I'm drowning in the hurt and betrayal. How can she think these things about me? How can she not see what it took to stay in that marriage, to slog through all those hurts and disappointments, just so that she would have a chance at something better?

Then my mom brain sends out a Lifesling. I put my hand over Liv's on the helm. "Baby. Are we talking about me right now, or you?"

Her eyes dart away from me, ashamed.

"Is this about what happened with your roommates?" I ask, sensing now might be an ok time. "Or with Grant Murphy?" I ask her.

"It's like you said," she tells me. "I dumped him for Manuel the zillionaire jet pilot."

I let out a laugh that's also a sigh. "We'll talk about it when you're ready?" I ask her, because even with that terrible shock, I still remember the kind of mother I've resolved to be.

She nods, wearier than any twentysomething should be. "After a good sleep in Provincetown."

"Which will be when?"

She tilts her head to the instrument panel. "Three or four hours," she tells me. "You can lie down if you want."

I look around us. The sky is getting pinker and pinker. The sun is making an aisle of ruby light from the horizon across the sea, the waves beginning to dance again. "Sleep sounds hard after all of this," I admit. "But I've got my sea legs now, so let's see what I can coax out of that little galley that might taste like comfort."

Liv nods. As I am going down below, I hear her call my name again. "Mom?"

"What's up, babe?" I ask.

"Whatever it is you're making, add chocolate chips," she says. And that is pretty much Olivia speak for "I'm going to be just fine."

12

We've been sailing for thirty-two straight hours now, and most of it has been impossible. Besides the cruise ship near miss, we also snagged a lobster trap on our propeller on the way into Provincetown, and I nearly fell in the marina water (you do not want to fall in the marina water) when landing *Becky Ann* on the dock. I am not good enough at piloting, you see, to park her, and whoever doesn't drive needs to be the one who leaps onto the dock as we're pulling into our slip to keep the boat from plowing into the boards.

In case you're wondering why this is all so hard, sailboats are nothing like small motor craft. They have this new factor to calculate for, this horrible thing called *windage*, which means basically that even with sails down and motor off, they are never gently floating in the water—they are just too big and have too much of the body of the ship sticking out of the water. The wind pushes on the hull and the mast all the time. Hard. Until she is tied up to something, she never stops being propelled in a direction you probably don't want her to go. So you jump onto the dock from the boat before the boat hits it, and then you, ah, swiftly, let's say, though *frenzied* better describes my state of mind, but, sure, you *swiftly* tie the fore and aft of the ship to cleats on the dock and start rigging springs—lines that go down the length of the boat to provide countertension and keep the thing from going back and forth as well as side to side. And a real sailor would do all this and then hop back on the boat and start derigging her before the pilot had even cut the motor, but I am not a real sailor, so I am still checking that I tied the line around half the cleat forward, around the other half inverse, and then made a backward loop around the front again and pulled tight. This must happen multiplied over six lines, and the whole thing probably takes me thirty minutes.

"Thank god for roller reefing," says Liv when she takes in my nautical ineptitude.

"Which is?" I ask her.

It turns out that not all boats have self-storing sails. If Alistair had spent a little less when he bought this puppy, we might have to pull down the jib every time we wanted to motor, fold it up, and cram it somewhere to keep it dry when we slept. We would have had to pleat the main after we let it down, secure it with special looped ties, and wrap the whole sail and beam in a sleeping bag of sorts. She points out the boats to our left and right, all with these boom covers. Our boat has a motor that rolls the jib into a tight spiral around the stay at the front of our boat and a folding arm thingy that packs away the main for us inside the boom.

"Tell your dad thanks for that," I say enthusiastically.

"I'll get right on it."

"For real, do you want to text him now that we have cellular? I'm sure he'll want to know you're ok."

"Pass."

"What? Did something happen between you two?" I ask her. As far as I know, they were having their weekly dinners together and getting along when we left.

"He . . . ah . . . asked me to help him out with something yesterday morning," she says. "I need some time to think about it before I get back to him."

Don't push it, I remind myself. But I'm wondering like hell what that could mean. Is he asking her to come intern at the firm? I know that's always been on the top of his wish list. And it's always been at the bottom of mine. "Ok. Then I'll send him an update. Otherwise he'll worry."

"Leave it, Mom." Liv is not joking. She is firm. "I do not want to be in contact with him right now."

I can be firm too. "I don't care. He's still your dad."

She turns to face me head-on and puts up a hand. "I need time to decide about what that means," she says.

Oof. Poor Alistair, I think, for the first time in, what, maybe ever? He has been a pretty odious husband, but he never came between me and my kid. In fact, if he were in my shoes right now, I am pretty sure he'd be telling her to send me a text.

But then, there's no universe where Alistair is in my shoes, is there?

"I propose a compromise," I say. "Activate him on your Find My Friends app while you're here in the marina. That way he knows you're alive, and you don't have to be the one to tell him. How long will we be here in this marina, by the way?"

"How long does it take you to shower?" she replies.

"No! What? We have to go again today?"

"We don't have to. We can live in Provincetown on a yacht and make a reality TV series. But if you want to get to Miami, and the weather window checks out, we should probably get through the Cape Cod Canal during the evening tides."

"No," I repeat again. "I need to sleep off some of the trauma of what I've experienced so far."

"You can sleep in Buzzards Bay," she says.

"Can you even hear the name of that place? Does it sound restful?"

Liv twists her curls. "I hear there are actually some bad waves over there."

"Not to mention the birds trying to pick your bones." I cross my arms. "It's decided. We sleep here tonight."

"Typically, the person who knows nothing about the weather, the route, or sailing itself doesn't make the travel decisions."

"Typically, the child doesn't attempt to tell her parent what to do," I tell her reflexively. I recognize here that we are on shaky ground. This isn't a fight, but it's the road to one. One we've been through more than a few times since she was a teenager.

"Mom, I'm twenty-one years old. Stop calling me a child!"

I take a deep breath. "I'm sorry," I say. "But I'm not the child here either. We've got to relate to each other like adults." I say this, but my mental fingers are crossed behind my back. This kid doesn't have the first clue what she doesn't know, and won't for years. "One adult to another: What kind of crazy person wants to keep sailing after the thirty-two hours we just had?"

"Have we met?" she jokes. "No sleep till Brooklyn!"

I pretend to sob and drop to my knees to beg. "I just want to take a long shower, take a good nap, and then eat dinner in a place where the table isn't sideways and doesn't move."

"I don't know if you're cut out for the sailing life," she tells me, but she's smiling.

"I can say with some certainty now that I'm not," I reply. "But that's ok. We've done our big crossing and saved a day of travel, not to mention at least a hundred bucks of diesel. Now we're in this big comfy marina, and we should live it up."

Liv shakes her head. "You know we're going to have to sleep at anchor, right? Because otherwise we'll just blow the hundred bucks on transient marina fees."

Sleeping at anchor means windage. Waves. Reliance on the pump on the marine head.

I put my hands up. "The fees are on me. We survived the Bay of Maine. Tonight we poop in flush toilets like the ladies we are."

Liv just laughs. "Ok, ok. When you're right, you're right."

I am so, so right. Despite the sun streaming into the cabin, we sleep for hours, stretch out our kinks in the cooling afternoon breeze, and plot tomorrow's course through the Cape Cod Canal and down to the tip of Long Island. Quietly, I make mental note of several bailout points on the trip along the coast of Rhode Island and Connecticut. Then we go up to the absolutely packed marina bar and grill, where the locals delight us with gorgeous fresh fish and chilly spiked lemonade served with pastel paper straws. We are seated at long picnic tables, ten people to a length, and to our right are three kings here for Drag Camp, getting ready for a late-late show nearby. After we all tuck into clam chowder, fried cod, and pie, we take directions from the gents and wind our way to a seaside club with a wall full of windows that open onto our very marina. The night is so fun, with so many of our favorite Motown tunes, that we seem to forget the long crossing and associated moments of terror and lose ourselves in sing-alongs and punny dick jokes until we are laughing so hard we are almost crying.

We stagger out of the club around one a.m. and seem to realize almost in unison how dog tired we both are.

"I'm really glad I sprang for the marina berth," I tell her.

"Same. Even if the tender was running from marina to moorings right now, I'm not sure I could climb up the ladder," she tells me.

"My bed is gonna feel so good tonight," I tell her. And indeed, when I am curled up in the owner's cabin, I drift off to sleep almost instantly. Only to be woken ten minutes later by Liv, standing right over my head, clutching a duvet around her. "It's colder than I thought it would be," she says to me, and drowsily, I say, "Ok, honey," just as I would if she'd told me there was a monster in her closet.

"Scootch over, I'm saying," she tells me. "There's only one warm blanket around here anymore, and you'll freeze."

Oh! Right. The Bedding Overboard incident. It feels so long ago already. I shove to one side, and Liv climbs into the bed next to me, using a throw pillow from the saloon and pulling the comforter around us both.

The shape of the peak berth I'm in means our feet are far closer than they'd be if we were in a normal queen bed, and at first, after sleeping alone for so long, I feel strange, crowded. But when Liv falls asleep and her face goes slack, I find the soft sound of her breathing to be the most reassuring sound in the world, almost like when she was an infant in the crib next to my bed all those years ago and I routinely put my hand under her nose to reassure myself she was still alive. Yes, I tell myself now. We are still alive. Alive and, somehow, happy.

Before I know it, I too am asleep, maybe dreaming of how this trip has already been hard, and scary, and somehow exactly everything I hoped it would be.

13

Admittedly, the next few days are . . . less wonderful than the marina night in P-Town.

First, we must get through the Cape Cod Canal, which has not only a speed limit—we are never in danger of approaching that—but also a minimum time in which you must traverse the distance. We would probably have made it, had we been able to motor right through the middle of the canal. Unfortunately, I now see why Grant Murphy called this boat *wee*. Under sail, technically, motor-powered boats of all sizes have to yield to us, but since you're not supposed to sail in the canal (it's very hard to go in a straight line when wind powered), we must yield to all manner of watercraft, some just because they are so much bigger than us, and some because they look like they are one big wave away from lining the bottom of the canal. I've never seen so much rust and rot in my life, and I get a moment's pride in how beautiful *Becky Ann* is, how majestic she looks cutting through the water.

The pride wanes fast enough when we run aground from steering too close to the side of the canal. Three times.

The first time I have a tiny conniption and want to call for a tow, until Google reminds us how to run up the mainsail and use the force of the wind to lean the boat over, thus reducing the depth of the keel—the draft, as they call it in sailor-speak. When we get out of the mud, we cheer and toast ourselves and generally feel brilliant for the entire half hour before a massive barge points directly at us, I steer out of the way, and we run aground again.

The second time, we use the same system of heeling the boat, plus a little of the time-tested reverse, go forward, reverse methodology I used to rely on when I drove a front-wheel-drive car in Maine winter. Again we break free, hear no crunching sounds, notice no visible damage, and exhale. And vow to stay far from the edge of the canal.

Then we run her aground right smack in the middle of the canal, and just five minutes after we do, we get a call from the VHF radio telling us, in no uncertain terms, that we've outlasted our welcome in the Cape Cod Canal and will now be greeted by a tow vehicle at our own expense. Yes, we did see the posted signs telling us we only had two and a half hours to get through what looked, on the map, to be an insignificant span of canal. No, we didn't realize it'd been three hours already.

"How did they even know?" I ask Liv after she comes back up from belowdecks.

"I guess they've been watching us on radar the whole time. They asked if we were in an unfamiliar vessel. Because you'd have to be clueless to run her aground this many times, I guess? I told them it was a delivery trip, not adding that we were delivering our own boat. Mom, the guy mocked me on the radio."

I have to admit, as we wiggle in the mud in our fancy six-figure yacht, that I'd mock us too.

So, we get towed the last five hundred yards out of the canal, and I dig further into my handbag profits. It's for the best—as I watch the depth finder on our way out, I see with certainty about ten more spots we probably would have been stuck.

The tow leaves us in Buzzards Bay, where some ugly combination of tide and wind gives us massive head-on waves to battle for the next hour. We're meant to get to Old Saybrook, Connecticut, by dark, but there's no hope of that, so we bail in Newport, Rhode Island, which has the dubious honor of being insanely expensive. We end up on a mooring ball far out in the water to save three hundred bucks transient marina fees, and then stay on board that night rather than mess with the costs affiliated with tender. Dinner is canned. Our enthusiasm is also canned.

—

The following day the weather looks fine and we seem out of reach of tides, but within an hour we are heading straight into the wind, what sailors call "beating." Probably because you'd rather take an actual beating from a professionally trained mixed martial artist than endure the bumpy, uneven Tilt-A-Whirl ride you get when you are trying to harness wind power to go into the wind. Liv, brilliant girl, gets us rigged properly, with sails close-hauled to the centerline of the boat, and we go up and down and up and down as we hit wave after wave, lucky to make half the speed we got when we were traveling the direction nature wanted us to travel. "The wind hates us!" I shout at her, just before I give up and start throwing up directly into the ocean.

We attempt an after-dusk landing in an unfamiliar marina somewhere in Connecticut, and forget to put the correct set of lights on, and generally scare the hell out of everyone watching—which is the entire town, it seems—before picking up a mooring ball that actually belongs to the sailboat coming in directly behind us, and getting another stern dressing-down over the VHF. By the time we are actually where we are supposed to be, I can't face the idea of going ashore even if they wanted us there, which I'm fairly sure they don't. More onboard dinner, though I take a little more care tonight—having thrown up canned salmon and greens all day, I whisk up some nice creamy parmesan polenta and grilled chicken sausages to try to put my stomach back to rights. The water in the shower is cold—I forgot or did not know that I should turn on the water heater breaker when we were motoring to charge it off the battery—and we fall asleep huddled together watching *Captain Ron* and finding it significantly less funny than in times past.

The next day we wake up in pouring rain, and though we were hoping for at least the East River today, we give up around Fairfield, after twice entangling lobster traps around our folding prop.

The day after that is spent motoring in circles, waiting interminably on the bridges of the East River with every other sailboat in the Atlantic. Somehow, though I am freezing, I get a sunburn.

Finally, we make our painstakingly slow, agonizing trip down through New Jersey at the height of tourism season, heading out to sea whenever we can to avoid Jet Skis, parasailers, and other things that are actually fun compared to whatever the hell it is we're doing. I have to admit, I am vaguely starting to tolerate the actual sailing part of our trip, when the sails are set and we are moving in a forward direction with the wind toward our backs. Everything else—the marinas, the food, the bathroom, the charting—is god awful. Somehow, it has been a week and a half at sea now, and we are still not to Norfolk, which we both thought would be only a week away when we left Maine. And that is with keeping on the move every day—we haven't had anything meaningful as far as heavy weather to contend with, just gusty breezes and occasional showers. In other words, we've had no reason to hole up at anchor, no reason to stop the relentless slog. We've learned we hate motoring, which is required in low winds. The diesel smell makes you sicker than you'd already be, and the minute you drop below three knots, flies the size of songbirds land on every available inch of your body, as though you are already dead of boredom, which you very well may be. We learn about marine toilet paper, which has the durability of a butterfly wing but the softness of sandpaper, and how you cannot, really cannot, use more than three squares of it per flush. Ask me how

I learned that. It does not matter what comes out of your body. Three squares will have to do, or you face a fate far worse than sandpaper butt.

I also find it remarkable that despite the fact that we are surrounded by water at all times, there is no actual frolicking in the sea, floating, swimming, or anything of the sort. Marina water is disgusting, with a skim of rainbow oil on top, and if you're not in the marina, you're not holding still. Getting in the water, no matter how icy it might be, sounds better and better the longer we go without a decent shower, and when we sail past Cape May and see the beaches crowded with people doing what mankind is actually supposed to do when confronted with the ocean—lying very still next to it—I find myself begging Liv to let us stop and spend a day off this godforsaken water RV.

She says no; we've got places to be. I call her a taskmaster. She tells me to get my head in the game. I tell her this doesn't feel as fun as a game should. She says "shut up and hand me the canned tuna."

———

That night, moored on the lee side off of Cape May, while Liv dozes next to me, I make a list in my journal: "Things we've talked about." Because we have talked about a lot of things since entering the Cape Cod Canal, and very few of them have felt meaningful or important. I look at the list carefully.

Marine toilet paper

Mnemonic devices to remember which side is port

Mnemonic devices to remember which one is the halyard and which is the sheet (halyard = heavy as hell / sheet = slippery as f***)

What VHF station we're supposed to be tuned to at all times

Which one we were actually tuned to for the first few days of sailing

What to do if we went overboard and saw a shark

How many mint sprigs go in a mojito

How many mint leaves are left before we need to resupply

Baked beans: delicious or toxic?

How to stand eating plain oatmeal for nine days in a row since mice seem to have eaten the raisins

What was the name of that lady in that show from that one time?

Things we've not mentioned, not even once, no way, no how:

How are we feeling about Dad?

How are we feeling about the divorce?

What happened with Grant Murphy, and why was Olivia dating her teacher?

Is my daughter going to be ok?

Is my daughter right that I am not going to be ok?

I contemplate this list as I worry myself into a fraught sort of half sleep each night. Though I am proud of what we're coping with, this is not the trip I thought we would be taking together. And I know that no matter how miserable this sail has been, I will need answers to each of these questions before either one of us can go ashore.

14

When I wake up the next morning, Liv is already going strong, coffee is made, and there's a plate with toast and an herb omelet, the thin, simple kind like I taught her to make, waiting for me in the saloon. I hear rain on the coach roof and see gray out the windows. We're supposed to be crossing Delaware Bay today and making for Rehoboth, but last night the forecast for wind was iffy, and I'm secretly hoping for a day without the vague blend of nausea and panic that combines to form my sailing experience so far. Maybe if it is too gusty, this is the opportunity I've been waiting for—a chance to sit belowdecks with my daughter and devote my attention not to telltales and apparent wind speed but to what her emotional weather forecast is reading right now.

But Liv has another plan. One that I don't see coming a mile away.

"Have some coffee. I spiked it," she tells me.

"Uh-oh," I say, knowing something is happening. "What's up?"

"Well, Mom, I'll tell you what's up. Today we're changing the music," she tells me while my mouth is full of toast.

"We are?" I mumble.

"On a scale of one to ten, where do you rate your current misery level?"

"Oh honey, I'm not miserable," I lie. "I'm in awe of what you are capable of and love spending time with you." I chew some more. "In fact, I feel like we've barely had enough time to just hang out."

Liv completely ignores me. "Scoring: one is a tickly foot rub at the nail salon, and ten is being eaten slowly by piranhas."

"I'm a four," I tell her, then take a giant swig of delicious Irish coffee.

"Mom, come on. I've seen you throw up over the side of the boat at least six consecutive days now."

"It's an innovative new diet plan!" I tell her. "Look, sure, I've been a bit seasick. But our berths are very comfy, especially when they don't smell too strongly of diesel. I sleep great thanks to all the sea air." I try to think of something else kind of good but falter. "Our toilet drains properly over sixty percent of the time, and I'm getting the hang of boat cuisine. When the sun's shining and we're sailing along with the wind at our backs and we don't have to tack or jibe or rig anything, life is good."

Liv's face is flat, unconvinced.

"It's like nothing I've ever experienced before," I add.

"That is basically the sailing version of what you said about my middle school interpretive dance phase. In fact, I can swear you commented on the auditorium seats being very supportive."

I blush. "That also was like nothing I'd ever experienced before," I admit. "And, I must point out, that was less generally nauseating."

"Thanks, Mom."

"Someday your thirteen-year-old will go onstage and pretend to be the female reproductive system in slow motion to adult jazz, and you can tell me how that goes for you," I tell her.

"I'm not having kids," she reminds me.

"Ok, what is even up with that?" I blurt out. Immediately, I wish I could eat the words back out of the air they hover in now. Like PAC-MAN. Nom nom nom. "Sorry," I add. "None of my business. I know."

"Mom, remember when Lisa Bonet and Jason Momoa got divorced?"

"Like it was yesterday. What a shocker that was." If anyone was good enough for Denise Huxtable, it had to be Aquaman, right?

"Well, it wasn't a shock to me," she says. "It wasn't even a surprise. Do you know why? Because successful people can't have happy marriages. They are mutually exclusive parts of life."

I gasp. "Where on earth did you get that idea?" I ask her.

"From you and Dad," she says, frank and unapologetic. "And Gwyneth and Chris, and Angelina and Brad, and Jeff Bezos, and the Clintons, and all the rest."

"I think Warren Buffett is still happily married to his wife."

"His second wife, who was introduced to him by his first wife," she tells me. "Who was dating her tennis pro."

"Whoa."

"Exactly. I don't want to be locked into something that's essentially doomed in its very nature."

I shake my head. "This is a silly way to look at marriage and family," I say, though there's a small part of me that wonders . . . was I right all those years ago when I intended to go after my dreams without some man? I suppose I'll find out now that I'm on my own. "It's a silly generalization based on a very few, very unusual data points. Outliers."

"Hang on . . . ," Liv says, sounding triumphant. "Look what we're reading next semester for econ." She holds up her phone with her fall syllabus on it. There it is, the famous Malcolm Gladwell bestseller, *Outliers*. I've certainly never read it. Alistair loves Malcolm Gladwell, and so I automatically assume the guy's a charlatan.

"You see?" Liv asks me. "I *want* to be an outlier. Do amazing things, change the world, be smart, rich, and successful. And I don't want to raise kids whose parents will just get divorced. So I am not having kids. Or getting married, for that matter."

"Aha," I say. "I see where you've got everything completely wrong."

"Just because I don't plan to have kids doesn't mean I'm completely wrong, Mom," Liv says disdainfully. "Read your feminism."

"Oh please," I say. "I didn't say anything of the kind. I said *you've* got everything completely wrong. You think that just because some famous people had crap marriages—"

"And my own parents, let's not forget."

I try not to wince. I think I deserve some real credit for what a nice normal childhood she did have. "Sure, a few famous people and one normal couple. Since they got divorced, you somehow jump to the conclusion that their kids are badly off. But that's not necessarily so. You might be hurting right now, but you're hardly *suffering*."

Liv sets her lips in a straight, sharp line, and I can see I'm now way out of the lane she's assigned me.

"Because I'm rich? Because of my trust fund? I can't suffer?" she asks me.

I take a long slow sip of my coffee to buy myself some time, not just to get what I want to say right in my head, but also to keep from admitting that yes, I believe her lifetime of wealth, her connections with the Larkins, her fancy college, and her paid-off car—those are all reasons not to moan and groan. Frankly, it's what I tell myself about my own situation whenever I feel daunted about the future. But if I voiced any of that, Liv would shut down so fast I'd lose any hope of reaching her.

Thank goodness this coffee's spiked. After I swallow, I say, firmly, "You can hurt. You can be wounded. You can be depressed, or alienated from your friends, or even rejected by a boyfriend. But those are all things that end, eventually. That pass. That certainly beat not having been brought into this world by caring, competent parents at all. I hope you learn that someday. It's like you comparing sailing to being eaten by piranhas. Yes, this trip has been hard. But I have a comfy bed, plenty of food, and mostly running water. In the end, the rest is gravy."

I want Liv to hear me, and I want these ideas to land in her somewhere deep. But she simply frowns and says, "I called Grant Murphy."

"What?" I ask her. She could knock me over with a feather right now.

"You seemed ok with him, to put it mildly, and I know he's broke. He needs work. If he calls back, I'm flying him out to Philly. You and I are going to go up the Delaware River to pick him up. And then he's going to sail the boat the rest of the way to Miami, and we can meet him there to complete the sale."

I don't even know what to say to this. I just stammer for a few moments. "But why, Livvie?" I finally manage to blurt.

"Olivia. Or Liv. Never Livvie."

"Sorry," I say, automatically.

"It's my name, Mom. I get to decide how to say it."

"Of course. I just forgot. Because I was being ambushed."

Liv looks skyward. "Now who's dramatic? Look. Grant's not the guy I was hoping he'd be, but he's a good sailor. He'll get the *Becky Ann* to Miami safely. Which is more than I can say for me."

I'm gobsmacked. I thought Liv was doing an amazing job, all things considered. "I thought you were doing an amazing job, hon!" I tell her. "Look at how many times you got us out of the mud or picked up moorings in just a few tries."

"Last night it took us fifteen tries to get on this mooring ball," she tells me.

"Well, that's my fault. You have an incompetent crew member," I say.

"You have an incompetent captain," she replies.

"Don't you talk that way about my daughter," I warn her. "You're an outlier!"

"Not, apparently, at sailing. Look: I couldn't sleep well last night. To be honest, I've hardly slept at all since we left."

I look up at her in shock. I have been tossing and turning all night, too, but I thought it was just me. I thought Liv was . . . well, being oblivious, like she often is.

"So I spent a few hours playing with the chart plotter. If you and I stick to our plan of going down the Intracoastal Waterway all the way to Florida, our arrival date is farther off than we promised the buyer."

"How much farther off?" I ask her, still reeling. I had a feeling we were more than a little behind schedule, but still thought we'd get to Miami in time. I left quite a large cushion.

"August," she says.

I cough on my mouthful of coffee. It's me. I'm the oblivious one. "A month? You've got to be kidding me."

"Experienced sailors call the ICW the ditch," she tells me. "And even they run aground a few times. Us, we're looking at some pretty slow going. We can't sail, we can't really use the autopilot with all the boat traffic, and we're going the wrong way on the current half of every day. We'll be lucky if we make three knots, and most of the shortcuts involve bridges that are too low for us or only open a few times a day. To make it to Miami in time to close your deal, we'd need to motor literally around the clock, sleeping in shifts."

I blink at her in horror. "That sounds . . . awful."

"Does *that* count as suffering?" she asks me archly.

"No," I say, with significantly less conviction than before. "But . . . it doesn't count as fun either."

"If Grant flies out here, he can sail offshore, and he won't need to do the ditch hardly at all. He'll be there in an easy week without spending much on diesel and nothing on marina fees. The sailing will be smoother and easier on him—and on *Becky Ann*."

I put my head in my hands. This is not how I planned it.

"Uh, I think the phrase you're looking for is 'Thank you,'" Liv tells me.

"I don't want to do this," I moan at her from my position of despair. "No, I won't do this." I sit up. "We can sail offshore, if that's what we need to do. I watched a couple of YouTubers who came out of the ICW when the wind was favorable, and then dipped back inside when it wasn't. And they were idiots. We can handle it if they can."

"I'm not doing that, Mom."

"But you're an *outlier*!" I remind her.

"I'm not suicidal. The hurricane season is jacking up. There are waves at six to eight feet out there most days. I am out of my depth when they get up to five."

I pale. Eight-foot waves. I remember, in flashes, being back at Alistair's and my old house, making muffins in the enormous kitchen, thinking I could sail to Florida. What a moron I was. My throat tightens.

"See?" Liv asks me.

"Grant Murphy is your ex-boyfriend," I remind her.

"He's also the only person I know who has been sailing his whole life, on the Atlantic, and needs a job."

"Won't it be awkward for you to see him again?"

Liv looks away but doesn't answer. Does that mean she's hoping this will be a chance for them to get back together? I can hardly blame her for pining for the guy. He's built like a model, and that lilting accent of his is icing on the physical cake.

I exhale. "Forget I said that. He's the one who will feel awkward," I tell her. "Having to think of what he's missing out on."

She smiles weakly. "You're not so bad yourself, Mom," she says.

"Oh yeah," I joke. "We're basically Doublemint twins."

Liv cringes. "Don't say things like that, though. That gum is from the Middle Ages."

Fair. "How much are we spending on this guy?" I ask her, having capitulated to Liv's plan fully now. "And will he take a postdated check?"

"I'm paying. This is my treat. Because I should never have agreed to this trip, and being stuck here now is pretty much my fault."

"Don't be silly," I say. "I'm the one who can't sail. I'll pay."

Liv frowns at me. "How? Won't he expect to be paid before the sale?"

I pause, embarrassed. "I can get an advance on a credit card," I say, but it's a flimsy answer. How do you get a higher credit limit without income? Is that still a thing, or has our culture learned better since I was in college?

Olivia, seeming to sense my vulnerability, says, "It's ok, Mom. You can pay me back later. Or never."

I put my face in my hands and moan. "It's one thing to let you buy me a drink," I tell her. "It's another to let you charter a captain for my boat."

"Think of it as an investment in my future," Liv says. "I would like to have a future, you see, and not die of old age on the ICW."

What can I do but nod my agreement? "Ok," I say. "Let's go up the Delaware. Like George Washington. In the rain. To get a new recruit."

"Washington *crossed* the Delaware," Liv reminds me. "In the middle of the night during an ice storm. For a surprise attack."

"See? Now *that's* suffering," I tell Liv.

The wind howls past the carriage windows, and the rigging pings madly against the empty mast. "Oh, that's what it is, then?" Liv says sarcastically. "I'll keep that in mind today when you're soaked to the bone, frozen solid, and yakking out the back of the boat."

15

I don't admit to any actual suffering, per se, but the trip itself is not fun. We make it to within a fifty-dollar cab ride of the Philly airport and then treat ourselves to a transient night in a random marina—no reversing endlessly to try to pick up a mooring ball that way. I don't feel great, either—I'm not sure how I would have picked up a virus on this trip, but I feel achy and run down. Maybe it's disappointment. I had such high hopes for this journey, and maybe, just maybe, I believed it would make me into the person I'm going to need to be to start my—what did Liv call it? My second act. Instead, we're throwing money at our problems and slinking away, just as if I'm still a Larkin, still the woman Alistair said could never live without him.

We have rather unexciting turkey wraps for lunch, and I fall into my berth exhausted, stealing a quick nap before Grant arrives. Somehow it feels like when he gets here, the party is over; we'll have to start operating like we're in the navy. Maybe he'll bring a whistle like Georg von Trapp. What's he going to think about my messy, unreliable knots on the fenders, our greasy hair and unwashed aroma, or the copious amount of bird poo on the front of the spinnaker pole that we've been delicately avoiding for the last five days?

Well, who cares, I guess. He's here to do a job. Get *Becky Ann* to Miami alive, on time. And then I will never see him, or a sailboat, ever again. Thank God for small mercies.

Five hours after I started my "quick nap," I am awoken by the sound of talking. Irish-accented talking. Grant is here, getting the tour from Olivia. Her voice is clipped. She sounds pissed at him. Or is it residue from being pissed at me? I'm not sure, and as I've experienced in the past, I find I don't care *that* much. She has her crabby turns—we all do—and mothers know their children well enough by this time not to bow to them. I wonder if Grant will be familiar with them too. I wonder again, How close were they? How could I not tell she was seeing someone? How well do I really know my own kid?

Then I curse, because in sitting up I have hit my head on three places in the low-ceilinged berth, and the last one was sharp.

"Mom?" says Liv.

"I'm alive," I say, feeling very self-conscious. I wipe my eyes and mouth, just in case. I straighten my two-day-old T-shirt. I scooch to the edge of my bed, put my legs over the side in the one-by-one-foot space for standing, and push the button to open the brass latch. "I'm sorry about that. I didn't mean to conk out for so long."

When I open the door, I see Grant at the charting desk and Liv standing in the galley, fidgeting but not cooking. She has a sour expression, but he is looking at me and smiling, just the edge of a laugh on his face. I look him over, trying not to, unable to stop myself. He looks different from before. Younger. But then, I know now that he's an infant, so maybe it's in my head?

No. It's the beard. He's shaved clean today, and before he had a week of dark stubble. The sharp bare chin and smooth lips give his youth away. And his green eyes are glistening when he smiles.

Why is he smiling?

"She's really a fantastic craft," he says to me.

Oh lord, here we are again with the boat worship.

"She's too big, too slow, and too hard to park," I reply. I'm picking up on whatever my daughter's putting down, and it's grumpy.

His smile fades, but only for a second. "That's why I'm here, yeah?"

"Yeah," I say. The room falls uncomfortably silent.

"I was telling Olivia, the two of you have done really spectacular," he burrs. "It's no easy thing, your first offshore, your first big trip, and look at ya."

I look down. I think there's drool on my T-shirt.

"Thanks," I say.

"Sorta thought you'd be dead by now," he adds.

I frown at him. Liv frowns at him. Tough room.

"Kidding," he says, putting his hands in front of his broad chest sheepishly. "Sorry, sorry. I can see you've been through it."

I refuse to admit that he's right. "Will you sail out tonight?" I ask him. "Are you making a distance schedule? How does having a captain work, exactly?"

He shakes his head and half shrugs. "I've never captained before," he tells me. "But we'll sort something out."

"What?" My head spins from Liv, who shrugs, back to him.

"I mean, I've been at the helm more than I've been on land, no worries there. But I, ah, I'm a teacher, not a boat-delivery service," he says.

"I think our crash course of the last week has been plenty of education. At this point, we just want you to get the thing to Miami in one piece."

"Well, sure, but there's tree of us," he says, and again my ear latches on to the way he pronounces his tee aitches, even more than the meaning of what he's saying, "and we're in a bit of a hustle, yeah? So we'll sail together."

Wait, what? Again, swivel head, like I'm watching a Ping-Pong game.

Olivia inhales. "About that," she says. Before she drops a bomb she should have made well clear before he flew down here, her phone bleeps. "Oh, crap, our rideshare's fifteen minutes away."

My head swivels to hers. "What? You ordered a car already?"

Liv crosses to the settee next to me, wraps an arm around me. "Grant, give us a minute," she says. He unfolds his long body out from behind the chart table and heads up the companionway to the deck. "No problem," he says as he goes. "Take all the time you need."

"You didn't tell him we were disembarking?" I ask her in a sharp whisper, the minute he's out of earshot. "What, are you nuts? He hasn't done a delivery trip before? What if he can't sail single handed?"

"He's won loads of races all over Ireland, and he'll sleep at anchor. The first time he'll need a crew is when we bring him into the dock in Miami."

"Liv, you can't spring this on people. You can't expect to hire them to do one thing and then have to do another."

Liv shrugs.

"No. No shrugging. This is not ok with me. We have to keep going on this boat now. We cannot in good conscience expect him to sail through . . . all that," I say, my hand just flailing in the general direction of the Atlantic Ocean, "alone, when he thought he'd have two deckhands to help him out."

"We can just pay him double," she says.

There it is again. Liv, throwing money at people to get them to behave as she wants. The Larkin way. I could scream. I think I'm madder at my daughter than I have been in . . . well, in ever.

"Mom, you need to calm down. You have to admit, if I told him he'd be alone, he might not have agreed to come. This is just . . . managing personalities."

"This is a lie. A lie by omission, and still a lie. We're staying on this boat."

"I just want to go home," is all she says.

"I want to go home too!" I cry. And to my surprise, it's not just a yelp; there are tears behind it.

"You don't have a home," she tells me.

I recoil. Did she mean it as a terrible slap in the face, or was it simply her being thoughtless? I don't know. But I don't like it either way.

"What made you want to talk to me that way?" I ask her sharply, though my voice is gluey with rising tears. "In what universe would that ever be ok?"

"I've been talking to Dad," she tells me.

My gut churns. "What? How?"

"He bought me a satellite link of my own when I didn't contact him in P-Town," she explains.

"But I thought you were angry with him. I thought you were freezing him out."

"I was. I thought he ripped you off. But he's been hounding me all this time, and I finally gave in and talked to him. Mom, he says he would have given you the house and alimony payments. If only you'd tried to ask for them."

My jaw sets. This is utter Larkin bullshit, and he knows it.

The problem is, our daughter does not.

"Olivia, that's not exactly true," I attempt.

Liv throws her hands up. "At this point, I don't know who to believe. You say you don't want our family money. It's too dirty for you. But you want me to take it. You don't care if I get dirty. You don't think I can survive without Dad. Without my trust fund. But you're the one with no money, no house, and no husband, stuck in the middle of the Delaware River. I don't know if this is some elaborate midlife crisis or what, but I am tired of being caught up in it!"

I put my hands up. "That is the last thing we wanted for you. That's why Dad shouldn't even be talking about me with you." I could kill him right now. The truth is, I want to throttle both of them.

"I'm going to go work for Grandma and Dad," she tells me, and the words knock the breath clear out of me. "I don't care what you and Grant Murphy do next, and I don't care if the *Becky Ann* springs a leak and sinks in this very marina. I am getting on a plane, and next Monday I will be at my new job. With my family. On dry land."

My mouth falls open. This isn't right. This isn't the kid I spent my life raising, protecting, teaching about love, and kindness, and decency. I would barely even recognize her—if I didn't know her father so well. I sit down heavily on the settee, too dazed to know where to go from here.

Her voice softens. "Come home with me, Mom. Grant will be fine. I'll pay him a bonus and meet him in Miami."

"You said yourself, there's nothing waiting for me back home. At least nothing up to your standards."

"I shouldn't have said that," she says. "I just want you to figure out what your life is going to be about, now that it's not about Dad anymore."

"My life will always be about you," I tell her sadly.

"Exactly. And that's not good for you. Or for me," she answers quickly.

The truth of her words opens a painful gulf inside me.

She squeezes in next to me on the settee and hugs me around the shoulders tightly, takes a deep intentional breath. "Let's reframe this, shall we?" she says. "We have done our mother-daughter thing, and there have been rough times, but through it all, we are still besties, right?"

I nod slowly, though I'm not sure she's treating me like a bestie right now.

"But I also love my dad, and we're close too. We've always been close. How do you think I learned to sail this boat? Why did you think it was getting all that touch-up work done? Why do you think I was taking sailing classes? Dad and I were gearing up for a big trip to Bermuda together this summer. Sailing was supposed to be his and my thing."

My mouth drops open. None of this ever occurred to me. I thought she and I knew everything about each other. I thought we were on the exact same page.

"Mom, I love you so much. Really. But I love Dad, too, and I believe him when he says he would never have agreed to a divorce if you hadn't demanded one. And sometimes I wonder, what was even the point?"

I want to tell her the point. I want to tell her all about the final straw, the thing that made divorce my only option. But that would ruin things between her and her father forever. I cannot, I refuse, to break my own daughter's heart. "I wanted to be free," I say at last. A fragment of a truth far more complicated than that. But a truth, a powerful truth, all the same.

"Ok, you're free. What are you going to do with all this newfound freedom? You act like you're ninety-five and next stop is Shady Acres, but you're not dead yet. And I cannot be the meaning in your life for the next sixty years or however long you keep ticking. You're the one who blew up your life. Now it's up to you to get a new one. One that doesn't revolve around me."

I open my mouth to protest this, but I can't. She's right. She's hurtful and cruel in the way I've learned that offspring will sometimes be, but at the same time, she's completely right.

But before I can tell her that, she's jumping up and looking at her phone. I'm realizing that this whole time she's had a duffel and two bags packed and sitting on the opposite settee.

"It's time, Mom," she says. "I can get the driver to wait, if you want to pack up. Are you staying, or are you coming with me?"

I should go. I should take her charity and get on the plane using the ticket she bought me, and go back to Maine. Help Liv through this, whatever this is. Face my uncertain future.

But . . . I don't have to do that anymore.

She's an adult now. And I am one too. And just like I always wanted, I am *free*. And what I want to do is see this journey through to the end, with or without my daughter.

"Have a safe flight," I tell her. I can't believe I'm letting her go without me. It feels like I'm giving up on the girl I spent twenty-one years sheltering, body, heart, and soul.

But it's time.

Liv looks at me for a long moment. Then she nods at me and vanishes up the gangway.

"Ciao, Grant," she calls as I hear her footsteps, feel the rock when she climbs off the *Becky Ann*. "She's all yours. Don't break her."

16

I wish I could say I handle this all gracefully, sit in quiet introspection, and make a plan for the future. But the reality is, I immediately blame the entire situation on Grant.

Because if the real reason Liv just left me is because of her feelings for Grant, then I don't have to face the fact that Olivia might be right about me. Or that I might be right about her, for that matter. Is it that Liv has become more entitled and reckless with other people? Or is that I'm finally starting to notice?

For most of my life, my daughter has been my North Star. She's my why, my reason for everything. I married Alistair for her, and when he did something I felt risked her safety, I divorced him for her. I've been getting up and living my life every day for twenty-one years—more, since you have to include the pregnancy—for this one person, and this one person just left me on a boat with no money and no friends and no idea what the heck I'm supposed to do next.

So yeah, sure, it's got to be Grant's fault, I tell myself lamely. Just so I don't spend the rest of the day crying in my berth.

But Grant seems not at all affected by my cold shoulder attitude. He is determined to sail a boat. My boat. And, admittedly, that needs doing too.

As I stand awkwardly to the side of the helm, trying not to think about the scene that just unfolded, trying not to let any tears out, Grant performs what can only be described as an inspection. He mumbles to himself a lot while he's doing it. I follow him around as he pulls on ropes and the cables that secure the mast in place—shrouds—and frowns at the state of *Becky Ann*. His eyes dart from one thing to another and he frowns, and I can just hear him thinking, *What did this idiot do to the boat I perfected for her?*

"I don't know what you're looking for, but it's all fine," I hear myself tell him defensively. "We did perfectly well up to now, and we'd have done fine without you too. Liv just got busy. She's got so much going on."

"It *is* fine," he says. But he's retying the fenders on the toe rails, all four of them. He's methodically unknotting them and reknotting them to meet his private standards.

Putting those fenders out every time we're coming to a dock is my job. I wasn't going to get any knot-tying badges, but they stayed on and did what they were supposed to do.

And then he's moving the dock lines around, even though the boat is hardly in danger of floating away. Dock lines: also my responsibility. He says nothing as he works, though I'm eyeing him like a hawk.

"What are you doing?" I ask him when I can't take it anymore.

"Hop onto the dock, I'll show ya," he says.

"I told you, I don't want a sailing lesson," I reply.

He shrugs his shoulders. "Well then."

But what is he doing? I watch as he takes the black dock lines off their cleats, moves them incrementally, and then resecures them. The boat's nose backs off the dock a bit, and I see now that *Becky Ann* is holding perfectly still along the dock instead of drifting over a few feet with the waves and then snapping back when the lines are taut.

"Oh," I say, aloud.

"Makes for a better night's sleep, I tink," he says. "Not a big deal, really. I can sleep in a pipe cot in a typhoon."

"What's a pipe cot?" I ask him.

He raises one eyebrow at me. "It really does seem like you want sailing lessons."

I cross my arms over my chest. "I'll google it."

A moment passes where he's adjusting the topping line, and another while he rerigs the traveler. I refuse to ask why, though I'm dying to know. Then he drops into the cockpit and looks at some instruments, shifts his jaw, contemplative, and pops over to the navigation tower. I still have no idea what he's doing.

"Did you really sail in a typhoon?" I ask him.

"Not intentionally, but yeah," he says. "Crewing in a Pacific crossing, before I came to the States. Brilliant trip, though, aside from the weather."

"How long have you been sailing?" I ask him.

"Couple, twenty years now," he says. Ok, so he's gotta be at least, what, midthirties, I tell myself. Because who sails when he's ten years old? "Only crew, though, until I was about fifteen. I was very into racing." Oh. Maybe *he* does.

"Sailboat racing," I say. I only now consider that that's a thing. I suppose that's what all those fancy events off the coast are, America's Cup and the sort, and isn't sailing in the Olympics now? I cannot begin to imagine the boredom involved in doing this as a sport. "That's like racing turtles," I say.

"What?" he asks. "Are you saying it's slow?"

"We could have driven down the coast three times over by now," I say.

He shakes his head with disdain. "Driving."

"Yes, driving," I say. "It's a mode of transportation where you don't get stuck on lobster traps, drenched in rainstorms, and lost in the dark, hours from the nearest shelter."

Grant stops what he's doing and looks at me. "So you're not in love with the sport yet, then."

I try not to bark out an ironic laugh and shake my head. "I am not. And to be honest, is anything you can do after three gin and tonics really a sport?"

Grant considers me, slowly. His gaze is long and critical. I haven't been looked at like this in a very long time. It feels, remarkably, like when I used to find myself standing naked in front of my ex-husband. Like I'm being evaluated. It makes me want to put on a poncho.

"You know, you don't look much like Olivia," he says. "She must favor her father."

Olivia is gorgeous, lush, young. I run slim, and my curves are only a quiet echo of hers. My arms and legs are skinny with little bumps of muscle here and there. The body of an underfed farmhand, Alistair once told me. But Liv and I have the same hair, silky, shoulder length, and rich red-gold, and the same watery blue eyes.

"Your eyes are different," he goes on.

"No, they're not," I say.

"They are. Yours are . . ." He falls off. "I just wouldn't have pegged you for mother and daughter," he says.

Oh, for Pete's sake. "She probably takes after her dad a little," I say, just to be friendly. "I think the resemblance is pretty balanced between us."

"Your ex-husband," he says.

I nod.

"The VRO."

"Sorry?"

"VRO. Very Rich Owner. The sailing world is full of them. Men and women, but usually men, who buy far more boat than they need, and then let us plebes do all the sailing, the care, the maintenance. Without them, there'd be no full-service marinas, no ship stores, no sailing lessons. No work for a guy like me."

"I thought you were an adjunct professor," I said. "Or was it a TA?"

"Eh. That's just working for the children of VROs," he says.

Well, he's got that right in our case, I think.

But then he smiles at me, and his eyes glimmer a bit. "Sure, you're the VRO now, though."

"Is there such a thing as VPO?" I ask him. "Very Poor Owner?"

"Not for long," he says, and the smile that was growing on my face withers and dies.

"Sorry. I just mean to say, boats can be expensive to own. They're a dear hobby. When the chips are down, they're usually the first thing to go."

"Certainly true in my case," I say, feeling a bit pathetic.

"Well, I'm sorry for you," he tells me. "It's a rough spot you're in."

"I'm fine," I reassure him. "I will be fine. Which is really thanks to you."

"Ah, you're the one doing me the favor," he says. "You've saved my summer."

I think: *What a lunatic.* I say: "Will we make it to Miami in time, do you think?"

"That's down to the weather, sure it is."

Oh come on. "Just say we will," I tell him. "After all, you sailed through a typhoon."

"You're right. We absolutely will make it in time," he replies. "And no typhoons in the forecast," he adds with a wink. "But here, let me show you something," he says.

He takes me down into the hull of the boat. The spot where Liv was sitting an hour ago still looks oddly empty. Her berth has been fully cleaned out, I finally see, with a heavy heart. And I suppose, now that I think of it, that's where Grant will be sleeping. How strange it will be to share such a tiny space with a near stranger. A stranger who's the ex-boyfriend of my twenty-one-year-old daughter, to make it weirder still.

He grabs our sat-enabled tablet, opens to the Garmin app, and shows me our next series of days to sail. "Here, here, and here," he shows me, pointing out anchor symbols on the map. "We can anchor off or grab a disused mooring ball, sleep the night, and carry on the next day. It'll get us there a day late at worst with good weather. But . . . if you're up to a few hours of independent sailing, four and four, then we'll be around here at the end of the three days." He gestures to a point far more southerly. "If the weather holds, we'll anchor there for a spell, wait out this storm here"—he gestures to what looks like an angry patch of rash on the radar screen—"and rest up. The rest of the path can be a bit more leisurely."

"Four and four?" I say. "As in, I'm only sailing alone for four hours at a time?"

"Right," he says. "Well, you do a four-hour watch, I do eight, and then you do four again."

"So you're only sleeping four hours at a time?"

He nods.

"Won't you be exhausted?"

He looks at me for a moment, truly considering it, and with a very honest look on his face, he simply shakes his head.

"I need to sleep for more than four hours," I tell him equally honestly. "Or I'll walk off the side of the boat in a daze."

"No, no. We can't have that," he says. "Twenty-four hours in a day, Rebecca Ann," he says, and for some reason—his accent is probably all it is—I don't hate it when he uses my middle name. "We'll have our lessons together midday. I'll snooze at sunset, you get your full beauty rest in the night, take the six a.m. watch while I grab another kip, and we do it all again the next day."

"Our lessons? Have I not made myself clear on the lessons thing?"

Grant shrugs. "I'm a sailing teacher, not a deliveryman," he tells me a second time. "Think of how nice it will be when you know what you're doing. What fun you'll have when you're confident at the helm. What do you say?"

I don't want to laugh in his face, but I feel I've had enough of this to know that me and sailing are not something I will ever describe as "what fun." But he's immovable. Finally I just tell him, "Ok, fine. If I have to take the lessons with the delivery, knock yourself out. But don't take it personally if I don't get a passing grade."

"Ah, well, offshore sailing is pass fail, love," he tells me. "You either figure out what you're doing eventually, or you drown."

And with that pep talk, I find my adventure beginning anew.

17

With all due respect to my daughter—and right now I'm not really feeling that much respect, to be clear—whatever we were doing before was not what Grant Murphy would have defined as sailing. Sailing according to Grant Murphy is a thing that is thoughtful, methodical, and precise. A dance, choreographed beat by beat. We are now underway, but what led up to it was nothing like the coffee-fueled frenzy of ropes and sails that Liv and I relied on. Instead, this morning I experienced what can only be described as a muster drill—a lesson in the safety equipment on the same boat I've been traveling on for the last two weeks. Then a lecture on the importance of tidy lines. Then a scolding for nonchalance in my use of my very expensive rapid-inflating personal-flotation device, which is too big and hot and rubs hard against my neck whenever I lift my arms. There's a right way to wear it, I'm told.

"Step one," he tells me, "actually put it on. All the time. One hundred percent of the time we're underway. With the buckles. If I see you without it, I will send you below."

"I like it down there," I reply, though in fact, most of the times I have gotten seasick have started with a trip belowdecks, where the air is stale and the rocking of the boat comes without visual warnings.

"If you don't want to wear your PFD right now," he tells me, "we can switch to the lesson on how to clean and maintain a marine head."

I gulp. The toilet in this thing is a mystery I prefer not to delve into. It'll be the heavy nylon vest, then, round the clock.

I buckle it and adjust the straps performatively.

"Next time, buy one in person, make sure it fits," he tells me. "Does everything have to be bought and sold online?"

I can't help but laugh at him. "You sound like my grandpa," I tell him.

"Must have been a smart one, your grand-da. Likely didn't drown at sea."

"Lived his whole life in Nebraska, so no," I say.

As he watches me work, and then repeats everything I do, only "the right way," we fall into some kind of power-imbalanced rhythm of work. I take off the dock lines in the wrong order. He makes me put them back again. I jump too soon, and he makes us repeat the launch. I leave knots in the fender ropes, and then call them "ropes" out loud. This results in a lengthy lesson on the etymology of sailing terms. It seems calling things "ropes" is a serious breach in Grant Murphy's navy. Even though they are, in fact, ropes.

For two long hours it's me taking orders, and then him telling me what I did wrong and saying, not cruelly, but firmly, "Try it again."

When it finally comes time to hoist the main, he sees the way I have to jump and pull, using all of my body weight to get the heavy white sail up those last three feet of the mast, and says, "We'll getcha on the helm soon enough, small fry."

I don't know if it's a promise or a threat.

Though I don't much like being ordered around under normal circumstances, there's something so frighteningly capable about Grant that I find I don't mind our lessons that morning. It's almost as though I'm a child, a fortysomething child who just longs to be given proper instruction. And it makes sense, after so much floundering, that I would enjoy finally starting to understand what makes this ship sail. When, together, we get the jib up, I marvel at how quickly it fills with air, and the turbo-boost of acceleration we feel when it's trimmed just right. Grant tinkers and tinkers with the main, the traveler, the jib sheets, and after all of his fidgets and adjustments, suddenly, magically, the boat seems to shift into something nimble and light. It's instantaneous, like pushing a button. Like shifting into high gear.

Where before we were in the water, pushing through it, suddenly we're in the wind. The boat almost seems to take off, like a plane just as its wheels leave the tarmac. The sails aren't just full: they're catching the air like kites. Imagine a waterfall made of air, the wind spilling in and over our sails in constant motion, the boat's massive keel simply a lazy foot dangling in the waves, while the sails become wings and take flight.

Grant calls me from the front of the cockpit, where I have been wedged near the port-side self-tailing winch. He gestures to the back, to the opposite wheel he's on, and when I make my way aft, he shows me the instruments, the readings, one by one, helping me to make sense of them. Somehow, incomprehensibly, we are making the same knots as the apparent wind speed. We're not just harnessing the wind anymore. We *are* the wind.

And I do feel free.

I look out to the horizon. The sky is almost a primary color today, the blue of a child's crayon. There are thin long strands of clouds rippling like their own kind of waves in echoing patterns, just off the coast as far as I can see. The waves, too, seem to have organized themselves from random roiling forces into a neat line, and the boat has taken from bumping over them to rolling across, like it hears something musical beyond my understanding. The telltales fly straight out, and Grant never lets go of the wheel. He is playing, I realize. Gaming the wind.

"How do you do that?" I ask him, and somehow, he doesn't say, *Do what?*

He simply tells me, "Imagine you arrive on a friendly planet full of distinct alien tribes. They show you to their library, packed with books in all their languages, but you can't understand a word any of them are saying."

"Uh . . ."

"There are as many languages being spoken on *Becky Ann*," he tells me, "as there are on any continent." He gestures to the wind instrument display. "When you sail long enough, you'll speak them all, and then, Becca, you can do anything." I cannot do anything—at least not on *Becky Ann*—I want to tell him, but something about the way he says it makes me want to believe him. "Start here," and he shows me the display that has a needle shaped like a boat as viewed from above. "Look from the hawk." He points up into the sky at the top of the mast, where what I would normally think of as a weathervane points the direction of the wind. "Then to the telltales, then to the instruments, and then to the weather itself. Read each one, in order, and then read them all again. They're all saying the exact same thing, in different words. You'll learn one language, then another, then another." He moves the wheel incrementally, and the boat gets even more speed. "Start with whatever feels closest to English to you."

"But how do I read weather?" I ask him, mystified. Perhaps he's mistaken me for some kind of nature girl.

"It's written in the water and on the sky," he says. "If you've never seen that language before, it will take the longest to learn, but you will learn it. See that?" he asks and points out to a line of waves that are out of sync with their partners. Just a ripple, where there should be a trough. It wouldn't have registered to me if he hadn't pointed it out, no matter how long I stared.

"That little blip of a dark wave?"

"It's a gust. Rest your hands on the wheel and feel it."

I don't know what he means, but I do as I'm told. And sure enough, there it is, a push and a bending and then the wheel moves itself, and the boat heels farther, and all I can think of is that we are a leaping horse, a horse that can fly, that what we are doing is at once the most natural thing in the world and the most uncanny.

And then Grant takes his own wheel and corrects us, and since I'm on the high side, I feel, just for a second, as if I'm totally weightless. My heart, the traitor, skips a beat.

He puts his hand on the compass and shows me the bearing. We're running southeast now, when we should be going south-southeast. I tilt my head at him. "Aren't we going the wrong way?"

"Take the wind. It's a light, light day. If the wind is on offer, take it."

"But we'll never get where we're going," I say.

"We'll get there, and in less time, I promise you." And sure enough, in a half hour, when the wind is fading, we tack in and zigzag back to our GPS line. Again Grant walks me through trimming each inch of each sail to perfection, and the boat takes flight again. And again I am amazed, exhilarated, to find he is right.

———

All day we sail this way, no autopilot, no lunch cocktails, no "that's probably good enough." Only "try it again." Grant is quiet unless he has something to tell me about sailing. After I've brought up puffy white pita wraps I made fresh on the stove, stuffed with red pepper hummus and salad dressed with yogurt, and he's eaten four servings before my very eyes, he finally puts me at the helm. Then he begins climbing around the deck, inspecting the jib and main—for what, I have no idea. Before me, the sun is setting, and for the first time on this trip, I have no idea where the nearest bailout harbor might be. We are on the water, and the weather forecast is clear, and we don't need to bail out, I realize, because we can sail all night.

And it is such a delicious realization that, for just a moment, I think I *get* sailing.

And then Grant is hollering back to me, "Just a bit more into the wind, Becca!" and though he is calm, I see we are about to swing around in an accidental tack—I lost the wind while I was marveling at the experience itself. In surprise, I hit the wheel too hard, the wrong way, and Grant hollers, "Toward me!" and then I correct and the boom comes back around and I watch Grant bend into an impossible position to avoid it, and the damn guy never stops smiling all this time, even though I almost hit him with a full boom, and it probably would have knocked him flat on his back, or maybe right into the drink.

And of all things to say to me after this, he calls, "Exactly! You've got it!"

"Got what?" I ask him, thinking he's a lunatic. But he gestures to the hawk, the telltales, and the near distance, and then he puts his arms out wide. And I see, without really trying, that I have perfectly corrected the boat back into the corner of the wind, the "close reach," as he calls it, where I am supposed to be, and almost without thinking, my hand is on the mainsheet, having given it just two inches more to reach out and gather every drop of speed without changing our course even one tick on the compass.

"Oh wow!" I say. "Oh, wow!"

"You're sailing," he tells me and canters easily to the cockpit, and for a second, I think he'll hug me, but then he sits and puts his head back and stares up at the sky, relaxing from his teaching duties for the first time in eight hours.

The wind stays steady, and while his eyes are on the heavens, I look at him carefully for the first time today. He is wearing long lightweight hiking pants in some kind of sporty gray/khaki color and a white T-shirt with a marina logo on the breast pocket. Over the top, fitted like a gun holster, is his sleek black neoprene PFD, looking as well worn and well fitting as a favorite leather jacket. How does he make a life jacket seem daring and sexy?

"How old are you?" I blurt out without thinking.

His head pops back up. "What now?"

"Your age, it's hard to read," I tell him. "You can't be that young, if you're an adjunct, but then, you and Livvie . . ."

He tilts his head at me. Curious. Cautious. "What about me and Olivia?" he asks me.

"Speaking as her mother, it seems like you shouldn't have gone there. Professionally speaking," I say.

He arches his eyebrows at me, the glimmer in his eyes graying out. "Gone there," he echoes. "For your information, I haven't gone anywhere."

"Oh, really? So you didn't date my daughter?" I ask him.

Now he pulls up and is sitting perfectly erect, staring at me, like I'm speaking in tongues.

"Why would you tink that?" he asks me.

I raise my eyebrows. "You aren't really one for the straight answer, are you?" I ask him.

He sets his chin. "I haven't dated Olivia, no. I haven't dated any student, ever, and certainly not your daughter. There's your straight answer."

I puzzle over this. This was not a lukewarm response. It was firm, and fairly convincing, and yet . . . still a lie? I decide I don't want to ask anything else, not, at least, when trapped in the ocean alone with this guy. I go quiet. "Sorry then," I say after a long weird spell. "I must have gotten mixed up."

But when I say that, I think for the first time in a long time about Alistair, about the moment just between what I thought our marriage would always be and what it actually became. The first other woman.

She was a girl in the office—I want to say *woman* for all the proper reasons, but she seemed so much a girl, just as I was, back when we first met. She was pretty but not breathtaking. Resistible, one would think, if he had been trying to resist.

Alistair's mother told me casually about her one day over coffee, almost like a test. She had no inflated sense of drama, was just "curious" if I knew my husband had gotten very close to a summer associate. And oh, my face, when she told me. I can only imagine my face. From my face, she knew she'd stepped deeply into a mess that would take hours to hose off, and said, "Or perhaps I'm thinking of someone else. Yes, yes. I must have gotten mixed up," with such icy emptiness that I had almost been angrier at her than at Alistair.

Now I can't even remember the poor associate's name. I remember raging at Alistair, I remember making him move into the guest room for a couple of weeks. I remember the apologies and the flowers and the promise it would never happen again. I remember, even, him talking to his mother about it, since she had gone out of her way to get herself involved in the mess, and that was back when there was still some pretense that it was me, and not the Larkin family, to which he owed his allegiance. But I know full well that neither she then, nor I now, "must have gotten mixed up."

"It's six p.m.," I tell Grant, new suspicions mingling with years-ago pain. "Time for you to get some sleep. Oh, and I'm going to use autopilot," I add. "I'm not confident enough on my own, and I'm tired from a long day."

"Of course," he says. "That's what it's there for. I'll set my alarm, see you at ten, but, Becca?"

"Yes?"

"You know to get me, if you need me."

I nod. "I know," I say. But I am hoping, like hell, that I won't need him.

Grant checks the instruments, pats me on the back, and tells me it's been a good day. I only nod and think back to what Olivia told me about Grant, what I thought I understood. Wondering, what exactly did I get "mixed up," and who meant it to go that way?

18

I get through the night with flying colors and sleep like a log for the first time since we left Maine. The next day when I get done with my six to ten a.m. watch, I make us both breakfast—fresh Boston brown bread spread with butter and jam, as we've run out of eggs—and bring it up to the cockpit, only to find all the instrument panels still obscured by their weather-protective vinyl covers.

Grant is sprawled on the high side of the boat, long legs stretched out, like he's sunbathing, not sailing. The air is warm today, and he's in a shirt and shorts, his stubble filling back in admirably. He has a water bottle in one hand, the other draped loosely on the bottom of the wheel, his eyes cast to the telltales or maybe to the horizon. He looks utterly relaxed, utterly happy.

It's a very pretty picture, I must admit.

And maybe yes, I did take a bit more care this morning after my alarm went off. Maybe I brushed my hair for the first time in a week, instead of tying it up in a bun. Maybe I'm wearing deodorant. It's hardly primping, even by my relaxed sailing standards. This is my daughter's ex, after all.

But still my face feels warm when I see him, and when I watch him see me. He looks from my face to the plate of bread in my arms, wolfish.

And then eats two-thirds of the loaf gratefully.

When he's done, he tells me some "fun" news.

"You're a quick study, you are," he says. "And I tacked before you came up, so we're heading almost due south, and the forecast is calm."

I look at the GPS to get my bearings, but the screen is off. Grant smiles.

"You're helming today."

I frown and shake my head. "Must I?"

"Don't worry, you're ready. All you need is here," he says, gesturing to the analog compass that's set into the carriage roof just to the right of the companionway. The black floating ball shows north behind us and just a hair toward my left shoulder. If it were a clock, it would be 6:30. "And here," he says, pointing up to the telltales.

I exhale. "What's wrong with using the instruments?" I ask him.

"You are using an instrument," he says. "What do you think a compass is? I could have you sail by the sun, love."

I have to laugh at this. "I mean, do you have a sextant?" I reply. "Or one of those, ah . . ." I telescope my curled hands from both at my eyes to one extended, as if I'm a pirate looking for enemy ships.

"A spyglass?"

"Exactly! Or why not sail blindfolded, just using the feel of the wind and the scent of the sea?"

Grant beams at me. "I think that would be a brilliant experiment," he tells me. "But not when we have somewhere to be. Today, just take your compass heading every now and again, and keep an eye on the horizon, as there'll be some big boats crossing our path into the ICW or out again. As long as we're pointed in the right direction, your job is simply to keep going, keep the sails full. Round three or four o'clock, we should get some wind, maybe a storm. You'll get to learn to put a reef in," he says happily.

"Oh boy," I say very quietly, because though I am not at all sure what that is and why it's fun to do in a rainstorm, I also don't want to dampen his sweet enthusiasm.

"What point of sail are we at?" he says as he cedes his high-side helm position to me.

I cup my hands over my eyes and look up at the sails. "Broad reach," I tell him, indicating that I did in fact study the chart Grant gave me when we traded watches last night.

He looks straight into my eyes and grins, as though I've just told him the best news in the world. "Yes! Yes, that's it. Oh, Becca Ann, you're brilliant at this. I thought, when I first saw you, *That's a sailor.* A woman comfortable leaning into the wind."

I have no idea what that means, nor why, coming out of those Irish lips of his, it feels like the most overtly sexual come-on I've ever heard.

"And where's Chincoteague?"

I look at him for a moment. We were in the Delaware River yesterday, so we'd need to have been in a car to be even in the vicinity of the barrier island that protects Virginia's coast. Vaguely, I point straight ahead.

Grant takes my frozen body, pointing like an Irish setter, and moves the whole thing until I am facing straight to the starboard side of the boat. West. As in, somehow we've covered so much ground that we're two states from where he and I started.

"What?" I ask him.

He puts his arms up in the air. "The wind is with us," he tells me. "I expect we'll be ready to start the ICW at first light tomorrow. If we even still want to."

"This round-the-clock-sailing thing is amazing!" I tell him.

He laughs.

"And also, this knowing-what-you're-doing thing is even better!" I add. "At this rate we'll be in Miami tomorrow!"

"Six days, I think," he says. "But yes, we'll beat that tropical storm coming in off Barbados by a fair shot."

Well, that's a relief.

"You slept ok, under sail?" he asks.

I think on that. I actually slept so much better last night on the water than I did when we were in a berth the night before, but then, that night was heavy with worries. Trading out Grant for Liv wasn't my ideal plan, but at least I know, thanks to a quick, information-only text back-and-forth on my sat phone, that she's safely back in New England, at her dad's Boston apartment, where she would be hard pressed to fall into the ocean at any given moment.

"It's weird to sleep wedged on one side of the berth and wake up wedged on the other," I admit. "But I was sleeping so heavily I don't remember the roll. Are you tired from the broken-up schedule?" I ask him.

He shakes his head. "In the Middle Ages in Ireland, lots of people slept in two short chunks for their entire adult lives. Not entirely clear on what they did in the middle of the night, assuming they weren't sailing to Miami. Probably prayed a little and drank a lot."

I laugh. "I bet they nursed their babes, stoked their fires." I say that and realize, of course, what they were really doing in the dead of night was having sex. Embarrassed, I add, "Maybe they started the rise on a loaf of bread."

He nods. "And then of course, during the famine, the coffin ships to America sailed all night and all day, and I imagine the fewer crew they took, the more paying passengers they could manage."

"Hardly the standard of travel we want to emulate," I say.

"They got here—or many did, at least," he says. "More Irish in America than in Ireland now."

"Irish-ish," I say, thinking of my cartoonish neighbor with his Guinness bar decor and touristy plaid family crest over the fireplace, though he's never put a foot out of New England. "You're Irish Irish. It's different."

"Difference of a twist of fate a hundred years ago is all. Sure, here I am in America anyway."

"Why *are* you here?" I ask him.

"Ah. I followed a girl, didn't I? Beautiful, smart woman, came to do her studies at MIT. And then she met a beautiful, smart man, before a year was out, and the guy had a Canadian passport. How could I compete? She lives in Ontario now, baby on the way."

"Hard to beat free health care and Tim Hortons," I say gently.

"Indeed, and well, she was my first love. You can't go marrying your first love all the time, now, can you? No adventure in that."

There's that word, *adventure*. It keeps popping out of the mouths of the people around me, and I'm not sure what it means, or what, exactly, it has to do with me. "I married my first love," I say. "You're right. Not the best way to do it."

There's a silence fallen over us now, and I check my heading, finding, to my surprise, that I'm helming the boat much as I would drive a car on a long tollway. Small adjustments, following the line of the wind just as I would follow the line of the road. "I think I'm sailing," I tell him.

"I know ya are," he says back. "Just needed a good teacher is all."

"Don't be so pleased with yourself," I tease. "I didn't say I like it."

"Didn't have to."

Ah, but I do like it, curse it all. I don't feel sick, or scared, or lost.

Oh dear. It seems I like sailing when I'm sailing with Grant Murphy.

"And what about your second love," I ask him, to keep those thoughts at bay. "Will you marry her?"

"I don't know. I haven't met her yet. Could be anyone. Could be you."

I choke and jerk the wheel, forcing the boat to wobble unnervingly before I can correct it. "Grant!" I cry when we're back on course. "You're my daughter's ex-boyfriend. It sure as heck had better not be me."

"Ach, there we are again," he says. "This nonsense. This has got to be cleared up, and now. I can't have you thinking I'm seducing college girls. That wouldn't be right."

I inhale, exhale, steady myself. "Ok, good," I say, now as ready to talk turkey as he is. "Listen, Grant, I'm telling you all this because we're going to be stuck on a boat together for some time, and I need you to understand the realities here: My daughter and I are very close. Best-friends close. I know what's going on in her life," I say, though, actually, once the words are out of my mouth, I wish I could take them back. Lately, they don't feel as true as I'd like them to be. "Olivia told me you were her ex-boyfriend, and your weird refusal to acknowledge that is not going to impress your honor upon me. And for that matter, your honor isn't really at stake here. I've been to college. I know how this stuff goes. There's quite a difference from a twenty"—I wave my arms around—"twenty-however-old-you-are TA taking a coed out on a few dates and some weird ick power dynamic between a professor and his student. So just . . . that's it. I don't care that you dated my daughter. I'm not going to call the school and have you fired or anything. Olivia's a grown woman, and she's hardly vulnerable when it comes to guys. She has to bat them away most of the time. Like, literally. My ex-husband makes her keep a baseball bat in the back of her car at all times."

While I am saying all this, my eyes are on the sails, so I'm surprised that when I look back to Grant, he's not on the cockpit bench but has climbed over to the weather edge of the boat, the side that is tilted low toward the water. He's sitting pointing out toward the water eight feet in front of me, his feet dangling off the side, his torso safe behind the lifelines. His body weight is enough that I have to adjust the traveler just a smidge so the boom is where I want it again.

He isn't even looking at me. He's looking out at the sea, which, thanks to the sharp tilt of the sailboat, he is considerably closer to than I am. I wonder for a second, just a second, if he's going to lean back away from the lifelines and let his entire body slide under them into the waves.

"Grant?" I shout.

"Yes, Becca. I heard you, all your whats and wherefores," he calls back to me with a dismissive wave. "I'm trying to decide if I am going to try to convince you to hear the truth, or let you think what you want."

"Oh, sheesh," I say. "If I'm so wrong, you might as well correct me."

"Ah, but will you believe me then? If I speak contrary to the word of your daughter, who's also your best friend?" Grant looks away from me and leans even farther forward on the lifelines, his legs bouncing with the movement of the ship. This, I realize, is about as far as he can get from me on this boat without going overboard.

I am silent for a moment, giving his words some genuine thought. Without a doubt, the last weeks have eroded my trust in my daughter. But could I ever let him see that? I refuse to betray her so. "Probably not," I tell him. "Because why would Olivia lie?"

After a long time, he says, "I think that, Becca Ann, is an excellent question."

19

To my great surprise, we make it all the way to the entrance of the ICW during my next watch. Instruments or no, there's no missing where we are when land rises out of thin air and the waters seem to propagate barges, motor yachts, fishing vessels, and cruise ships out of nowhere. This is it. I have done it. Just me, with a good teacher and a great deal of courage. Guess what, Alistair? Rebecca Ann Larkin has learned how to sail.

And then, when I have made the most minute of adjustments to the points of sail and we are running alongside the coastline of Cape Charles, where the Chesapeake opens to the Atlantic, I get another clue of my success: my phone springs to life, not on satellite—which is slow, expensive, and laggy enough that I have all push notifications off—but on a regular old cell tower nearby.

My watch buzzes, and then the screen fills with messages, and I realize just how completely enmeshed I've been in this process, in the rhythms of the water and wind, because every notification comes as something of a surprise. Chatter from a group chat; Natasha twice, asking for updates; and three messages from Liv with updates on her doings. I take in her messages and realize that for once in my life I haven't been wondering what Liv is up to in every second of her day.

Because my day has been so full of sailing. Because I have truly lost myself in the work.

The thought actually gives me some guilt. Aren't moms supposed to be thinking of their children every moment of their day? Isn't that the standard I've been holding myself to?

But that's ridiculous. Why on earth shouldn't I just let her be? She's left of her own volition, and she's got people looking out for her, and she's got her own choices ahead. Choices I've tried to guide but I certainly can't make for her. Or somehow will her to make by way of psychic connection. It's ok, I tell myself, to just let her be. And the idea of that feels so incredibly good that I know I'm on to something.

I put the helm on autopilot so I can fill Natasha in on the general gist of the trip, omitting the drama between me and Liv, the struggles of the previous legs, and the simmering sexual attraction I can't seem to ignore between a guy who may or may not be my own daughter's ex-boyfriend: Trip going fine, almost to VA beach, more tomorrow. I send something equally vague to Liv, but just seconds after I hit send, the phone starts to ring with her number.

"You're alive!" she says when she picks up.

"Of course I am," I tell her. "You're right about Grant, he's an excellent sailor."

"Are you still mad at me?" she asks.

"I was never mad at you," I tell her, but then I realize that actually, I was. "Well, ok, I guess I was mad, now that you bring it up. I don't think you handled the situation that well."

"I'm not like you, Mom. I can't just keep going like nothing's wrong when everything is wrong."

"You mean keep your commitments? Power through the hard times? I'm proud of that trait. That's just who I am."

"Well, I'm a person who knows when to fold 'em. That's just who I am."

I try to hold my tongue. And then fail. "You know what is driving me nuts about you right now?" I tell her. "Your insistence on making grand proclamations about who you are. You're an iconoclast, you're an outlier, you know when to fold 'em. At the age of twenty-one, those are all just stories you tell yourself. They can be limiting stories."

"Ok, fine," says Liv. "But what stories are you telling yourself, then? What kind of stories did you have to tell yourself to stay in a loveless marriage for twenty-two years?"

Normally, I think, I would just take this lip from her. But today, for some reason, I don't feel totally normal. Today, I feel like speaking a little of my truth.

"When you say things like that, you sound every bit the trust fund princess I don't want you to become."

"So you are still mad at me," she supplies.

"No. Mad is not the word. In fact, I think you did the right thing leaving."

"You do?" She is shocked. I am, too, actually. Something key is dawning on me. Something I wasn't ready to understand until now.

"You should have been more honest about your plans with me and with Grant," I tell her frankly. "But I'm starting to put together the pieces of this puzzle. I think while we were sailing together, we were on top of each other and both trying to figure things out after a huge shift in our family circumstances. And I think just as you have your own stories about yourself, I have stories about you too. When I was your age, I would have given anything for a mother who had all the time and energy I have for you. I would have loved to sail, or fly, or hell, take a walk with my mom. My greatest dream was to pack all my necessities in one little bag and see the world. And to feel like someone was cheering that dream on? It would have changed everything." *Everything.* I don't regret those first wonderful years with Alistair. But staying a Larkin for far too long? That was something I did because I believed I wouldn't survive without that support.

"But," I go on, "I am starting to see that this was *my* dream, not yours. Being held to someone else's wishes, being the center of someone else's expectations, that can be a lot of pressure, and that pressure might even lead you to try to be someone you're not."

Liv is quiet for a moment. "What do you mean?" she says at last. Her voice is hushed. It could be dangerous, the territory I'm in. But this could be my only chance.

I decide to go in for the kill. "Tell me more about what happened between you and Grant."

Now the silence is so long that I start to wonder if she hung up. "Livvie?"

My daughter seizes on this moment of forgetfulness. "How many times do I have to tell you? It's Liv. Olivia if you have to. Livvie is a pimply girl with bad hair who goes to community college."

"I'm just going to ignore that idiotically entitled remark, because obviously I've hit some kind of nerve asking about Grant."

"Oh, so now I'm an idiot?"

I want to scream. "No, but you sure do sound entitled. Your ideas about your name are your right, but you should know they're just another story. And here's a story for you: after I had you, I had the worst hormonal shift—as in, bad hair and blackheads. I was very proud to go to community college to finish my prereqs at the same time as I was raising a baby. And for your information, I loved the heck out of your dad back then, and he thought I was even more beautiful than when we first met. I couldn't keep him off me. If I wasn't very good at taking my pill at the same time each day no matter what, you'd have four siblings, the way we carried on."

"Uhhhhhghhhhghhhh," says Liv into the phone.

"And through school and life and love and loss, I took good care of that little girl. And I called that baby Livvie, and now that she's grown, she has the right to call herself whatever she wants, but she'd better have a bit of patience for the woman who gave her life, you hear me?"

"You're acting weird."

I *am* acting weird, I realize. I am treating Olivia like a real person and not my perfect angel. Because I suddenly see she's had that honor for a bit too long.

"And you're being deceptive. What is the truth here, Liv? What aren't you telling me?"

Olivia takes a deep breath in, so deep it sounds loud even over the miles. Then she says, "I met Grant right after you and Dad went public with the divorce."

I nod to myself. We filed between semesters so she wouldn't be under extra pressure from exams or midterms when the news went out. "Ok," I say, when I realize she can't see me nodding her onward.

"He's cute, obviously. He's friendly. I thought . . ." Her voice drifts away. "Ugh, Mom. This is too embarrassing."

"You've seen me almost fall off a boat a large number of times," I remind her.

"True. Well, I guess I just misread the signals. I thought we had a thing. A flirtation thing. And then after sailings, we'd all go to the student union and have beers, and he'd come, too, and it started to feel like we were really connecting. I thought . . . well, I guessed the reason he wasn't making a play was because I was his student. Mom, this is going to sound kind of cocky, but I've never really liked a boy and not had him like me back. I didn't know what that looked like."

I think this through. Did I ever teach her about rejection? Maybe her father and I protected her from that lesson a bit too much, with all our smoothing over of life's wrinkles. Maybe we have a little catch-up work to do there. "Ok, that makes sense. So then what?"

"So then I started texting him."

"About what?"

"Just anything. Like you do when you're dating someone. Normal stuff."

"And what did he text back?"

"I guess not much, looking back on it. I mean, he was very businesslike. I even teased him about how I wasn't going to turn him in to the dean." She lets out a clipped laugh. "God, this is embarrassing."

"I think this situation is pretty normal, babe. Cute older guy in position of authority? Nabokov had a lot to say on the matter."

"And Sting," she adds. "But it wasn't a Sting situation. It wasn't like 'Don't stand so close to me,' it was like, 'No, literally, go over there, I'm not interested.' Oh Mom."

"Oh babe," I echo. "That sucks. I'm so sorry. He's a fool not to adore you."

"Mom, listen to you! You are like a track on repeat. He's not a fool. Sometimes, believe it or not, a guy isn't going to want to date me. And he tried to let me down easy, and I kept pushing it and pushing it, and then, ugh!"

She's right, I realize. He's not a fool. It's time to dismantle Liv's pedestal, just a tiny bit. "So then what happened?" I ask her.

"Then I texted him a selfie."

"So?"

"A selfie, Mom. A . . . you know . . ."

Oh. Oh no. "A naked picture? Of yourself?" I try to keep breathing, but I feel like I'm going to jump into the black waters of the Chesapeake to avoid this reality. I grip the helm tighter. "Honey," I start.

"Don't. I know. I am never, ever, ever, ever going to do that again. He took me aside after class and told me I had to stop. He told me I could take an excused incomplete, or transfer to a different section, and he was sorry, but I had gotten it all backward, and . . . anyway he never looked at or spoke to me again, until that day at the marina. And that was like, the second-worst day of my life. I wanted to die right there."

"Oh," I say, my heart poured into that one syllable as if it can reach to Boston and wrap my poor embarrassed daughter into a huge hug from here. "Oh Liv, that is . . . you poor thing. That is . . . painful."

"I thought I was actually in love with him, Mom. But none of this had anything to do with him, and everything to do with . . . just the whole situation. You and Dad. Wanting to be, I don't know, grown and away from it all. I had this fantasy we'd fall in love, go to Ireland, I wouldn't have to put up with all the people who hate Larkin and Larkin, or with taking care of you now that you're alone—"

"Now hold on. Who said you have to take care of me?" I ask.

There's a long pause, and then finally, she says, "Daddy. He says you can't manage on your own. He asked me to be . . . his proxy."

A barely stitched-up pain inside me rips wide open again. That is it. "ALISTAIR," I shout into the nothingness of the water and sky. "FUDGE YOU!"

"Just say fuck, Mom."

"I will NOT," I insist. "I will *not* say fuck. I will not be reduced. I am not a child, and I don't need you to be his proxy, and frankly, he was terrible at taking care of me, so please do NOT step into those horrible, stupid two-thousand-dollar bespoke Italian loafers, if you don't mind." I feel rage coursing through me, and it's familiar. In fact, being angry at Alistair might be the most familiar thing I've known over the last decade. The anger is like being home in my old house, angrily cleaning the air intake on the fridge, scraping soap scum off shower tiles, using a toothbrush to scrub each inch of the oven rack until it shines like new.

If I just had some teak oil around right now, I would polish those handrails until they turned to dust in my hands. That's how angry I am right now.

"Mom, are you breathing?" she asks me.

"Kind of," I admit.

"Should I have told you that?" she asks.

"You absolutely should have. You are not a child, but even so, the whole ball game in a good divorce is to not get the kids involved in the drama. Your dad and I agreed on that. That was the deal. That was the reason I waited so long to leave him." As soon as the words are out of my mouth, I realize what I've done.

"What do you mean, waited so long?" she asks me.

I am quiet for a second. "You've been honest with me, and it can't have been easy. You deserve the same courtesy. The truth is, I have been trying to leave your dad for years, but back then I just couldn't figure out how I could make it work without his financial support. I was too scared, and Dad knew that. One day, after I started to believe I would be in that marriage forever, something came up that I couldn't tolerate, and I finally told him to fix it or I was gone for good. He didn't fix it." I exhale. "But even then, it was hard to finally give up the marriage. Harder than it should have been. You're not so wrong about me, Liv. I am afraid of what's out there. Anyone in my shoes would be." I think for a second and add, "Where you're wrong is that it's your job to take care of me now."

"Well, I tried anyway," she says. "And I sucked at it. I left you in the middle of the ocean in a huff."

"Now that I know what you were up to, your huff makes a lot more sense. Look, I will gladly accept your friendship, but I don't want you or your father's pity. Sharing your twenty-first birthday with your aging mother was, truly, the sweetest thing. It made a very hard day so much better. That's where it should have stopped."

"You're not that old, Mom," she says, a reflex. "And if you want me to believe you can take care of yourself, stop acting like you're a hundred and about to die in your sleep."

I think about this, wonder if she's right about that. After all, I did just sail the Chesapeake without instruments. "You're not that old, either, honey," I tell her. "What happened with Grant, that was just . . . it was just part of growing up."

She sighs. "Did you already know?" she asks me. "Did Grant tell you everything on the boat?"

"No. He didn't say a word. But he didn't let your lie stand either. He . . ." I look for words to describe his quiet but firm denial, his insistence on letting Liv tell her own story when she was ready. "Aside from his terrible taste in girls, he seems like a decent guy. If you're going to have an imaginary infatuation with a teacher, at least you picked a kind one." One whose status has just lifted even higher in my estimation.

"He's really kind. I can't even pretend he led me on. I'm just . . . I'm an idiot."

"We've all been there," I tell her.

"You haven't!" she exclaims. "You were married by the time you were my age. You have no idea."

I think back to a moment about five years ago. When Alistair was seeing a casual friend of mine. Our friendship vanished quickly—not because I knew what was going on, but because she chose him over me. But then one day I came home from the grocery store with my arms full of bags, and her car was parked in front of my house, and something deep, deep inside me said, "Do not go inside the house."

I couldn't pretend anymore if I went inside the house. And I preferred, back then, to pretend.

"I have some idea," I tell her. "Just trust me on that. And if I could have one wish, it would be that neither of us has to feel that kind of shame ever again."

20

I wake the next morning in the very middle of my berth, arms spread out wide as if to take up as much of the bed as possible, and a little part of my brain puts a pin in the fact that I'm not wedged in one corner or the other. But it isn't till after my first beautiful cup of coffee that I hear the ting, ting, ting of shackles on the mast and I realize we're not under sail. No motor, no sail, no waves lapping against the bulkhead. We're at anchor. Where are we? Why did we stop? What does it mean?

I twist my hair back and pour a cup for Grant before heading up the gangway. "What's happening?" I ask him.

He doesn't have to answer. I see what's up right away. What's up is that when I went to bed, we were in the middle of a vast bay, and now we're in paradise. To the aft of the boat I see long narrow strips of land, dotted with just a few brightly colored homes, boathouses surrounded by white railed porches, long piers on stilts poking out into a sea that is ten different blues and a few greens besides, depending on where you look. The bright sky stretches farther than it should, streaked by pink and orange ribbons of cloud, and the air smells sweeter, the sun heating the brine and the warm breezes carrying it inland like a fresh-baked gift.

"Welcome to the Outer Banks," says Grant as he accepts his coffee. Do our hands touch? Does the music swell when I look out on the stunning expanse of beach and grass, of navy-blue water and lavender horizon from the sunrise behind us?

I don't know. Something zings between us, and then as soon as I can turn on my senses to try to figure out what, it's gone. Surely it wasn't . . . but then, knowing what I know now, about what really happened—or didn't happen—between Grant and Liv, would it be so bad if it were?

I let myself consider him for a moment. Now that I know more about his character, I can see him with fresh eyes. Or rather, the old eyes that first saw him at the marina. More beard coming in, darker tan, sunlight glinting in the lightest strands of his rich brown hair. Wow. He's delicious. No wonder poor Olivia lost her mind. No wonder I'm losing mine.

"How old are you?" I ask him, and this time I'm ready to dig deep to get an answer. If he evades, I think, I'll find his license, or spend some of those precious sat-phone minutes googling. I need the straight truth. If he could be old enough, could I . . . ? I hardly want to let myself think it.

But this time, he doesn't evade. "I'm twenty-six," he says plainly. "My birthday was last month."

Oh my. I try not to choke on my own tongue.

"I'm forty-two," I tell him, before I think it through.

"I figured around there. I thought early thirties, when you came to the boatyard that first day in your wee sweater. But then you would have had Olivia when you were ten."

"I looked very different in my early thirties," I tell him. Just for one vain second I consider that I might actually look *better* now. I have, in the passing years, gotten cheekbones and a handle on my eyebrow situation. "You're a terrible judge of age."

"And what about you? Am I older or younger than you thought I'd be?"

153

Thought? I wonder. Or *hoped?* "Younger. Actually, a lot younger." Wouldn't it be lovely if he were thirty-five, even? I would settle for thirty.

"Ach, age is meaningless," he says, and I think, *Spoken like a youth.*

Instead I say, "Olivia is twenty-one. Not so different. Yet you kept her at arm's length."

"You talked to her? Is that why you were shouting about chocolate confectionary into the empty ocean last night?"

I blush, remembering how I had fumed over Alistair's meddling, forgetting that maybe I would have woken the sleeping man in the berth directly below. "Partly, yes. I think . . . I think I don't know her every thought quite as well as I proclaimed to. I'm sorry about that. I really had the wrong idea. But I still can't see why you weren't interested, when she's so close to you in age."

"Her age isn't the point. She's my student. She *was* my student."

"She's not now," I say.

"Yes, but . . ." His voice trails off, and he simply shrugs.

I puzzle this through. "You're seriously telling me you were never interested in her? She's gorgeous and smart too," I say. "And from a good family," I add as an afterthought. This is WASP code for rich, and I feel like that would have to be on the mind of a young man starting over in a new country, no matter how upright he might wish to be.

"Your daughter is very pretty, truly," he says, with absolutely no conviction.

"Well, then, why didn't you fall for her?"

"Don't take offense. It's not personal. I don't think her feelings were personal to me either. We'd never had a conversation, beyond sailing instructions and course assignments. She hardly knew anything about me. I get the impression she was going through something."

I look out at the shore, unwilling to discuss Olivia further without her permission. And maybe I'm startled by the depth of this young man's insights. Twenty-six, two years younger than Alistair when we first met. It's ridiculous to compare the men but impossible not to. When Alistair and I met all those years ago, the age difference between us was far from either of our minds. If anything, Alistair enjoyed that extra bit of authority between us that came from the combination of seniority and status over me. Yet Grant wouldn't touch Liv with a ten-foot pole. He had no interest in that kind of dynamic.

What kind of man will he be when he's nearing fifty? I steal a look at him, tanned, strong, completely engrossed in the care and workings of one solitary sailboat. Whatever his future holds, I don't imagine life as an infamous defense attorney in ten-thousand-dollar suits is in his future. No, this man reminds me of someone else: a younger, more hopeful version of me.

He catches me looking, and I cut my eyes again to the beach. It's early, and we're maybe three hundred feet away, but I can make out people walking their dogs and even a few tents up on the sand. Judging by the lack of development, this might be a preserve or a state park. *Campers?* I wonder. What a spectacular view to wake up to.

Or perhaps I have the best view, I realize. Perhaps I'm the one who has it made. I have a soft bed, running water, and a fridge. I suddenly feel that I'm in the lap of luxury, here at anchor, in my beautiful *Becky Ann*.

"Why did we stop?" I ask Grant.

"Partly just to check the anchor chain. I wanted to see that it was long enough, and dependable, if there's a storm down south."

"And is it?"

He nods.

"So shall we, then?" I ask, even though in truth, I'd like to stay here, bobbing around in this perfect blue dream and talking to Grant for the next three days. Reminding myself that this kind of life, unhurried, adventurous, inspired, even, is, at least for this moment, real. But that's not the task at hand.

"I was also waiting for you to wake up. It's time for us to decide if we're going to enter the ICW."

I think this through, looking from the GPS screen to the coast. "Is it, though? Or wouldn't that have been about three hours ago, when we were passing Norfolk?"

Grant gives me a sheepish smile. "Aye. Yes. I decided against it, and then got cold feet about making such a unilateral judgment. Wanted to go over it with you while there was still a choice to dip inland."

"Oh, well. That's actually lovely. Thank you for bringing me into this conversation." He's the skipper here, and he didn't have to. I'm unused to having my feelings taken into consideration before major decisions, I note with some regret.

"I can make a strong case for offshoring." He puts up a finger. "One thing, it's lovely out here. I've never been south of Washington, DC, before. This landscape's like nothing I've ever seen. And for another, the ICW has tides to manage, and shallows. I can guess we'll spend half the day backing off shoals of mud. Third, the weather is perfect for about eight more hours, easy. We'll be in a broad reach down the coast. Then we can dip into the channel in Pamlico Sound, miss tonight's rainstorm altogether that way. Or, you know. Sail through the rain."

He's a madman.

Still, he knows what he's doing, and I've learned enough that I know exactly what he's talking about. How cool is that? "The first plan is fine," I tell him. "The one where we miss the storm."

He nods at me. "Thought you'd say that."

"How are we on time?" I ask him.

"Good. Great, really. I think we're within five days' sail."

"We're still on schedule?" Part of me that hasn't been relaxed since that first offshore day in the Bay of Maine finally exhales. "Grant. You're amazing."

"Cheers to that. I have to tip my hat to you, though. I couldn't have made this time on my own. You're really catching on. There's just one major issue," he tells me.

I steel myself. I still risk backfilling the sails sometimes when I overcorrect. Or is it how I tied some knot or something?

"We're out of eggs."

Eggs? "Well, ok. Sure. Not a huge deal."

"We'll need to go on land, get some eggs at some point."

"What? Why?"

"I've got to make you an Irish breakfast. Sooner than later, preferably."

"What? Don't be silly. We've got things to do. We can have cereal or toast."

"Ach, no. I won't get off this sailboat till I've made you a proper fry-up. Eggs, beans, rashers, and fried bread. At the very least. Mushrooms and tomatoes would be nice too."

I can't tell if he's kidding. "O—kay? We'll get eggs, then. And . . . to-mah-toes," I add with a smile.

"That bread you made. That wheaten bread. You can make that again, yeah?"

"The Boston brown?" I say.

"It's Irish bread. Tastes like home."

"I can make it again," I say. "If it keeps you sailing like this, I can make it every day."

His eyes positively sparkle at that. "Could you really?"

"I can make some now, if you want."

"No. Now we pull the anchor, get back to it. Then, after that, aye, some bread would be just the thing, don't you think?"

"Ah, ok?" I agree, feeling nebulous. "You really like bread."

"I'm Irish," he says by way of explanation. "I really like bread. And toast. And soda bread. And potato bread. And potatoes."

"Understood. Kid needs carbs."

Grant's voice goes deep. "Not a kid, Becca. I assure you."

Oooh. "Right. Sorry," I say. Though I think it is a sign of his youth that he bristles at the idea of me commenting on it. If he were Alistair's age and I called him a kid, he'd just laugh and preen.

If he were Alistair's age, I think, as I follow Grant's instructions to start the motor and give her a bit of gas in reverse to back the anchor out of its hold, he wouldn't be able to drop everything and sail me to Miami. No, I have stumbled across Grant Murphy at the absolute ideal time in his life. Free to travel, to adventure, to get into trouble and have plenty of time to get back out of it.

And he has met me at my absolute worst time. Settled. Staid. In a rut almost as old as he is.

But then, maybe that's not entirely true. What would Natasha say? She'd say it was exactly the right time to adventure. I look at Grant's broad shoulders as he opens the anchor hatch and begins the heavy work of pulling up at least thirty feet of galvanized steel chain, plus the aluminum alloy anchor itself. Twenty-six though he may be, he is not hard to look at, or to talk to. And he is certainly *not* my daughter's ex-boyfriend either. Not even a little bit.

In fact, he's not technically off limits at all.

21

Near Roanoke Sound the sky goes gray, and under motor, we cautiously dip in behind the barrier islands for the rest of the day's miles. The hours pass almost too quickly, between stories of Grant's past sailing exploits and brainstorming aloud to help me create a new, post-Alistair bucket list. I thought I had youthful ambitions, but Grant puts young Becca's wildest ideas to shame. He suggests cruising to Antarctica, sailing through the Galapagos, scuba diving amid the Great Barrier Reef. I tend slightly more landward, with a dream walk on the Great Wall of China, a road trip to Uluru, Kruger National Park in the north of South Africa. I know life is taking me in a very different direction after this—administrative assistants in the state's Office of Ed have very little time or spare change for such elaborate journeys—but still, every time we hit on something really lovely sounding, I pop the idea into my phone, just in case. And then, every time, I remind myself: Safe, sweet, cozy house. Window boxes. A good, stable, independent life ahead. Certainly that is more than enough.

Within Pamlico Sound, we enjoy plenty of depth and only mild rain, and we anchor around eight p.m. in a cove within view of the Cape Lookout lighthouse. It's a truly beautiful sight. In the dark, the black-and-white-diamond pattern on the silo makes it appear as though someone has knitted it into a giant argyle sock, and the light flashes around every fifteen seconds, the most reassuring kind of rhythm on this dark rainy night. Our dinner was a creamy pasta with olives and sardines I whipped up a few hours back, eaten by Grant as if he'd never seen such a feast before. Now that the sails are down and the hatches shut tight, I rustle up a bottle of Mount Gay I found stashed inside the table storage in the saloon, add strong ginger syrup and plain soda with plenty of lime juice, and pour us each one perfectly spicy Dark and Stormy in the stainless wine tumblers I brought from home. Grant googles the Cape Lookout lighthouse and reads me a quick history—it dates to 1812 and got a rebuild just before the Civil War, then was disabled by the Confederates and soon after put back into service by the Union, and it's been lit ever since. It's seen things, in other words. Now it's a national historic site and part of the protected seashore, available to guests only by boat. Like us.

The allure of using lighthouse motifs in coastal decor has always eluded me, but now I am enchanted. I have plenty of sat-phone data left, so an hour goes by with both of us reading to each other from our online discoveries about the landmark—the story of Confederates attempting to bomb it, the installation of a Fresnel lens, figuring out what the heck a Fresnel lens even is. Then we both navigate to a website called "Great Lighthouses in Ireland," and Grant begins telling me about all the voyages around the island he's made by sea, while I call up pictures of the lighthouses he would have seen on his adventures. I hold up a picture of a squat silo with two thick black stripes on a white background. "Ah, that's Hook," he says. "Capsized maybe ten nautical miles from there on a crossing to Wales. Helmsman blamed mayonnaise."

"Mayonnaise?" I ask. "What, now?"

"He hated mayo. Big angry guy—you didn't mess with him. And he was terrified of a condiment. Wouldn't so much as step on a boat that had mayo on it. After we were safely right again, drowned like rats, cold as ice, he shook us all down. 'Who had mayo? Was it you? Was it you? I know there's mayonnaise on this boat,' he said." Grant shakes his head.

"He was right, actually. There was a packet of it, one of those small ones from the chip shop, in my mate's jacket pocket. We were fourteen years old and scared witless. Me mate didn't dare admit it, when we found it, but somehow the skipper knew he'd been betrayed. Barely spoke to the crew the rest of the trip out."

"Betrayed by sauce," I say thoughtfully. "I hate to tell you this, but we have mayonnaise on this boat. I make the most fantastic grilled cheese sandwich, and that's the secret behind it."

"Grilled cheese sandwich?" he asks.

I describe it to him, and a light dawns in his eyes. "A cheese toastie. Oh, I could murder one of those right now."

"Guess the next lighthouse, and I'll fix you one."

"Would you now? Oh, that's brilliant. Make it a hard lighthouse, though. I need to earn it."

I show him a tall skinny lighthouse practically dangling off the side of a craggy isle.

He shakes his head. "Too easy. Fastnet. That's the site of a famous yacht race. Stump me."

"Hm," I say, thumbing through. "How about this one?" It's a pretty white house with a tower coming out of it, set onto a rock that's impossibly green.

"Fanad," he says. "Sure you know my mum was born in Don-e-gall."

"I did not know that," I reply, though I realize after a beat that this is just how he talks sometimes. "Does your . . . *mum* . . . speak Irish?" The website says the lighthouse is located in an Irish-speaking area.

"Aye. Me, barely a word anymore. You're meant to learn it in school but, ah, my mind did wander. Ok, try one more lighthouse. This one's for the toastie."

After a bit of scrolling I show him a close-up of the top of a very nondescript, mostly white lighthouse.

"Hm," he says. "Could be anywhere. The red fence around the top is all I have to go on . . ."

I tap my fingers in mock impatience.

"Ballycotton?" he tries. "Which is Irish for, uh, town of . . ." He squints. "Town of common town, I guess?"

I laugh at his faltering translation, recognizing the power of a millennium-old history to create, and then erode, things of great meaning. "Nope. Ballycotton's black beneath the red fence," I say. "This one's called Loop Head."

He raises a glass to me. "Ah, so it is. Where the demigod Cú Chulainn was forced to leap when he ran from the witch Mal, who was trying to make him fall in love with her. Well done you. I would never have gotten there, not if I had all the guesses in the world. Which means, now I make you the toastie."

I shake my head. "Oh, no, I'm not hungry. I'm dead on my feet," I tell him.

"I make me the toastie, then."

"You sure I can't—"

"You just said you're tired."

I did, I realize. Is this what it means to have someone truly listen? Even I sometimes forget to listen to myself, but here is someone who is *paying attention.*

"Off you go, clean your teeth, wash up, and off to bed with you."

I smile at him weakly, the exhaustion rushing in now that the door has been opened to it. It's the most delicious kind of tired, one where the fatigue of your body meets the weariness of your brain, and you know when you climb into bed, the sheets will feel like heaven and your cares will melt away. "Aye-aye, sir."

The sheets do feel like heaven—I put fresh ones on my mattress midday, the only clean things left on this boat. Each vertebra seems to relax into the bed in turn, as if my spine is saying thank you. But just a couple minutes after I'm settled in bed in my favorite soft-as-silk T-shirt, I smell browning butter, and my stomach wakes up. I try to deny it. After all, midnight snacks of bread, butter, and cheese aren't the secret to health, as I try to remind myself. But then, my stomach argues, there's no one back home waiting to make sarcastic suggestions about juice cleanses if one morning my pants fit incrementally more snugly. And that is a very good thing.

I open the door and pop my head out of my berth, thinking I'll ask him if it's too late for me to have half a toastie, too, but find him stretched out long on the settee next to my door, a plate on the table with grilled cheese triangles, crusts removed, stacked high atop. "Oh!"

"Don't get up," he says. "Hungry after all, aren't you?" he asks me.

"Starved," I admit. "I had no idea until I smelled the melting butter."

He doesn't even sit up, just grabs his plate of food and balances it on his stomach. Under his plate, there stands a second clean one, nested there apparently for this very eventuality. "Sailing's hungry work," he says and loads me up with four little triangles that look as warm and nourishing as anything possibly could right now. "There you are, now," he says as he hands the plate to me around the edge of my door so that I don't even have to leave my cozy bed. "No secret ingredient, but a bit of melty cheese sure is nice after a day like ours."

I nod. "Thank you." I think, but don't say, *This is amazing*. I have been a caretaker for twenty-odd years. And completely forgotten how nice it can be to let someone else take care of me.

"No trouble," he answers back, and I appreciate his finality. There's no need to carry on with gratitude. It's as though he's saying, *You make me food all the time; I'm simply returning the favor.*

Like we're equals.

We eat our toasties, with our tired legs outstretched, our eyes half-closed, in a dreamy, rolling silence, as the dull, rain-diffused glow of the lighthouse runs over us from head to toe, again and again and again.

22

When my alarm goes off the next morning, I am wedged between the wall of my berth and the mattress. We are already underway, and somehow I slept through Grant single-handedly hoisting the anchor and the sails. How did he do that? How did I sleep through it? How, for that matter, am I sleeping so well in such strange circumstances in the first place? But I am, and each day I seem to think more clearly, even *see* more clearly, than the one before. The air seems to be clearing the fog of the last decade, freeing me from all those Larkin-built ideas that have locked me in place so long. What I eat, how I dress, the way I spend my days. It's all down to me now, and it always has been. And I can only see that because I'm on this boat, in the middle of nowhere, doing something I don't think I truly believed I could have survived.

So when I manage to crawl up and out of my berth, walk goat legged through a morning pee and freshening, and come up to the deck, I see the situation we're in right away.

"Are we going upwind?" I ask Grant, and he startles from the windward helm.

"Whoa! Where did you come from?"

"Bed," I say. "I'd say I slept in, but it's so freaking early. What are we doing up?"

"Looked at the forecast last night, and my mind was racing after that," he tells me. "Must have taken me twenty minutes to fall asleep."

I try not to laugh at him.

"Finally got to sleep, and then what, I wake up at first light thinking about our passage."

"Passage?" I ask. "I thought we were going into the Intracoastal Waterway today."

"I don't think we can—and we're not crawling down the coast either. The wind is not with us. Nothing but doldrums from here to Charleston if we stay inland. We're heading out to sea, if you're game for it, of course."

"Wait, by doldrums, what does that mean?"

"No wind. No going anywhere."

"Oh, I didn't realize that word really meant something," I say, stupidly. "Besides boredom. Sorry, I haven't had my coffee yet."

Grant is ignoring me for the moment, adjusting the heading, and I realize he's more focused on sailing than usual. It seems most of the time to be an involuntary act for him, like breathing. Today he looks intensely focused, like he's trying to breathe underwater.

"Is there a storm?" I ask him, though the sky is a bright neon blue and the sunrise is blazing two inches above the horizon.

"I wish," he says lightly. "No, just a shift in the wind, meaning we'll have to beat for hours."

"Beat? As in sail into the wind?"

"Afraid so. Probably all day long. Bound to happen eventually."

In our quiet moments over the last couple of days, I have noticed how most of the time on this trip, the boat has been in some form of "reach"—in other words, the wind is to our left, our right, or nearly behind us. Now the wind seems to be blowing straight into our faces, hard, and the boom is set just a few degrees off from being a straight line with the length of the boat. The end of the mainsail is only about two feet to my left, and the end corner of the jib is so close-hauled it almost follows the arched contour of the bow. More to the point, the ride is bumpy, like the boat is going over an old potholed ocean, instead of fresh-paved highway as usual.

"Oh dear," I say. My stomach is already unsure about this situation.

Part distracted by the work of sailing, Grant tells me we are sailing very close to the "no-go zone," a distinction that describes when the wind is straight into your face or anywhere from about eleven to one on the face of a clock. We are close-hauled, but if we let the sails come in even a little bit too tightly, we'll quickly be "in irons," which means exactly what it sounds—shackled to the wind, blown backward. In that case the rudder does no good, so you can't steer out of it; you have to maneuver the sails in ways that sound tricky and also maybe kind of dangerous. In other words, I am highly motivated for us not to get in irons. "I won't distract you, then," I tell him.

"We'll be at it for hours, I'm afraid. I'm going to send us out and straight south, and then we'll triangulate into shore for the night. Unless the wind changes, it's not a night to sail through."

"Will we lose time?"

"Nah. Reckon not. We'll just not get into irons, will we?"

"Good plan," I say.

But the plan is not foolproof. Sailing this way makes the water so choppy that going below becomes an exercise in seasickness tolerance. We need food in our stomachs, so I go down, put ingredients in a bowl, start to feel green. Come up, stir ingredients, start to feel better. Go back down, pour them into a pan and bake them, get a little sicker, come back up and wait for the timer, feel a little better. I challenge myself not to complain to Grant. If he's going to keep helming through this, and single-handing almost everything while he's at it, I can at least feed and water him. And when we do at last have a basket of fresh muffins and defrosted frozen orange juice and sweet maple sausages to feast on, it's clear we both feel a lot better.

But eating at this lean, with this lurching motion, with waves breaking over the hull and spraying our already cold selves again and again, it's hardly relaxing. I have my legs pushing against the base of one cockpit bench while my torso is being pushed by gravity into the back of the other. If one, for some reason, decided to eat cinnamon oat muffins on the back of a mechanical bull, then it would feel almost exactly like this.

"So . . . ," I say, after we've been eating for a while. "This is fun."

"What?" says Grant from the cockpit. The wind rushes in my ears, and I realize there's no point in shouting back and forth. I fix my eyes on the horizon and will myself not to be sick in front of Irish Adonis. We hit a bump, and the basket of muffins topples over the deck, and I rush to corral the goodies again, though they have now rolled through all manner of ickiness. Seeing no bug carcasses on the food itself, I tie the towel that lines the basket into a pouch and will myself to take everything down below, where the fresh breeze and calming horizon will disappear, but the rolling and rocking and lurching will not. I'm unable to talk myself into it and instead just throw the whole bundle in the basket down the steps, aiming vaguely for the galley sink. It's come to this, I think. For the first time in ages, I wish Olivia were here to make gentle fun of me, to make this something to laugh about, to be the lightheartedness I cannot convince myself to feel.

I've been thinking about my daughter a lot since she left, of course I have. When we get into Miami, there are things I'd like to say to her. About who I am. About who I want to be. I want to tell her that my whole life is ahead of me, and I'm going to be someone she's proud to know and call her mother, someone fascinating and delightful and yes, adventurous. The problem is, if I say that now, then it will truly be a lie. When I search my heart for what I want next, it's a mess of contradiction. First it tells me this is the time to be safe. To hunker down, away from Alistair, away from his noise, away from the noise of his world. To sit in my pretty shuttered house with my pretty vined garden and let the whole universe go on around me, like this wind. With the rocking and pitching nonstop, I am longing for land more than I have since Grant stepped aboard.

But then, from time to time, I start to feel fine again. And then my heart changes its mind. It tells me this is just a shift in the wind, one of thousands in a long and promising life. This is a chance to do something new. To try something brave. To be someone you thought you'd given up on long ago.

And then we hit a wave, a big one that washes over the entire deck. I turn to ice again, and thoughts of my uncertain future swirl around in an eddy I cannot escape. After all, I am bouncing around, literally tossing my muffins, while trying not to figuratively toss my muffins. Perhaps this adventure business is not for me.

Grant calls louder. "Need the toilet," he shouts. "Can you take the helm?"

I can, I suppose, but must I? "Course," I holler and slowly climb my way back to him. He shows me what to watch for on the hawk, the sails, and the monitor and then clambers to the transom, ties a knot to his waist and then the other end to the rear stanchion, and kneels to face the water. For a minute I wonder if he's going to jump in. I watch in surprise as I realize he is peeing off the back of the boat.

Ok. I guess that makes sense. It's weirdly intimate, sure, but then, this whole trip has been. We've been living together in the belly of a boat not even ten feet wide.

When he returns, he says, "Sorry, but I couldn't bear to go below. Too choppy. 'Sides, what sense does it make to use the head? Waste of pump water."

"It must be nice," I say as I hand over the helm again.

"Why?"

"Well, I have to pee, too, but I can't go off the edge of the boat. I have to go into that hot, tiny bathroom; try not to slide off the toilet, which must currently be at a forty-five-degree angle; and then lean over and pump out the bowl while I try not to fall in headfirst. Or maybe just wait till I barf and then pump that too."

"That's silly. I'll tie you out, and you can use nature's bathroom too."

"Uh . . . my mechanics are different from yours," I tell him, feeling as stupid as he sounds.

"Becca Ann, I have sailed with many, many women. I am clear on the mechanics. Take down your trousers and your pants. Clip your waist in a harness. Climb over the lifelines and hold on to the backstay, and squat enough that you don't pee in the boat. It's a life skill."

I stare at him.

"I won't look," he insists, as though that's the only issue holding me back.

"I'll fall in," I say.

"Don't do that. It's a hassle, and the water is cold."

"I'll just use the head."

"Suit yourself. If you're sick, and there are any . . . uh . . . *chunks*, you'll probably need to fish 'em out with a cup rather than try to flush them down. Those heads are so sensitive."

I stare at this horrible man for a very long time. He looks at me, grins, and gives me a shrug that starts at his eyebrows, flashes over his smile, and takes over his whole torso. It is a shrug that says, *Welcome to sailing, baby.*

I decide to hold it. For about ten seconds. Then I hear Liv's voice in my head, and she is making fun of me.

"Ok, I'm peeing off the boat!" I announce. "But if you so much as turn your head to the side . . ."

"How will I know if you fall in, if I don't watch the performance?" he asks.

"I can scream pretty loud," I tell him. "Turn to look and you'll find out."

"Just in case, I should probably have you keep one hand on the harness line."

"If you touch the rope I'm using to keep myself from falling out of the boat while I pee standing up in high winds with my undies around my ankles . . ." I look for an appropriate threat. "I'll pee in the boat. Just watch me."

"Understood. I'll leave yourself to yourself, then. Have at it."

"Tell Olivia I drowned doing something besides peeing," I tell him.

"I'll tell her you were saving an endangered turtle from a fishing net," he says smoothly.

"Perfect. With no pants. It'll be a story for the ages."

And I climb back, follow the outlined steps, stick my naked rear a foot out over the open sea, and let go. That, in my opinion, is the moment when I truly become a sailor.

23

The wind gets worse, and the day gets long, and at Grant's instruction, I spend much of it sucking salt off of pretzels to settle my stomach. Sometimes I take the helm, and sometimes it goes well. We make plans for a bailout spot at Topsail, North Carolina, so we know what we'll do if the seas get worse or if I just can't take it anymore.

Then, thank the saints, the wind shifts, moves to our side, and we are able to tack, take a beam reach and head south on the emphatic gusts that puff up and die, puff up and die. I'm hardly about to dig into a four-course dinner, but I feel just stable enough to take my eyes off the horizon for a few moments, and soon I'm asleep on the low side bench and dreaming of—what else—being in a rodeo.

I wake to Grant stretching the bimini out over me, but it's too late—I'm soaking wet. Someone has scrolled the brightness setting on the sky down to 10 percent. Rain is driving into our faces, and the wind is shifty, requiring constant adjustments to our sails. It curls around in front of us, and I see the jib backfill, and pow, we're in irons just like that. The wheel spins uselessly, and the boat stops in its tracks, and then, slowly at first and then alarmingly quickly, begins to spin perpendicular to the wind. Soon the wind on the sideways hull will push us backward, hard, while the keel drags. I don't have to be told just how dangerous this situation could be, but to my surprise, I'm not freaking out. I'm getting focused. Grant hollers instructions at me to stay in the cockpit and let off the jib sheet, while he climbs up to skirt the jib and guide it till it flaps completely loose, holding the sheet in one gloved hand to keep the back corner out of the water. Then, almost by instinct, I let the main off, duck the boom, grab the other jib sheet, and winch like hell.

That's it. It works. Grant whoops, and the boat swings around like a ballerina *en pointe*, and we're sailing forward again. We hug, we high-five, and then we get back to sailing, wet, tired, barely fed. Strangely exhilarated.

The day continues this way. When we see the sun start to dip, we head into shore, knowing without having to say it that this is not the kind of day to keep sailing through the night. I feed us both a simple, comforting mix of veggies and rice topped with spicy sautéed shrimp from the freezer, and we collapse in our berths at eight p.m., doors latched open for air circulation, talking about the day we lived through even as we are falling into that wonderful, tired, spent kind of sleep.

The next day feels similar. Rain showers, gusty winds, constant sea spray. But today I'm dressed for it in rainproof overalls with a reinforced seat, heavy jacket, hat with a clip to my collar to keep it from flying off, and a big dose of ginger pills from Grant's luggage. I look, and feel, like a black-and-white picture of the Gorton's fisherman, and I feel freaking great about it. Wind, rain, spray, flying sheets, and stubborn halyards: you have all met your match in Rebecca Ann Larkin.

Grant gives me the pep talk: We are going to kick that ocean's ass today, he explains with infectious confidence. We are going to conquer Poseidon's fury. And guess what: today, in virtually the same conditions as yesterday, I have *fun*. The two of us laugh and holler and make bad puns. I pee off the transom twice. We toast our lunch with a couple of bottles of Allagash White and play a short beer-bottle concerto before Grant shows me where to wedge an empty bottle on the coach roof so the wind turns it into a self-operating flute. I learn to tie four new kinds of knots, and immediately forget them all, and Grant talks me into spending some time riding at the very front of the bow, sitting with my legs dangling off the front of the boat, riding up and down, up and down, my stomach feeling some cross between tobogganing down a mountain and bouncing at the bottom of a bungee jump. Grant unapologetically steers into waves while I scream from the thrill, and I laugh so hard my obliques start to ache.

Today I feel I could sail forever, but I happen to know we are going to make landfall somewhere very special, somewhere steeped for me in memories of happier times. Tybee Island. This is where the Larkins, way back when, spent every Christmas as a family. It's where Liv bounced in her first baby gym and met the ocean's waves for the first time in her life. We haven't been here in years—Grandma Larkin didn't feel it was convenient enough anymore—and I've missed it more than I realized. I remember how I felt back then, a young mother, forming a new family all my own. I felt strong and sure of who I was. I felt my dreams were right around the next corner. On Tybee, I thought we had all the time in the world.

We find the marina at the entrance to Lazaretto Creek with surprising ease despite the borderline depth (thank you, detailed chart apps) and take a day dock, and when I step out onto the land, my body seems to be mystified. My knees bend and straighten, and my sense of balance churns, and I realize that somewhere in the last week I got my sea legs. Now the ground feels like it's waving, undulating, ever so slightly. Phantom waves.

"Whoa," I say to Grant, grabbing hold of a post on the pier anxiously.

"It's weird, right?" he tells me. "Goes away quick, though. Just keep walking."

The air ashore is hot, and we've swapped out our offshoring gear for island clothes. I'm in capris and a linen shirt that is only mostly wrinkled, and Grant is wearing jeans and a light chambray shirt rolled to the elbows. We can walk to a gumbo spot right next to the marina, but I want oysters, and savory bread pudding, and ice cream—Sugar Shack ice cream—so I start to take out my phone to order a rideshare. But Grant has already spotted a Vespa rental, and this late in the day, they're discounted half off. He looks at me with a hopeful expression on his face, and his youth comes through. I can't say no, even though a scooter ride will be a first for me, so we hop aboard, him driving, me panicking slightly behind him, focusing my entire energy on holding on without actually touching him.

This is a lost cause, so he reaches behind himself and finds first my right hand and then my left, depositing each in turn on his waist.

My mouth goes dry. I try to focus on the fabric of his shirt, tell myself I'm touching soft washed chambray, not Grant. But this is the closest we've been, for the longest. By the time we get to First Street, I am fighting with my body not to lean in tighter, not to follow my want for this man, not to notice his smell, the muscles under my hands, the place where my knees touch his thighs. If I have developed sea legs over this trip that I only noticed when I got to dry land, I have likewise developed a desire for Grant that just felt like easy companionship on *Becky Ann*. On Tybee, it's something more dangerous.

We park. I resolve to stay sober, to stay back a couple feet from here on out. I can tell if I'm not very careful, I'm one good cocktail away from kissing Grant Murphy. Two away from something altogether more. And at the same time, with the strange sensation of solid earth beneath my feet and the joyful anticipation of a night eating perishables on the stunning Tybee beach, I feel as if the cocktails are already coursing through me. We luck into a table at the Sundae Café, and I order brewed sweet tea, thinking some combination of caffeine and sugar might jolt me out of my haze. But Grant, his eyes, the way he's looking at me. It's wolfish. Hungry. He's feeling it too. Isn't he?

The very thought, frankly, makes me question his judgment. It's one thing, a very silly thing, for a newly divorced, longtime celibate woman of a certain age to lust after a trim, fit, sexy-as-hell Irish sailing captain fifteen years her junior. It's another thing entirely for him to look at me and think anything besides *Old*.

I inhale deeply and think of something to say. "Hush puppies," I come up with at last.

"What now?"

"They serve them here, and I haven't had them since the last time I was on Tybee, which was . . . a long time ago."

Grant looks from me to the menu and back at me. "Hush, puppies," he tries out. "Is it like a variety of hot dog?"

"Not even remotely. It's fried, and"—I gesture with my hands, like I'm forming a ball out of Play-Doh—"uh, it's a fried orb . . . I'm not sure what it is. But it's good. I'm definitely getting some."

"Can I have one?" he asks me. "Of these tasty fried orbs?"

"Absolutely. We can have nothing but hush puppies for dinner, if we want," I say. "We've certainly been working hard enough."

"Before I agree to that, I'd like to find out what they actually are."

When the server comes, he helpfully describes them as deep-fried cornmeal and buttermilk dough with low-country seasonings. Slightly more descriptive than fried orbs. I order a special of shrimp, oysters, and succotash to go with them, and Grant decides to have crab cakes with fried green tomatoes, which he has never even heard of, much less tasted. I can't resist the urge to get out the Fannie Flagg book on my Kindle app and read my favorite quote, one that was my guiding light during the latter half of my marriage to Alistair:

"'Remember, if people talk behind your back, it only means you are two steps ahead,'" I tell him. "Isn't that positively brilliant? I survived on those words during the Gorman case."

"The what?"

"Barry Gorman?" I ask. "The Boston newscaster-cum-serial-abuser?"

Grant makes a grossed-out face, but there's no sign of recognition.

"Oh my gosh. It's nice to have dinner with someone who doesn't know who he is," I say. "That means you don't know who Alistair is either."

"Ah. That I do have some idea about," he says. "He's some fancy barrister—"

"Lawyer," I supply. "It's a bit different. Lawyers are hired directly by the client. And my ex-husband specializes in truly awful clients."

"Right. Well, that's what I read about him. High-profile cases, we'll say. Where the public have already made up their minds about the guilt of the accused."

"That's him. Or rather, it's his family. Three generations of lawyers, making a fortune by standing on what I would call 'the wrong side' of justice. Mobsters. Profiteers. Even, before we were born, supremacists. Alistair's no prince, but for years, I believed—well, I think we both believed—he would be different than the other Larkins. He had a balanced mix of clients. He stayed back from the most egregious cases. He set himself apart."

"So how did he end up representing someone like Gorman?" asks Grant.

I shake my head. "He was the proverbial frog in the boiling pot of water, working in that firm, answering to his parents' legacy. Only, by the time it was too late, he thought he was in a really great hot spring or something. Tried to convince me to get in too."

"And did you?" Grant asks gently.

"I did," I admit. "For almost ten years. I didn't like the man he was becoming, but I wasn't sure about the woman I would be alone. And, even more, I worried for Olivia. I saw how that family could change a person. I thought . . . I guess I thought I could be the grounding force between her and all of that."

Grant raises an eyebrow. "That's a lot for one woman to accomplish on her own."

"And yet I thought I'd been successful. Right up until this trip. Now I'm not so sure."

A silence falls over the table. Grant shifts around in his chair and then says, "I know what it's like to be tangled up in family obligations."

"You do?"

He only nods, doesn't elaborate. "I do. And I think you've got to let Liv have some of these revelations on her own now. Let her decide for herself what's right, what's important."

"And if she doesn't decide well?" I ask him, putting voice to my nagging fears. "If she follows in the Larkin tradition?"

Grant shakes her head. "I can tell you have the capacity to love her for exactly who she is," he says. "No matter what that looks like. I can see it in your eyes when you talk about her. You have dreams for her, and hopes, but you're brave enough to keep loving people who don't live up to every hope."

"Brave enough, or dumb enough?" I ask him, trying to joke when my heart feels heavy.

Grant tilts his head and looks at me for a long time. "In some cases, I guess, both."

I have to laugh at his honesty.

"You'd have to be pretty dumb to think you couldn't survive on your own, I mean," he amends. "When you're actually kind of a badass."

Now I just shake my head at him. If this guy thinks I'm a badass, he really doesn't know me at all. Still, I preen; it's rather a lovely thing to hear, especially coming from someone who saw me at the beginning of this trip, when I didn't even know how to load a Lifesling. A time that feels very long ago. "So . . . you read up on Alistair?" I ask, flattered and eager to let him keep believing I'm a badass for as long as possible.

He shrugs. "A fella gets curious about the woman he's sharing quarters with."

How did he make two separate berths on a forty-foot boat sound somehow suggestive? I wonder to myself. Maybe it's just that I badly want to be . . . uh . . . suggested.

I try to steer the conversation back to less date-like subjects. "One spin on what Liv's dad does is what you said—the client has the constitutional right to be presumed innocent, even if he's already been tried in the court of public opinion. Another is that every American deserves the best possible representation during his day in court. Those things are both true . . . and yet . . ."

"Sometimes the court of public opinion gets it right," he supplies.

"Exactly," I say. "In Gorman's case, he gave internships to young men in their late teens, asked them to come to his house in the evenings to work, and then drugged them. Six teen boys, strangers to each other, described the exact same scenario to the police, and I can't imagine that was an easy day for any of them. His guilt isn't a matter of opinion. It's a fact."

"But your ex-husband took his case, even so."

"And won it, yes, by tearing the boys down piece by piece over twenty grueling days in court." A choice so galling I couldn't even look at my own husband for months. I couldn't stand the sight of him. And yet, for Liv, always for Liv, I pretended everything was fine.

"Ah. That's . . ."

"Disgusting. I know. And as far as anyone in my neighborhood acted, it might as well have been just as much my doing as his." I pause for a moment. "Well, I felt that way, too, if I'm being perfectly honest. I certainly never felt like Fannie wrote—that I was two steps ahead."

"Ach, how could your husband's behavior be your doing?"

I shrugged. "I fed him dinner every night. I stood by his side at parties. I never said a word about my thoughts in public, and played the part in his life he needed me to play. Instead of drawing a firm line in the sand, I cajoled him about how he could use his talent for the greater good, and wheedled that we didn't need any more money, and then even threatened to leave if he kept setting violent predators free."

"And you did leave, sure you did," he says.

I fall silent. For a moment I'm back there, in that awful time, being the dutiful wife, the quiet daughter-in-law. That cocktail of heavy responsibility and fear in every step I made. "Eventually," I say after a moment, fighting back emotion. "And only after he gave me no other choice."

Grant's eyebrow pops up again, but something stops him from asking me what I mean by that, and I'm grateful. I didn't want to go there. I don't know why I did. Quiet falls over the table, and my mouth feels dry. I sip water and wish we were back on the boat, sailing into the wind so that it would be too hard to talk.

And then, when I think I'm getting composed again, Grant reaches across the table and oh so gently squeezes my hand.

Mercifully, the hush puppies arrive.

"Oh thank goodness," I say with exaggerated relief, yanking my hand away. I pull a hot one out of the basket with the tiny enameled tongs they came with, break it in half on my plate, and watch the sweet, smoke-scented steam rise out of the middle. If there was ever a moment for comfort eating, this must be it.

The cornmeal-and-flour dumplings are so light, sweet, and spicy I audibly swoon.

"That good?"

"Try one," I tell him, desperate to change the subject.

"Oooh," he says. "Fabulous. Where's the butter, though?"

"Butter?"

"It wants butter, don't you think?" he asks.

When the server comes back to check on us, Grant asks for a wee pot of butter, and the server's eyes light up at Grant's pretty lilting speech. He returns with a small metal dish of whipped maple butter with a dash of hot sauce. The hush puppies go from great to orgasmically delicious instantly. *Don't moan,* I remind myself. *No actual moaning.*

I can't help it. Some overtly sexual combination of a sigh and a moan escapes from my lips against my will when I taste the rich hot butter melting into the fluffy dough.

"It's sooooooooo good," I say to cover my embarrassment.

"I wish you could see yourself eat that," says Grant. His tone is light, and I try to figure out if he means I look like a farm animal or if he's suggesting I am . . . sexy while eating hush puppies?

"Hunger is the best seasoning," I say, laughing nervously, but I can feel the heat of a deep blush rising up my collarbones and climbing onto my face.

"What do you mean, you had no choice but to leave your husband?" he asks.

Even the low-country flavors can't make me eat after that question. I set down my bite in progress and look up at Grant. "I'm not sure where to start to answer that," I tell him.

"Start at the beginning, of course," he tells me.

I inhale. "The very beginning is when I was just a bit younger than Liv. My mother did the best she could with me, but I was a latchkey kid with a lot of alone time and not a lot of opportunities. And then, in the ninth grade, I joined our school choir and sold candy bars to earn money to travel to a music festival in Spokane, Washington. And that's when I fell madly in love."

"With Spokane?" he asked.

"Oh no. I don't even really remember Spokane," I admit. "It was with the travel. The independence. The freedom. I loved everything about it. I loved the airport full of grouchy people, the baggage claim conveyor belts disappearing into who knows where, the way the ground drops away when you're taking off, the way the city zooms in when you're landing. I loved the people on the flight, and all their potential, and the flight attendants, and the pilots. I thought I had stumbled across my true destiny."

Grant grins at me. "You wanted to fly on planes?"

"I did. I wanted to be a flight attendant for United Airlines, based primarily on their outfits at the time."

"You would have been a brilliant flight attendant," he says, raising his glass to me.

"Thank you, sir. However, I got waylaid on the path to glory. I met Alistair, and my mother was ailing, and family started to feel more and more important. I thought maybe with the Larkins, there'd be travel and adventure around every turn." I sigh. "I loved Alistair very much back then, but even so, I mistook money and privilege for security and choice. I thought I could still have everything I dreamed of, only do it with a family." I shake my head at myself. Maybe I could have, indeed. But the Larkins probably weren't the right family to try with. "Believe it or not, back then, I was ready to spread out every experience available to me on a plate and take an enormous bite."

"You don't seem very different from that now," he replies, looking puzzled.

"Are you kidding? No. There is no more plate. And I certainly don't need any more giant bites of life." I think of what Alistair said, about me always getting stuck with the crumbs. "I am very happy now to nibble around the edges, as long as I have peace and a good heading on my moral compass."

"That's not true at all," Grant protests.

"I don't have a good heading on my moral compass?" I ask.

"Oh, well, you certainly seem to have that," he says. "Having walked away from what looks from the outside like a pretty comfortable life for moral reasons. But even after a week I can see you are still very much a big-bite sort of person. You attacked sailing like banshee, you'd kill a man for looking at Olivia wrong, and I just saw you reach orgasm over a corn fritter. I'd certainly say your passion for life is still going strong, just below the surface."

"Passionate is literally the last word I'd use to describe myself," I say. But after I've spoken, my mind replays his words like an echo.

"What word would you say?" he asks me.

I think to what my daughter told me, but I don't want to come out and say I'm boring out loud. Instead I say, "Steady. Twenty-two years in a declining marriage, staying home with my daughter most of that time, always dependable, always . . . predictable. That's who I am."

"Ach," he says. "Ridiculous. If you're predictable about anything, it's that you're predictably easy to be around. You can turn boring old lighthouses into a game, or throw down jokes about sextants. When you're baking, I can hear you singing old Motown, and even when you were absolutely clueless about what you're doing on *Becky Ann*, you'd crack jokes nonstop, never taking yourself too seriously. With all due respect to your daughter, many women in their twenties that I've met— especially the American ones—take themselves extremely seriously. It's all this talk about thigh gaps and phone dating and how social media is a plot against humanity, which they post about on social media. There's not a one I've met who would survive the sail we've had. We'd be stuck at a Four Seasons in Philadelphia, FaceTiming a life coach to recover from yacht-related trauma."

I have to laugh at this. "That's a gross exaggeration," I tell him, although I can now visualize Liv in a marble hotel bathtub filled with bubbles, talking to her friends about how awful the trip had been. How we had to eat cold tuna from a pouch.

He squints at me. "Is it really?" he asks. "And then there's you. I know you better than you realize. You had a chance to get off this cruise to hell, as Liv called it on the phone. And you stayed."

"I did stay," I think aloud. Maybe I am a badass.

"And I'm so glad you did. You've got me in a smile all the time we're together. You're good *craic*."

"Crack?" I ask, even while I'm savoring these kind words like melting maple butter on my tongue.

"It means fun, vivacious, full of life. But that's not exactly it, because it's sort of . . . ethereal. A good party where everyone has just enough Murphy's but not too much, that's craic. The guy who always makes time for a coffee or a pint to cheer a mate up, that's craic. When you're all setting off on a big race, or coming in from one and about to hit the pub, and you know there's a wild night ahead, that's very good craic."

"Cheery and lighthearted?" I ask.

"Yeah, sorta like that. It's hard to translate."

While the server puts down our dinner plates and Grant puts in an order for a Southbound Mountain Jam, I consider the last time I felt that magical lightness of spirit Grant's describing. Certainly, I felt it as a kid all the time. And I felt it on that trip I told him about, and when I first went off to college, and when Liv was a year-old baby and our days were patty-cake in the grass and long stroller walks and library story times. And I felt it at the bar, that day after my divorce. In fact, maybe it was exactly the feeling I had after Liv and I decided to go sailing, but before we actually started on the logistics of it. It's the first moment when an adventure begins . . .

Exactly like this moment.

And just like that I decide.

I'm 99 percent sure that Grant is actually flirting with me tonight. And he knows who I am, who I was married to. He knows how old I am. He knows what Olivia's advances were about, and he had no interest. For some reason, though, he's interested in *me*.

And there's no reason whatsoever I shouldn't take him up on that interest.

24

After dinner, a walk on the beach. Sun low, light crowds, a rising tide pushing us closer together on that thin strip of sand that's perfectly packed for a stroll.

After twenty minutes our hands brush. I say, "Is this happening?"

"Is what happening?"

For a moment I think I've misread things. I feel like an idiot. Then I remember I'm forty-two damn years old. "You *know* what," I reply to Grant.

"Oh," he says. He's quiet for a moment and then says, "No. Of course not." Another long pause, then, "Well, could it?"

I have to laugh. It's been twenty years since I flirted with someone new. Then there was uncertainty, anxiety, fear of humiliation. Now I feel . . . pretty bulletproof, I guess.

"Here are the terms," I tell him.

"There are terms?"

"Yes, of course there are terms," I say. "You're my daughter's . . . um . . ."

"Former sailing instructor," he supplies.

Yeah. That's true. Not an ex, or not even a genuine interest. I know what Liv would say if I asked her right now. She'd say something like, *Hit that.* "Ok, well, you're my *current* sailing instructor. And we still have a few days to travel. If we kiss now, and you don't like it, you still have to sail me to Miami."

"I'm going to like it," he says. He seems to feel none of the panic I felt all those years ago. And come to think of it, I don't feel any of that panic now. My main concern is trying to figure out if I can have sex with this beautiful young man without having to take off my shirt. Probably yes.

"Also, neither of us are drunk," I remind him. "We can't wake up tomorrow and pretend it was a mistake."

"Good," he says. "Consent is my biggest turn-on."

"Oh, that's cute. I like that."

"It's true. Drunk girls are a boner killer for me."

I try not to get hung up on the word *girls*. Or the words *boner killer*. "Even so. If we . . . go there . . . there's no escape valve. Not for a week or so."

"I don't want one. I'm not afraid of you."

"Oh sheesh," I say. "You don't have to romance me."

"But I *would* like to be romanced, if it's all the same to you. I like you, Becca. Since you walked into the commodore's office. But I don't want to be a boy toy."

This stops me in my tracks. I turn to look at him, to gauge his seriousness. His face is set firm.

He goes on. "I don't want terms, I don't want rules, I don't want lifelines."

"Lifelines?"

"To keep me aboard if it's rocky."

My mind creates an image of us, in the cockpit, in flagrante delicto. "Oh boy," I say, trying not to blush. "I'm not sure I'm a good enough sailor to use boat metaphors that deftly."

He laughs at this, and thank goodness, the mood gets a bit lighter now. "Can we just kiss?" he says. "And if we have to negotiate more after that, fine."

But now I'm a bit nervous. I shake my head. "It just seems like our relationship is unbalanced," I say.

Grant throws up his hands. "Ach," he says.

"Ach?" I laugh. "Ach?"

"Aye. You're maddening. It's sunset on the beach with the tide rising to our toes. I've had a crush on you since I saw you first. This is when we kiss. It's now."

"The very first time you saw me?" I ask.

He puts his hands up in surrender. "Can't we just . . . I don't know, what would Olivia say . . . *mash faces* for a minute?"

Now I really am laughing hard. "Mash faces? I don't want to mash faces."

"So then I do have to romance you," he says.

"Uh . . . ," I say. I'm lost in this conversation. I thought I was taking charge, playing the role of Mrs. Robinson. Now I'm tongue tied and wondering if this is such a good idea after all.

"Becca," Grant says and stops walking. He takes me by the hand and stops me midstride as well. "Come here."

I turn to face him, but I can't quite make eye contact.

"I'm not going to kiss you," he says.

"You're not?" I ask him. Now my eyes seem to slide to his, and they lock.

"Not yet," he says. "Not until you're sure it's a good idea."

I sigh. "I'm not sure there's a universe where you and I are a good idea," I say. "But I was willing to overlook that—"

He puts up a finger, like a warning. I stop talking. My eyes follow as that hand moves to the side of my face, where my loose hair is whipping in the sea breeze. He wraps his hand around a lock of hair and then tucks it neatly behind my ear. It's easily the sexiest thing that's ever happened to me. Unbidden, my eyelids close and my mouth waters.

In the dusky dimness, I feel as he runs that one finger from the back of my ear, to my jaw, to my mouth. I feel it trace the full skin of my lower lip. I swallow hard. The finger turns to a hand gently dragging down my jaw, softly caressing the front of my neck, the skin between my collarbones. And then it returns up, again, tilting my face toward him. My eyes flutter open, and he's staring at me intently.

Hungrily.

I feel light headed. I let my lips part and beg him to kiss me. But instead, he takes his hand away. "Let's go back to the boat," he tells me.

I just stare. I thought he was about to . . . I thought . . . I wanted . . . and now I can only think about his lips finding mine.

"Now?" I ask him.

He runs his hand down my arm gently, and when he reaches my hand, he cups it in his much larger one and uses both our hands to gesture past me to a bruise-colored cloud on the horizon. "There's a storm coming," he says, and it's very hard not to reply, *Tell me about it.* "We need to get *Becky Ann* to a mooring ball if we mean to sleep tonight."

Who said anything about sleep? I am thinking.

"Right," I say.

But it's not right to stop now, just as I've gone from thinking about Grant—and Grant's body—not just as a night of liberation but as a need, like air or water. A long line running through my body, from the back of my skull through my solar plexus to the base of my spine, seems to be vibrating with want. And why? Because of the way this man touched my face? My neck? The way he brushed the hair out of my eyes?

Climbing on behind him on that scooter this time is sheer torture. I can't seem to crack a joke or even make a sensical comment. Grant, too, is uncharacteristically quiet. We return the scooter to the rental place, walk to *Becky Ann*, and ready ourselves to move her. The wind is picking up now, and the light is fading fast. Without the usual course of instruction, I take off the springs and the stern line, and hold the bowline in place on the dock while Grant starts the motor. "Let it off," he calls when it's time for me to jump with the bowline from the pontoon onto the edge of the ship's deck, and the small hop feels, for the first time, as natural as a breath. I climb over the white wire-rope lifelines strung around the boat's perimeter, thinking of what Grant said earlier. He doesn't want them around us. Do I?

Within minutes, I'm at the helm and Grant has the hook he'll need to tie our lines to a loose mooring ball among a large group of sailboats. He's seemingly in a hurry, and I wonder. Is it the storm?

Or is it me?

And in the hopes of the latter, I am the perfect crewman. I cut the motor, store the keys, pull up the fenders and stash them in their locker. Put the covers on the instrument panel, secure the boom. When Grant gets back to the cockpit, he takes in what I've done and the neat coils of ropes I've made for the mainsheet—very out of character for me. Hopefully a turn-on for him.

He smiles at me, and it's the most wicked smile I've ever seen on his face. In his eyes, I see the unmistakable confidence of knowing.

My body goes completely slack.

And then he reaches behind his head and pulls off his shirt by the neckline.

Everything inside me wakes up. As confidently as I possibly can, I stride right up to him, take him hard by the shoulders, and reach up, up, up for that promised kiss.

25

I don't keep my shirt on.

When the kiss, hot and demanding, isn't enough, and Grant's mouth slides down the side of my neck, and his hands slide up to wide spans just below my rib cage, I push him away, thinking of my middle-aged midsection. His midsection is, ah, not soft. It's muscles, not huge or bulging, but firm lines under my hands, and I explore every inch, the bulk of his shoulders smoothing into strong biceps into busy forearms and then onto pecs and obliques and abs, a topographical mapping of the body of a man who could have modeled for a Renaissance master. When I reach the line of his jeans, I think about leaving them alone, going slowly, taking my time.

Instead, I unfasten his belt and the top of his jeans, too greedy to wait for a slow methodical reveal.

We kiss again, and this is becoming delirious, and I realize that I'm not going to worry about my soft midsection or the shape of my ass. No, that would be a total waste. A waste of a kind of alertness and aliveness I haven't felt in so, so long, and that kind of aliveness leaves no room for me to doubt myself. Grant wants me, he's tearing at my clothes, we're in the cockpit of a rocking sailboat at sea, and I'm going to let him have whatever he wants, and I'm going to love it.

He strips me down, and then just stares, open mouthed, and there is no question he likes what he sees.

And then, with me naked and his jeans falling open, I hesitate, my mind a spinning wheel of ideas: of what I'd like to do to him, of what I'd like to have done to me. But he is not uncertain. He pulls me in close, presses my chest against his, runs his hands over my breasts, and kisses me deeply. He slows me down. Now he is the one exploring, and as he kisses me, those last drops of inhibition fall away. I step back for air, and when I do, he falls to his knees and pulls me down, too, and now we are wrapped up in kisses and arms and heat, and he is tangled in his jeans, and he sets me on the bench and frees himself, and all I can think is *Now, now, now.*

But not now. He's got other plans. All I can do is arch my back and slide my hips forward and moan in pleasure, for a long time, and then I feel him take my hand and pull me down to the deck.

"Now?" I ask. I beg.

"Condom," he says and fumbles in his jeans, his wallet. Until this second I have forgotten I'm a real woman, this is real sex, not some elaborate, unbelievable fantasy. And when the condom is in place, I look him in the eyes and say, "You sure?" because while I am very, very sure, I have no idea how long this certainty can last for me. I have never, in my life, felt this safe with a man, and I have never felt this greedy. Like I'm going to explode if we aren't together, but that even then I'm not sure it will be enough.

"I'm sure, Becca Ann," Grant tells me. "I want this. I want you. It's all I've been doing, wanting you, since the minute I saw you."

And who can say no to that?

We slide together, lock and key, a perfect fit with a slight adjustment here and there. And like that, there is a rhythm, natural and easy. My body seems to know what to do on its own, so I let every neuron light up with sensation. And in those moments, I don't care about age, or wealth, or what weird face I might be making, or really anything except the awareness of being in my own body, having it be truly mine, in a way I can hardly remember feeling for so, so long. It's freedom, it's bravery, it's something else, something ageless.

And when we meet each other's eyes, I see he's feeling it too.

And I'm not sure if I've ever felt this good before. As we tumble back to earth, I let my eyes close and savor the feeling, quaking slightly. When I open them, Grant is sitting back on his knees, watching me with bright eyes in the night. And I love it. I'm not feeling shy anymore. I'm feeling alive.

And then, because he is Grant Murphy, twenty-six years old and made by the gods, he falls into the foot-wide space next to me on the deck, still breathing hard; presses a weak kiss to my shoulder; and falls straight to sleep.

26

I wake to rain. Rainwater falling on my hip bone, and then on every inch of me. It starts in drips and drops and then becomes a steady downpour. The storm we were rushing to avoid. And now I'm lying naked, in the middle of a sailboat, rocking in a wild sea. The water rushes over me. It rushes over Grant Murphy, who is on his side, pressed against me, fast asleep.

A month ago I was alone in Alistair's house, which was once my house, baking muffins. I was surrounded by his clothes, his collectibles, his nanny cam. A ward of his very considerable estate.

This is very different.

This is pleasure, and sensation, and satisfaction. This is contentment mingling with surprise. And though I am sort of shocked at myself, I'm not upset or regretful. I'm delighted.

Which makes no sense. Grant is sixteen years younger than me. He's from a different country and a different time. He is of one moment, and I am of another. But on this boat, named after a woman I haven't been in years, our moments have collided. Sailing has made me young again, I realize with a start. Why should I have regrets?

As quietly as I can, I ease up, pad naked to the bimini, and stretch it over the cockpit enough to cover Grant's upper half. Sleeping through a cloudburst is something only a kid could do, I think. But then I correct myself. There's been no time in my life that I would have slept while it rained on my face. And there's been no time in my life, not when I was nineteen or twenty-six or thirty-six, that a man like this would have seemed like a possibility to me. Have I ever met anyone in real life who moves through the world with Grant's style of quiet calm, or his inner confidence, or, for that matter, his chiseled oblique muscles?

But then, there's never been a time in my life I've been ready for someone like that. Not until now.

When I first met Alistair, I had my life all worked out. I knew what I wanted; I knew where I was going. And falling in love was never a part of any of that. In fact, I was kind of scared of men. I rarely dated, I didn't know my father, and I had no brothers leaving stinky sweat socks all over the place. Males were as foreign as—or maybe more than—all the places I dreamed of flying to. But they were less appealing than those places, by far.

The first time I met him, Alistair sat in my section at the bar and grill where my roommates and I all worked, using fake IDs that our manager seemed very unconcerned with at the time. Alistair came in one day wearing a suit, a tie, and a kind of confidence I'd never seen before. I treated him like I treated all my tables—one more tip, one step closer to my big plans. In fact, I probably wouldn't have even remembered him at all if he hadn't left his phone number on his receipt. I didn't call it, so he came back a week later and tipped twenty dollars, a lot at that time, and put his phone number on the bill again.

I still didn't call it.

But, after that day, he became the subject of great discussion with me and my roommates. He was such an adult by comparison to us; it was like a sideshow curiosity to guess what he might be like. We discussed his looks—he has always been very easy to look at—and who he might be, and where he came from. We knew he was older than us, and that was a huge plus to our minds. Boys our age, ew, right?

I steal a look at Grant. The TAs at my college never looked like him.

Even if they had, I had a certain healthy suspicion of men of any age, seeded deeply by my mom's heartaches. I felt certain that love was an impediment standing between me and my ambitions. So I gave them all a wide berth, and Alistair was no exception. In that odd way of men and women who don't know what the heck they're doing, my nervous fear at his advances read to him like rejection. And Alistair is not someone who gets rejected very often. Never was, probably never will be. He kept pursuing, and I fell for his laugh, his style, his confidence, and his insightfulness. I fell for his razor-sharp intelligence, the way he made me feel a part of something—something I didn't have to travel the world to find. Something that had walked right into my section at the grill. And he fell right alongside me. That what we had was real, I will never doubt. I refuse to take that away from myself, no matter how we turned out in the end. I gave up much to be with him. But the love I did it for was powerfully real.

Without it, my life now would be totally unrecognizable. I probably wouldn't have gotten a daughter as amazing—and turbulent—as Olivia. I probably would never have had the privileges, the friendships, the joys and triumphs of my life. Or those very happy, very hopeful first ten years of marriage.

At the same time, I probably wouldn't have been cheated on quite so callously. I probably wouldn't have lain awake twelve years into my marriage wondering, with hot shame, if my husband might die early enough that I could one day have a chance of a happier life. I probably wouldn't have signed such a ridiculously unbalanced prenup, and I probably would have entered the workforce, and probably would have earned my own money, my own retirement accounts, my own identity outside of my husband's.

I probably wouldn't have overheard a call Alistair put on his home-office speaker earlier this year, when one of his disgusting clients told Alistair he found Olivia "eminently fuckable."

I wouldn't have told Alistair that *this, finally*, was the final straw. That he could either fire his client or find a new wife.

He wouldn't have told me it was long past time for me to go.

My throat tightens. I haven't loved Alistair for a long time, and I have never been so sure that I was right to leave him as I am this very moment, on the deck of the *Becky Ann* off the coast of Tybee. And yet I don't know if there will ever be a day when that memory doesn't hurt me.

It's raining too hard now to keep lying here. I'm too cold to be above decks. I grab up my sodden clothes and take them down below, find the waterproof sleeping bag Grant brought along, and take it back up to drape him in some protection. He shifts, rolls into the space where my body just was, and sleeps on. I go back into the sheltered saloon, towel my body off, and slide into clean underwear and the coral-colored bamboo pajamas Olivia bought for me two Christmases ago. Still chilly, I wrap up in a heavy knitted cardigan from home and let a few shivers run through my body before I exhale, invite my shoulders to sink deep into the settee, and relax.

I was so afraid that day, the very last time I asked for our divorce. Afraid of what was ahead without my husband and his family to rely on.

Now, I can barely remember why.

With Alistair, over the twenty-two years we spent together, I learned how to carry my body, to dress it well, to become a wife who would make other men jealous. I learned that my flat chest would fill out just enough with motherhood, and my genetically slender frame would become the envy of my friends. I learned that I had the clothes hanger look to wear pretty things, and that, by and large, beauty could be bought in the atrium of Saks and at the registers of the best hair salons.

I learned that I could be an incredible mother, partner, friend. I learned how to laugh at anything and how to survive endless client dinners with just one good glass of wine and a perfect goat cheese salad (and a *pot de crème* for dessert). I learned how to get by in French and

Spanish, to find the perfect gifts for every soul in our orbit, and how to get Celtics tickets at the last minute on the half-court line. I learned how a child will crack open your heart, build a whole new chamber inside it, and then fill it to bursting with love. It has not, for one second, been a waste of a life.

Nor has it been my entire life.

Because in a week, I have learned to sail.

In an hour, I learned about passion.

In the last ten minutes, I've realized that my life has only just begun.

I have had a litany of things I believed about myself. Things I thought I *knew*. But these things we believe, they can stay buried just far enough down that you can't see how ridiculous they are. It is only when you're capably helming a forty-foot sailboat that they surface, angry, betrayed. They say, "You can't do this. This isn't you. You're a wife, a mother. You're *just* a wife and mother."

They come up again when you see a man who makes your mouth water like you're gazing into the window of the finest Parisian patisserie. "You're too old. Your prime is over. Actually, you never even had a prime."

They arise when you wake naked in a warm Georgia rain lying next to someone new. "This isn't your husband. This isn't your life. You don't belong here. Remember Alistair, in that restaurant, asking, and asking, and asking again?"

I shake my head and clear these thoughts away, the last time I'll ever indulge them. These aren't truths. These aren't facts. The facts are the helm, the sails, the hunger in a man's eyes, the push of his lips on mine. Those are the only incontrovertible truths anymore.

And in this moment, I decide that no matter what tomorrow holds, I will never let myself forget them.

27

In the late morning, I hear footsteps on the coach roof, and then a knock on the fore hatch—the large window that opens from the roof of my berth to the front deck of the boat. It's cracked about three inches to let air circulate without rain coming in, but the rain has stopped, so I throw it wide open and lean back. Instead of Grant's face through the window, I see a pair of feet pop through the hatch, and then the rest of him lands in my bed. Naked.

He is smiling at me like a nitwit.

"Good morning!" he says cheerfully.

I wasn't really sleeping anymore, just lying in bed, marveling at my life, but still, I am a bit groggy. Last night's sleep was restless. Grant sliding down into my bed feels otherworldly, and I'm not really sure what to do. Luckily, he seems to have a plan.

"Eggs," he tells me.

"What?"

"I'm taking a tender in and getting eggs. And a few other things. I'm going to make you a perfect breakfast. Your job is to lie here looking beautiful and thinking pleasant thoughts about me."

I sit up and look at him, confused.

"Yes, just like that. You're doing an excellent job."

"Grant," I say, my head lagging behind my body by a few seconds. "Why are you so cheerful?"

"Are you kidding me?" he asks. And then he puts his arms around me and gives me a passionate kiss. "Look at you," he says when he's finally pulled away.

"Look at *you*," I say. The kiss has woken me up. I come back to him and pull him to me. His bare arms are still a little damp but warm and solid under my fingers. I push his hair out of his face and cup his rough, stubbly chin, the contour of his neck, the place where his collarbone and shoulder meet. "Let's forget breakfast," I tell him.

"Really?"

I press my lips to his mouth and convince him of my seriousness.

Somewhat later, we break apart again. I am no longer groggy, and in fact, my brain has decided to take all that oxygen I just panted into it and use it to try to make sense of what's going on here. I sit up, watch Grant who has fallen, yep, back to sleep.

I imagine what it would be like to show up back in my old neighborhood, at the local wine bar, with Grant on my arm. Yeah, that's not how this ends. It's been a long time since I watched *The Graduate*, but I don't remember that being a happy movie. In fact, wasn't she kind of a predator? I remember when it was popular to call women who dated younger men "cougars." Minerva and Liv wrote a one-act play together in high school about the misogynistic history of comparing women to animals. The takeaway was that dehumanizing women's sexual appetites was a sophisticated way to keep us glued to hearth and home.

That said, I feel very animal right now. Normally, I am a fairly self-conscious person, never one to use, say, a gym sauna in the nude or wear a revealing bathing suit on the beach. But those gorgeous sex hormones I'm pumped full of now make me feel like a lioness sprawled on a rock, contentedly licking her paws after a feast. I don't need to pull my clothes back on, or tie my hair back, or even curl up on my side to give Grant more space on the mattress. If I am a cougar right now, I'm a very contented one.

Grant stirs, and wakes, and gives me a quick kiss. Then he is away to make us this breakfast he's been talking about for so long. He leaves me in the berth with my tablet and asks if I can have a look at the weather. Our sailing time today is already halved by our shenanigans, and the days between now and the delivery deadline are numbered.

Even so, I find I have no desire to go anywhere today.

What if we stayed here, I wonder. *Just for today. What if we spent the entire day tangled in my sheets?* I succumb to this daydream for a while, but then consider the buyer, standing on the dock in Miami, looking for his expensive sailboat. The imaginary check he's holding is the key to what comes next for me.

"We have to go," I call out into the kitchen when Grant returns an hour later, and then, realizing it's not that helpful to be shouting around the boat, I walk out into the saloon in just my skivvies. "Grant, we have to sail today," I tell him.

"Is there an issue with the weather?" he asks me. He is fishing around the galley, making an unholy mess.

"Is that baked beans?" I ask him back when I see what's cooking. "For breakfast? Oh, no. I haven't even checked the weather yet. I'm just . . . I'm worried about making it to Miami in time. I feel like I have a lot at stake."

"I expect you do," he says and puts down his wooden spoon to look at me. "Your entire future . . . Olivia told me this boat is all that's left from your marriage."

I look off into a corner. "I wish she hadn't."

"I'm glad she did. When we first met I was intimidated by your . . . stature."

"My stature?" I ask him.

"By the fact that you were loaded. A Black Watch is not a boat just anyone can afford, much less from new. And the jewelry you were wearing that day."

I think back to the day I went into the marina office. Was I still wearing my diamonds? At the boatyard? That's embarrassing to consider right now. I blush deeply.

"Big diamond earrings?" I ask.

"Each the size of a small car," he says.

"What you must have thought of me," I say, cringing.

"I thought, my god, that woman is beautiful. Then I thought, forget it, Murphy, she's way out of your league, and probably married to boot."

"You didn't really think that."

"On my mother's grave."

"Your mother's passed away?" I ask.

"Oh, no. It's just an expression. She's alive and well and shouting at me da in the front room even now, I'll bet."

I smile at that, and then suddenly a thought crosses my mind. "How old is your mother?" I ask him.

He furrows his brow at me, and then when he realizes why I'm asking, he rolls his eyes. "Older than you. And the one of you has nothing to do with the other, neither."

"How old," I ask again.

"Hm. Well, she had me when she was thirty-two," he says. "So that'll make her fifty-seven or eight now? I was fourth of us, and my little sister's fifth."

"Good Catholics," I say.

"Once upon a time. I'm afraid her children haven't followed in her prolific footsteps. My brother had his snip after two kids, and my eldest sister's childless by choice. My little sister is a ways off from settling down. Now, my second sister's getting married to her girlfriend next year, and she's baby hungry as can be. Maybe she'll come through with the flock of grandkids."

"Or maybe you will," I suggest.

He shakes his head. "I don't know. Kids are great and all—I love my nephews to bits—but it's not high on my list."

I look at him, considering this, wondering how much of it is about him being twenty-six. "What is high on your list?"

"A lot of things, and not many of them exactly conducive to child-rearing. I want to sail across the Atlantic and the Pacific. I want to open a sailing school in the Bahamas or the British Virgin Islands and, one day, fix up a fleet of dinghies for the local kids' sailing club. I want to spend at least a couple months a year back home, but I don't want to actually live in Ireland—it's just too small anymore." He thinks for a moment. "Someday I want to cruise the Med for a season, and I want to live awhile in one of those overwater houses in Oceania. Oh, and I want to go to Svalbard, where there are more polar bears than people, and Patagonia's islands, and I want to sail alongside the whales off of Vancouver. Oh, and go back to race the Scottish Series every year, or maybe the Fastnet. Or both. And I want to write a book, or four, and learn to make perfect Thai curries, and dive the Great Barrier Reef and eat an entire tower of cream puffs."

I laugh at that last one. "A croquembouche?"

"Exactly."

"I can make you a croquembouche," I tell him. "The next bad-weather day. It'll take hours, but I'd love to see you try to demolish it."

The sparkle leaves his eyes. "I'm not sure we have that many days left," he tells me. "It's onto Florida next, Saint Augustine by tomorrow night, and then from there . . . another day or two at most."

"Oh," I realize. "We'll actually be early." I can't hide the disappointment in my voice.

He sets down his spatula. "Are you sure you want to sell this boat?" he asks me. "One hundred percent sure?"

I laugh gently. "You've asked me that so many times, Grant."

He holds my gaze and says, earnestly, "But never with myself attached."

Oh. That's very different. I must be careful of his feelings, I tell myself. I might enjoy the idea of being a lioness, but in fact, I do not want to predate on anyone, much less lovely Grant Murphy. Carefully, I cross to him, a comforting hand extended. "After we sell the boat, I'm going to go back to Portland to find a little house and a little job and make a little life. You have much, much bigger plans than that."

"But you would love my plans," he says, like a kid. "You'd love the adventure."

I shake my head. "I'm sorry. This is my big adventure."

"This?" he asks, gesturing to himself and then me.

"All of this," I say. "The boat, the trip, and you too. This isn't my real life." Not that I know what is, for that matter.

His eyes cast downward. "But you had a real life," he says. "And you left it."

I press a kiss to his forehead. "It's so much more complicated than that."

He shakes his head and narrows his eyes. "You're patronizing me," he says.

Well, maybe I am. He's twenty-six years old, after all. But that would be an even worse thing to say out loud in this moment. "To be honest, I'm trying to have my cake and eat it too," I admit. "I'm being greedy. I know we're in different places in our life, but I want to do that"—I wave vaguely toward my berth—"and that"—I point up to the cockpit—"about a thousand more times between now and when we get to Miami."

Grant frowns, but he still wraps me tight in his arms. He speaks right into my ear, his voice a growl. "We could have that, and more," he says as he takes a nip on my neck. "If we never got to Miami."

28

As if Mother Nature herself is in support of my tryst, the weather forecast looks ominous enough to keep us on our mooring ball. Grant hitches in again with someone on a fishing boat, gets us provisions for the rest of the trip. I stay behind and clean belowdecks, getting her ready for her next owner. Every inch I wipe or scour or neaten is a little act of reconciliation with *Becky Ann*, a boat I so disdained just a couple of weeks ago. Now I can see her better. I can see how ingeniously she's designed to make use of every cubic inch of storage, how seamlessly her endless stretches of teak nestle together, how she handles the never-ending wet and waves and weather. Grant has explained some of her efficiencies to me, and others I am discovering on my own, like the way the stove burners are on gimbals, allowing saucepans to stay flat even when the boat does not. How all the handrails are rounded off so there are no sharp corners to hit your head on. How the lights dim to red to preserve your night vision on round-the-clock sails.

It's just a thoughtful thing, this vessel. Fine, yes, I am starting to admire it. *Her.*

I will miss her terribly, I realize at once. She has become a friend to me. The kind of friend who you can rely on to show you what you're truly capable of.

As I tidy her chart table, I let my eyes roam over the atlas open there and imagine the possibilities. I even let myself, for just a moment or two, contemplate setting our heading just a few degrees too far east when we sail again. It would be the tiniest shift, but the error would multiply over the miles, until we found ourselves smack-dab in the crook of Grand Bahama Island.

It's a thought so tempting I have to force myself to look away.

———

The next morning, we wake tangled together, still pleasantly satisfied from the previous night's rich Irish lamb stew with creamy black beers on the side—and an entire loaf of my wheaten bread. I reach for the tablet. The weather forecast passes muster.

"Only just, though," warns Grant. "We could stay another day."

I consider the prospect with some longing. I've had more sex in the last forty-eight hours than in the five years prior, and better too. Much better. But I need to be real. I can't stay in bed with a twenty-six-year-old forever. I shake my head a little sadly, and we start readying for a long sail. We'll take watches, as before, only now I am more independent. At six that night, I tell him not to set his alarm. I'll come get him when I'm sleepy.

Best-laid plans. Around nine p.m., the winds rise and the water starts to churn beneath me. There are still stars visible in the sky, but it's blowing harder and harder. I keep trimming the sails and realize soon I'll need to put a reef in the jib to reduce its size so we can withstand higher winds. I look over the rigging and instruments, reminding myself of the reefing process, and make sure to keep the boat on course. I needn't panic. I will stay calm and stay as close as possible to our original route.

But before much longer, clouds roll in. As I am shaking the jib halyard to get a kink out while it reefs, a soft rain starts up. I have what

Grant calls my "oilies" on, reinforced overalls and a sturdy raincoat with a rigid brim on the hood, and I feel mostly weatherproof in the thick waxed canvas. Still, the weather keeps getting angrier and angrier. The wind shifts, the autopilot adjusts, and I trim the jib again. Now we are bumping straight into the waves, rolling and rolling. My stomach begins to churn. The night is pitch dark now, the only light coming from us, and I see lightning a mile or more out to my right.

"Look at you. You're brilliant," comes Grant's voice from the companionway.

"Oh thank goodness you're up," I say, relief coursing through me. "But—you're supposed to be sleeping."

"I did sleep," he protests. "It was very lonely."

I have to laugh. "We're sailing in a storm," I tell him. "No flirting."

"I promise nothing. You're doing perfectly, though. We'll reef the jib again, or maybe take it down all the way soon."

"I think we should bear off toward shore. In case we need to bail out."

"Forecast says we're good as is."

"My gut says bear off," I persist.

Grant's eyes catch mine. "Ok, gut it is. Only . . ."

"What?"

"Is it your gut or your fear?" he asks.

What's the difference? I wonder. But I consider it for a moment. As I do, a wave hits the bow hard enough that a spray comes up over me. The force and the wet deck combine, and I am knocked off my feet.

"There's lightning," I tell him from my place sprawled out on the deck.

"*Becky Ann* is made for storms," he tells me. He is muscling his way to me, and handing me up and onto a bench, where I use my feet to brace myself. The boat is heeling so high I might as well be standing sideways.

"Really? Is this ok?" I ask him.

"This is a heavy weather," he tells me. "But not deadly weather. Tell me again: What does your gut say?"

205

I get quiet and listen. "It says I'm afraid," I admit.

"Then we sail on. We always sail on through fear."

I furrow my brow. "Hold on," I say, thinking of all the things Liv thought were good ideas that I now know enough about to see they were dangerous. "That philosophy sounds like a way to get killed."

To emphasize my words, lightning cuts through the dark sky. I'm no good at estimating wave size, which is lucky, because right now I'd say they were ten feet high. The boat is lurching over each wave, not cutting through any of them anymore. There are moments where I catch air and then hit the bench hard.

"That's true—if you don't know what you're doing. Or can't trust the people you're with," he says.

I open my mouth, about to ask him if he knows what he's doing—because this is well outside my experience, and I have completely out-grown blind trust on this trip. Grant puts up one hand to silence me as he watches the lightning and counts the seconds before the thunder. "Ok, forecast confirmed," he says after the claps of thunder finish booming. "Storm is blowing in from the south. We're going to catch the tail of it in a half hour or so, and that is going to be amazing—in a good way, not in a deadly way. I'm not doing this without your say-so. But if you're in, let's get ready."

Something new—no, something long quiet—inside me sends up a little thrill. "Let's do this."

Grant works fast. The first thing he does is check that my PFD is secure. Then he shows me how to climb into the harness, ties a cara-biner to a line off of a handrail, and clips me in. He shows me how to clip in and out to navigate the shrouds, and together we work to tidy up above and below, making sure doors are locked open and dishes are tied down. Then we reef the main and Grant alters course, not toward what I thought might look like safety but just a hair off from due south. I see now how the storm is moving far too fast for us to make for land even if I wanted to. Grant has taught me that these storms move from sea to shore, always, and as they do, they make a wedge of strength that could trap us in the shallows and knock us over if we're not well clear.

Then he furls what's left out of the jib. I think we're going to sail without it, but he hoists something else just behind it—a small thin triangle of thick material I remember finding in one of the storage lockers before we sailed. This, he shouts, is the stay sail. Compared to the jib he just removed, the stay sail is minuscule—the difference between a grandma panty and a thong. "That's what we're sailing under?" I ask him. The main is reefed down to a sliver, the stay sail is even smaller, and we might as well be holding up wind socks from the dollar store at this point. I tell Grant so, and he smiles.

"We can go down to bare poles, but what's the fun in that?"

"FUN?"

"You'll see, the fun we'll have," he tells me.

"Am I having fun now?" I ask him, and the wind is coming up enough that I have to shout to be heard. I have been put in charge of helming and am pitching and hurling with the boat, while Grant seems to loosen and tighten his grip on whatever he's holding on to in time with the waves, like a sandpiper dancing over a beach in high tide.

"You ARE!" he shouts back gleefully.

Ok, I tell myself. *I'm having fun.*

"Just keep heading right into the waves," he tells me.

I don't want to do that. I want to sail in the troughs of these monsters, as if we are a keelless surfboard that can ride a wave up and into shore, where we'll gently step off the boat; go into a warm, dimly lit pub; and dry off. Of course, that would shatter *Becky Ann* into a pile of sticks and probably drown both of us, but it sure does sound pleasant. Instead, I steer us straight into the waves as I've been instructed. I know when I have it just right, because the pitching and lurching becomes a roll, the way you'd feel if you were skiing directly over moguls, riding over lots of little bumps on a roller coaster. Up and down, up and down, and now I feel the rhythm. And yep, the rhythm feels like sex.

Well.

That's not a comparison I would have made a week ago.

"That's it," I hear Grant call through the wind. "That's perfect. Hold it right there, and watch the water for the gusts."

I am clipped into a harness hooked to a line tied to my boat. I am half a mile from shore, on the Atlantic, in a thunderstorm, and I am thinking about sex. I laugh out loud. Like a lunatic, I laugh. Am I actually having fun? Is this fun? What is it exactly that I'm feeling? It's a cocktail of adrenaline thrill, oxytocin daze, and that staticky aliveness you can feel in the hairs on your skin—a kind of holistic *awareness.* The rolling, the gusts, the wheel in my hands, the rhythmic coming and going of gravity underneath me.

Holy crap. I AM having fun. Here comes a gust; I can read it on the water. I can read the water! I steer straight into it, and whoosh, we lift up, up, up and surf down and do it again.

This is amazing!

"I'm having fun!" I shout.

"Ya-hoooooooo!" shouts Grant.

"Did you hear that, Ocean?" I shout. "I'm having fun! I'm having a great freaking time. You and I are, like, a thing!" I shout, and the ocean, in return, raises the bow of the boat again and then drops us off. I laugh and steer and laugh, and when Grant tells me to adjust the bearing, I do, and when the water tells me what's next, I listen, and the lightning stays on our side, and then behind us, and then, who knows how much longer, the thunder falls away far away from the flashes of light. The storm is gone, and the wind is still high, and we are still on course, somehow, and Grant is at my side. We are taking the reef out of the main, removing the preventer, and flying at eleven knots over the water. My heart is flying over my body.

We take every bit of wind the storm has left to give us, gobble it up greedily, on and on we sail, until at last the main starts to flap a bit, and we must let it out the rest of the way. The weather is over.

Grinning, Grant unclips me. He gambols to the fore hatch, opens it, and readies the regular jib, and at his orders I let the sheet off so he can switch the sails. When it's time to hoist the regular jib, I realize I can see everything he's doing now, whereas before he was in an inky haze. It's dawn; the sun is coming up. We've been sailing this storm for hours, sailing through an entire night on the thrill of it alone. And now, in the pink-orange glow, Grant is coming back to help me hoist the jib. We sail up into the wind, then swing around, hoist the jib, tie it off, and reset the autopilot. And then Grant turns to me and wraps his arms around me and says, "You were PERFECT. THAT was perfect."

The look on his face right now is exactly the same one he had in the seconds he was awake after the first time we made love.

I start to laugh again now. I laugh at all of it. I am laughing when he kisses me, laughing when he pulls me to the deck, laughing when he strips off my oilies and starts kissing down my body. Though the sea has calmed and the storm has passed, when Grant is above me, I can feel the echoes of the high waves, and he seems to feel them too. We move in unison in the exact same rhythm as that ocean we survived together. And when we tumble into a twin finale, it's as though the lightning has finally found me, run through my entire body, lit me up, and never been a danger after all.

29

I am in the head showering off five hours of midday sleep when I find the box of condoms.

It's not a small box. It's a Costco-sized box. What I would describe, prior to this week, as a lifetime supply. They're in a small sliding locker above where the showerhead is mounted. I never saw the storage there before, but then, I've never spent ten minutes under the cold anemic spray of the crappy pump shower remembering hands on my skin and waves under my back until now. There's been quite a lot of sleepy, satiated staring.

I rinse off my conditioner best I can and turn off the hose. The Turkish towel I crammed into the medicine chest to stay dry covers all of me but is too thin to mop up my hair—I wring it out into the sink instead. Then I lotion up, mop the shower with the soggy towel, and grab the condoms, emerging from the bathroom damp, naked, and amused.

"This many condoms?" I ask Grant when I come up to deck.

He looks at me, all over my body, and then to the box in my hands. "I think that's a great idea," he says with a playful grin.

"Were these purchased with *me* in mind?" I ask him.

He blushes, and it's irresistible. I'm two seconds from crossing over to him and pressing myself into his arms. But then he shakes his head.

"Well, I assume you're the one who brought them, so I certainly hope so." He looks a bit worried now. Does he think I was going to find a man in every port?

"So wait, you didn't bring these aboard?" I ask him.

"No. And you didn't, either, I assume."

I shake my head.

"So then . . ." He has the good taste not to finish that thought.

"Liv," I say. "Oh my."

Grant tilts his head. "You think?"

"I'm going to text her and ask."

Grant's eyes soften. "Maybe don't . . . ," he suggests.

I nod. "I see your point. After all, do I want to know why she had a jumbo box of condoms on a boat for a trip with her mother?"

Grant grimaces. But after I say that, the penny finally drops.

"Oh," I say.

Grant nods.

"These aren't hers," I realize aloud. For one thing, I was there when she packed her bags. She could have sneaked them in, but then wouldn't she have sneaked them out? She had every opportunity. For another, I am starting to recall this particular brand.

It would be rather an odd coincidence for a twenty-one-year-old girl to use the same sort of condoms as her father used to use, wouldn't it?

Before Grant can reply, I go down below and fire up the sat phone. I have to know, to be absolutely sure. I can't spend another moment in this boat without knowing.

What brand of condoms do you use? I text Liv. It's only after I hit send that I realize this is the first we've talked in a couple of very eventful days. That's quite a change. She writes back right away. **The abstinence brand,** she replies.

No really, I send back. **It's kind of important.** I follow up with a photo of the box, too upset to care about data limits. **These?**

There's a pause, and then she writes back, **Not those.** I notice she doesn't ask why, and it's a relief not to have to tell her that I just realized her dad was probably cheating on me even more than I already knew about. Is there something wrong with this kind? I ask. They work, right?

Hey, Mom?

Hey, Olivia.

This is the weirdest text string we've ever had.

Weirder than when you asked me to explain circumcision to your entire ballet carpool of five year olds?

That wasn't via text. I didn't have a phone when I was five years old. Nor could I spell circumcision.

Sadly.

So . . . , she prods. Now is the part where you explain why you're texting me about condoms.

I set down my phone for a long time. Look at the expiry date on the packaging. The stub of emotion where my feelings for Alistair used to live, like a phantom limb, aches wildly. I wonder, will it ever stop? Here I am, miles from home, in the middle of a steaming-hot affair with a gorgeous guy who couldn't be more different from Alistair . . . and yet he still has the capacity to hurt me. Will it be like this for the rest of my life?

The phone buzzes again.

Mom. Are you okay?

I'm not okay. And Olivia is not an idiot. I found these on the boat, I admit to her. And they weren't meant for me.

There's a long pause, and then she writes, simply, Oh Mom. I'm so sorry.

I inhale and force the air slowly out of my lungs, as if I'm reminding them how to work. I'm sorry I told you. I've been trying so hard to keep you out of this part of our life. But I just . . . I couldn't stand not knowing for sure.

You don't have to apologize. He should apologize, she writes back quickly. I can't believe he did that to you. On the boat named after you. I'm just so sorry for you, Mom.

I let my shoulders drop and then text back. Thank you. And just so you know: it's all in the past, now. Water under the bridge.

The expression reminds me of the waves that pounded the deck last night. The fierce howl of the wind and the exhilaration of the rising sea. Grant told me each wave brings hundreds of pounds of water aboard the boat. But over and over again the weight of the keel balances the force of the wind and water. The balance never failed to put us to rights. I'll find my balance again too. I always do.

If he was cheating on you, then I'm really glad you divorced him, types Liv. And I guess that it makes sense if you don't want to live in his house anymore. I guess I wouldn't want that either, in your shoes.

My heart gives a little squeeze. She's getting there. It's taking a long time, but she's finally getting there.

Which means it's time for me to drop an even bigger bomb.

There's something else, I tell her. I steel myself. I can do this. Just a long week ago, I thought my daughter was the reason for every single thing I did. Then she told me to back off and get a life . . . and *I did!* Grant and I are . . . I fish around for the right word. Hooking up.

There's a pause, and I hold my phone with a death grip, as though I can squeeze Liv's response out of it. Finally something comes.

Ten vomit emojis, one after another.

Then, after another beat, she adds, Ok. Sorry. Just had to die there for a minute. I guess that makes sense. He's hot, and a really nice guy. Annoyingly nice. I guess it's ok.

For the record, I don't need your permission, I tell her. And holy crap, it's actually true!

How about my blessing? she asks.

Yeah, I say. Your blessing is awesome. Your blessing means a lot to me, I reply.

Ok. Blessed. Just never use the phrase "I'm hooking up" to me ever again.

I laugh. That's very fair. In fact, I hereby request the same of you.

30

Saint Augustine will be our last port until Miami. The buyer's representative in the area has been in touch with instructions, and when I update him with our location, it's clear we're not to delay, not even by a day, much to my chagrin. It's time for my great adventure to come to its natural conclusion. Time to pack up, fly home, and start my life anew.

We'll be sailing into a popular South Beach marina, and *Becky Ann* already has a berth there for her transfer. They are waiving the normal process of craning the boat out of the water for a dry-land inspection "for expediency."

This strikes both Grant and me as very odd. There are a lot of zeroes on this check not to wonder about what kind of condition the hull is in. After some discussion, Grant shrugs it off, saying, "Trust me, being able to afford a yacht doesn't necessarily correspond with intelligence. In fact, if anything, there might be a negative correlation. Look at your ex. Obviously a moron."

He pulls me in tight to him and kisses me. I laugh at his boyish flirtations. It's childlike to assume that a woman you've known for less than a month is a catch, or that her ex is a fool to let her go, and I tell him that, though not in so many words.

"Are you warning me against something?" he asks absentmindedly. He is at the helm, steering us toward land. He seems to be able to sail without paying any attention whatsoever. It's second nature.

"No," I say. "Well, yes. When you are in your forties, half the people you meet are divorced. And every single one of them is a hundred percent sure their ex was the crazy one."

"You don't have to be in your forties to see that," Grant tells me. "We start vilifying our exes when we're twelve years old."

I laugh at that. "You had an ex-girlfriend when you were twelve?" I ask him.

"Oh yes, actually. I was a consummate ladies' man in lower school. I never ran away when the girls wanted to kiss me. And there was this one wee girl, so pretty and shy about her freckles, I pretended to trip one day, and then she caught me and smacked me one on the lips and said, 'We're getting married now.'"

I laugh. "Those were the days."

"Right?" He smiles. "But then she met Charlie Royce, and he was very good at football, and that was that."

I tilt my head. "And did you vilify her after that?"

"Oh no. I'm the exception that proves the rule. She and I became very close friends. We're still thick as thieves, actually. Charlie was already a mate of mine, and I stood up at their wedding. Actually that's where I met the girl who brought me here."

"Oh, and that's the girl you vilify, then?" I laugh.

"Yes. She is the worst. That said, she's pregnant and did already ask me to be the godfather."

"You're kidding!"

"Alas, no."

"Will you?"

"Of course I will. It's an honor. And I adore kids. I'll be the one to teach him or her to sail."

"But you'll have to be around to teach this baby to sail," I said. "I thought you were going to see the world."

"Time for both."

"But not time for a kid of your own?"

"Not if it's up to me, no."

I try to laugh him off, though he seems fairly serious. "That's ridiculous."

"Why?"

"You'll miss out on parenting!" I say. "The best thing in life."

"I haven't missed out on anything," he tells me. "And I'd definitely beg to differ about the best things in life. As would millions of other people who live their whole lives without having kids."

I frown at him. "How can you know, if you've never had a baby?"

"Well, for one thing, I have, after a fashion. My little sister, Nora, is fourteen years younger than I am. She came along when I was about to leave for a summer to crew in the Med."

"Well, then, you probably missed her whole infancy."

He shakes his head. "Ach, no. That's not the case. At first we thought it would be fine for me to go for the summer, new baby or no, but then during delivery, me mum came down ill."

"Oh no," I say.

"Sepsis in the hospital, and then an infection, and one thing after another, and finally postpartum depression something awful. I mean, the poor woman was almost fifty."

"The poor woman," I echo, trying to hide my horror at the thought of how my own body or mind would handle a pregnancy in that stage of life.

"And my dad. He was a wreck, couldn't think straight from worry. He brought wee Nora home when she was healthy, gave me the pamphlets from the hospital, and was gone again. Lucky I hadn't sailed yet or it would have been the cats watching her. My auntie came over after work, checked up on everything, made us dinner. Dad slept at home a few hours here and there, and then up to work and the hospital."

He frowns deeply. "Three months I minded that baby round the clock, and then after Mum came home, I cared for both her and the baby every moment I wasn't in school. She was so sad all the time, sad because she was sick, sick because she wasn't doing what she felt she should be doing, and then Nora was a sobber, tummy aches, growing pains, and ach—when the molars came in . . ." He makes a horrified face, and I can see he's scarred for life. "I took on the job of not only caring for Nora whenever I could, but also trying to make it look easy on me so my mum didn't feel worse. And you know, my sisters helped when they were back on holidays, and the extended family pitched in, but my older brother was a big fat nothing. Git drove me nuts. It was a lot to take on for a teenage boy."

"I can imagine."

"Maybe it's why I was hot to travel after I finished uni. Maybe it's why I'm not that into having my own kids. I'm mad for Nora—she's got me wrapped around her little finger still—but that experience changed me." He shakes his head sadly. "I see my mates when they're expecting a wee babe. They have no idea what's headed their way. What bomb is about to detonate. And that's as it should be—that's as nature intended it. Me, I can never have that mindset back, never feel unequivocally excited about the arrival of a baby I'm responsible for. I may feel differently later, but right now I feel there's nothing so wonderful as a wee one I can hold and lay kisses on and then put back in her father's arms when she starts to cry."

I exhale a breath I didn't know I'd been holding. "At this moment in my life every hormone I have is put there biologically with the goal of making me want to procreate, and I am baby hungry, as you call it—but it's for other people's babies. It's all I can do not to tamper with Liv's birth control pills."

He laughs. "You know, we're the same that way, then."

"We are."

"We're alike in other ways too," he says. "We've been through stuff, happy and sad. We've had our hearts broken, hard. We've put up with things that were less than perfect for the love of our families. Maybe put up with less than what we deserved. And we've, ah, decided the time is right to do things for ourselves."

"Yes," I agree. "But we're different too. I'm coming out of a twenty-two-year marriage. I have a grown child and a notorious ex-husband."

"It's true. If we . . . gave it a real go," he proposes, "there'd be a lot to navigate."

I don't know what to say to this. Give it a real go? What can he possibly mean by that? He knows this thing between us has an expiration date. He *has* to know, right?

Uneasy, I try to fake a laugh. "Understatement of the century, Grant. What about that matter of sixteen years' difference? Can you imagine me taking you to parents' weekend at Liv's college? Or running into my old friends from Larkin and Larkin?" I shake my head. "I don't think I could survive people asking me if you were my son."

He rolls his eyes at me, as if I'm being silly. "Who said anything about returning to Maine?"

I blink at him. "Maine is my home."

"Sure, but it's cold there, with rough seas, and you've already told me you've got nothing waiting on you."

"That's not what I said. I said I have smaller plans. That doesn't mean they're not plans."

"Ok," he says. "But, and I'm not trying to freak you out here—it's early days and we're just . . . you know . . . having a very nice time."

I nod. I do know. I very much enjoy "just . . . you know." But that's all it is.

"Plans can change, Becca, if you want them to," he blurts. My eyes widen. I can try to laugh it off, or roll my eyes at him, but there's a part of me—a foolish part, no doubt—that badly wants to hear what he has to say.

"What exactly are you suggesting?" I ask him.

He takes a hand of mine and puts it on the helm, puts his own over it, so we're steering together. "After we've delivered *Becky Ann*, we could . . . I don't know. Give it a shot. We could travel around and not make babies together. Use up these condoms together and sail the world together and then come back and cuddle our godchildren and nieces and nephews and who knows what other little miracles lie ahead on our path . . . we could love on them all and then, you know, sail off when the nappies need changing."

For a moment I can see it all in my imagination. I lay my head on his shoulder and let out a longing sigh. Patronizing though it may be, I see no point in bringing down such a lovely image with an overabundance of actual facts. "That sounds really, really nice," I say. "And you have to admit, it also sounds really, really unlikely."

"Hm," he says. Under my cheek I feel his muscles working as he adjusts the bearing.

"Hm what?" I ask him.

"Well, it's just that I happen to be very good at unlikely," he tells me. "In fact, I think it might be my very favorite thing."

31

That evening, as I am sailing my watch through slow, flat seas, I make up a funny table in my mind. "Ways Grant is too young for me," says the label over the first column. "And ways he is not," says the second. When we're together, we're talking, and when we aren't talking, we're naked, and when we're not naked or talking, we're sailing. And there have been a few times where we've been doing all three at once.

Now that I'm finally alone with my own thoughts, I find myself replaying the earlier conversation, wondering—does he really want this to be more than a sailing fling? And do I?

It's not an easy question. One part of me is dying to chase after Grant when the trip is over, trying to tell me I don't know enough about him to make up my mind one way or another. That I like what I know so far, and I need to learn more.

And the other is quite sure I do know him, that he is a good man, smart and strong and kind and capable, and that he is far too young for me.

With a skill I can barely believe I now possess, I set both those thoughts aside and let the jib sheet off its cleat, swing the boat around head to wind, and winch in the other sheet, then trim the main. A perfect single-handed tack in the dead of night. Look at me. *I will not be chasing after anyone,* I remind the thirsty part of myself. *I'm independent now, and free.*

And I deserve good and strong and capable, I remind my other, more fearful side. *In whatever age or package it happens to be in. When the time is right, and I know I'm ready.*

Which will be when? both sides demand.

My brain feels like it's smoking from the back-and-forth. *Both of you, be quiet!* I tell the warring factions. *I am trying to make a list!*

1.   He Is Too Young for Me:

He is hotter than me. He is in better shape. He hasn't had an entire life already, like I have. He hasn't ever had a job where he works indoors. He eats like a field horse. He very well may wake up at thirty-five and decamp for a youthful Irish fertility goddess who knows how to say the rosary and wants to settle down in a pretty house near Howth.

Though . . . I wouldn't mind settling down in a pretty house near Howth. So close to the Dublin Airport. An easy sail to the Isle of Man, or Belfast, and from there, why not Scotland, the Orkneys, even farther? Would *Becky Ann* be able to handle the fjords of Norway, I wonder?

Would I?

2.   He Is Not Too Young for Me:

He grew up fast. He has had loves, and lost them. He knows how to end a relationship on good terms. He knows how to care for his parents. He is brave and bold. He is fearless. He can sleep in the rain. He understands hard work. He would never let someone threaten my daughter. He would never let someone hurt me.

And that thing he does with his tongue.

NO, I shout at myself. That thing he does with his tongue is not a decision factor for the rest of my life. Tongue things are nice, don't get me wrong. But they are not a reason to throw aside everything.

What, exactly, would you be throwing aside?

That is a very good question. And a snarky one. That question feels as though it was voiced by the part of my daughter that has come to live inside me after all these years. The part of her I carry with me always.

The daughter, I've come to learn, who is a bit too entitled, a bit too reckless. A bit detached from reality. It would be easy for her to tell me to go for it, to live it up. It's not her that might wake up at forty-five or fifty having to start all over again.

I fish around for the sat phone. I have one more day to travel and plenty of data left, and it is only nine p.m. I call Natasha.

"I've fallen for a twenty-six-year-old Irishman with a six-pack," I tell her instead of saying hello when she answers.

She just laughs.

"No, really."

"Wait. *What?*"

"That guy that helped me sell my boat, Grant Murphy. He turned out to be my daughter's former crush. And then he came aboard in Philly and sailed me to Tybee Island and then we had sex in the cockpit and it was amazing and every time we talk I like him a little more, and now I'm wondering if I should chuck my entire life and go wander around the world with him."

There's a moment of pause, but it's Natasha, and it doesn't take her long to get her feet under her. "Liv had a crush on this guy?"

"Monster crush. She sent him a picture of her boobs."

"And then you slept with him?" she asks.

"Oh—no, it's not like that. Liv said it was ok," I tell her.

Natasha coughs pointedly. "Well, what else could she say? You're coming off a dry spell that's older than her retainer. Besides, Minerva says she found out about her dad's, uh . . . side projects."

"Oh yes. That was my fault actually."

"You told her that Alistair was cheating?"

"Well, I told her there was a jumbo-sized box of condoms left behind on this boat that I knew nothing about. And that they were pretty new. And half used. And not hers or mine."

"Oh man," she says. "So you just spilled it like that."

"She's been very erratic, Natasha," I say in my defense. "Almost bratty. And she outright admitted that Alistair told her to babysit me."

"So this is your no-drama divorce, then?"

I cringe as Natasha's emotional scalpel hits bone. "There wasn't supposed to be drama," I insist. "But drama found us. It started right up alongside our trip, about some meaningless quote I'd given my lawyer." And, I mentally add, about me wanting to sell the house. About the challenges we faced sailing, even when she should have seen them coming. About having to take care of me, and then about me smothering her. There's been quite a lot of drama in the Liv department, and it's not that she's always been wrong, but it's not that she's always been kind either. When we're together again, we'll have a lot to figure out.

Natasha clears her throat. "I would rather be penniless than spend another day as Alistair Larkin's wife," she quotes.

"Well, it's true, isn't it. I AM penniless. It's not like I didn't live up to my words."

"Liv adores her father," she says.

"Even more than I realized," I complain. "She moans all the time about his work. But she's dependent on him in a thousand ways, and now she's thinking about interning for their firm." I rub my forehead, wearied by the thought. "I stayed with Alistair for too long believing I could protect her from his influence. How was I to know she was playing both sides like that?"

"Becca, she's not playing both sides. She's living both sides. Walking every day between the two paths laid out in front of her. Trying to figure out what kind of woman she's going to be. And she loves people on either end."

"When you say it that way, it sounds impossible. And now I'm boning her crush." I put my face into my hands. "Oh no. I think I've lost my mind."

"It kind of sounds like you have. I mean, I didn't even like twenty-six-year-olds when I *was* twenty-six."

I breathe as deeply as I can and then go back to watching for oncoming sea traffic. "The thing is, Natasha, the last week of my life has been the most fun I've had since . . ." My voice trails off. "Since ever." I lower my voice. "I have been with this Grant guy twenty-four hours a day, and we make an amazing team. I can sail now. Like, I am literally sailing right now while we talk. And it's hard. It's athletic, and scary, and everything has weird nautical names, but I'm still kicking ass. And now Grant's asking me to come along on his next adventure. Me! A forty-two-year-old empty nester with more SPANX in my closet than lingerie. When I started this trip, I thought . . . I thought I was nothing besides Liv's mom. A middle-aged, broke, invisible nobody."

"And now?"

"Oh, I'm visible now. I'm a badass now. I'm a badass, a sailor, and I'm even good craic, whatever that means. More than that, I am pretty sure that whatever comes next, I'll be able to handle it. And that's an amazing feeling."

I swear I can hear Natasha's smile coming through the phone. "Heady stuff," she says. "You kind of sound like you're in love."

I laugh. "I love *you*, Natasha, but it's only been a week with Grant."

"Not with him. Well, maybe with him. But definitely with yourself."

Oh my gosh. She's right. That's exactly what's happened. "You're right! You're exactly right! When I last talked to Alistair, he told me I always settle for the crumbs in life."

"Ouch. Fine thing coming from him," she says.

"Right? But actually, I'm glad he said it. Because it's true. No. It *was* true. Now . . . now I am digging into the most delicious layer cake filled with berries and covered in buttercream icing. And Natasha, let me just tell you: I am eating way more than the crumbs of that cake. I want the entire freaking thing. I want to pull up a chair to the table and get a fork and just eat and eat until I'm sick."

"That, my friend, is amazing. That makes me incredibly happy for you."

"It is pretty amazing," I admit. "It's making me very selfish."

Natasha takes a deep, audible breath, and I wonder if she's about to deliver another big fistful of hard truth between the eyes. But what she says takes me entirely by surprise. "Rebecca Ann Larkin, it is time for you to be selfish. It is time for you to eat some freaking cake, and damn the consequences."

"And if it blows up, and I have to start over again?"

"So what? You just told me you can handle whatever comes next."

I did, didn't I? And I meant it. I can handle whatever. Grant, no Grant. Land or sea. Maine, Ireland, Bora-Bora for that matter. It's entirely up to me. Whatever comes, I will be fine.

So I choose Grant, I realize with astonishing certainty. At least, I do for tonight.

And my daughter?

"Have you seen Liv, since she went home?" I ask my friend.

"She's sleeping on Minerva's futon," says Natasha. "The one in Cambridge, not here at my house."

"Oh? I thought she was staying with her dad in Boston," I say.

"She was, until the last time you two talked. She says she needs time now, to forgive Alistair."

My heart gives a squeeze at what she must be feeling right now. "First your parents get divorced. And then your friends realize your bills are paid by child molesters. And then you find out that the jerk's been schtupping randoms on the very sailboat you thought was just for the two of you to hang out on. Oh, and your mom is sleeping with your college crush. It's a lot. Do you think she'll get through this?"

"I think she'll need time."

"Just think if she knew about the other thing. The 'eminently f-able' thing," I say.

"But she'll never have to know that, right, Becca?" asks Natasha. "That's just . . . too much."

"Oh my gosh, no. Never in a million years. I don't care how mad I am at Alistair or at her. I would never say a word. I love her way too much to do that to her."

"You are a very good mom," she says. "In really unusual circumstances."

"Thank you, Natasha," I say. "I'm really glad I called you."

"Me, too, sweet friend. Now go have a big slice of that twenty-six-year-old cake."

32

It's eleven p.m. by the time we finally anchor off, ten nautical miles from Miami. Grant and I exchange a look of fatigue and clean up the boat just enough to keep the bugs at bay. The buyer plans to meet us at the marina office at noon tomorrow, and by that time we'll need to have the boat clean and everything we want to take with us in suitcases. Tonight is the last night of this adventure. The end is here for me and *Becky Ann*.

"I'm tired down to my bones," I admit to Grant, when we're down below in the dim light of the saloon. "I feel like I'm too tired to sleep."

Grant sits carefully down next to me and then stoops to pull off my shoes. "I'm tired too," he says. "But I don't want you to go to bed without me."

I look down at my hands. They look different from a month ago. They're chapped and red and calloused from wet gloves, and the knuckles are sunburned. A lot of me is sunburned, or roughed up, or changed. I am achy and bruised from banging legs and arms whenever we tacked or jibed. I have a cut near my eyebrow where a block and tackle swung back and clipped me in the face, and bandages on a finger that I put too close to the reefing mechanism one day. One of my toenails split from crushing it on the instrument panel, and I've lost a pound or two, first from nausea, then from activity. And then there is that ethereal limberness that comes of making love, those tender spots from bites and touches and the stretch in my inner thighs. Even a little raspiness in the back of my throat—a souvenir of the sounds Grant has coaxed out of me when alone on the water with no one around to hear.

Grant brings those calloused hands to his lips, gently. "Come on to bed," he says. "I won't bother you."

I shake my head even as I rise and take his hand. "You're not bothering me."

"But you look so sad. Tomorrow you're going to be a wealthy woman," he says as we climb into my berth. "At least by my standards."

"I have been a wealthy woman before," I tell him, honestly. "It's not all it's cracked up to be."

He eases me out of my shirt, kisses the bare shoulder he's exposed. "I know."

"I'm going to miss this boat," I admit to him. "Well," I add, thinking of the condoms. "Not everything about this boat. But I think I'll miss sailing."

"I know that too." He lowers me down to the bed and smooths my hair on my pillow.

"What . . . what would you do next," I ask him, "if I told you this thing was over between us?"

He frowns. "Spend a lot of time and energy convincing you otherwise."

"But what if you couldn't," I persist. I need to know what would truly make Grant happy, without me as a factor.

"Ok, if you blew me off for good? Well, that would suck, but I'd probably still not go back to teaching in Maine. The administrators know I am a maybe there, and they can't really pay me enough to demand a commitment. They do handle my visa paperwork, which is a big deal. But if there's no you, maybe it's time to go back to Ireland for a while. Crew on a racing yacht, sock away some more cash and new connections."

I nod. "That doesn't sound so bad," I tell him.

"Oh, it'd be brilliant. But then, it could be a lot better too."

"With me?"

He just laughs and puts a kiss on my forehead. "Of course with you."

"You know," I tell him, "it's your very certainty that makes me doubtful. It makes me wonder if you're thinking things through."

"No one thinks things through as much as you do, Becca Ann. But I'm doing my best."

I try to find a smile in my voice. "The thing is, I'm sixteen years older than you are," I tell him. "I'm sixteen years more sophisticated and experienced."

"You're not that experienced," he says. "You'd never even had sex on a boat until me."

I laugh.

"And you've been doing something else with your extra sixteen years. Having a family. Raising a child. You still haven't gotten to have all your fun, all your adventure. You've missed your entire twenties. If anything, you're actually behind me."

"Not everyone gets to have an entire decade of fun and adventure," I say.

"Sure. That's true. But why couldn't you at least have, what, a year of it?"

I say nothing. Do I clam up because Grant is being ridiculous? Or because I can't help but agree with him?

"Becca?" Grant says.

"Mmm?"

"You're thinking hard."

"I am." I'm thinking about the road that led me to this moment in time. About all the times in my life, up to now, that I have taken the safe route. Done the sensible thing. Settled for the crumbs.

"I think you're thinking hard about me," he says.

I nod. "Yeah."

"Tell me what you're thinking."

I sit up, in nothing but undies and my sports bra. I take him by the hand, unable to hide my growing excitement. "What if we did, you know, go for the adventure together. What if after we sell *Becky Ann* tomorrow, we took the money, or at least a little of it, and just . . . went. Where would we go? What would we do?"

Grant cracks a smile that runs straight to my soul. "Ah! That's the beauty of it, though, Becca Ann. We wouldn't sell the boat after all. We'd sail her to the Bahamas."

What? The record screeches inside my brain. I look at him aghast. "Grant, unless you've been hiding a trust fund this whole time, we cannot afford to sail her anywhere besides South Beach, Miami."

"How do you know that?"

"Because I can do math?" I say back quickly. "I need the money from that sale. No matter what we—or I—do next, I have to have that nest egg."

"But you don't know the numbers," he says, gaining steam even as I am deflating. "I've been saving for years. I can certainly handle financing our trip to the islands, and once we got there, we'd live aboard, on a mooring ball, or even at anchor—the inlets are very well protected if we know where to go. We could rough it and live on the cheap."

"This sounds a little half-baked, Grant."

"No, no. It's fully baked. Listen: I've got a mate from my old sailing club who lives in the Exumas. He runs a sailing charter—takes tourists out on his old catamaran a few times a week, teaches lessons, does overnight sails. Last time we spoke, he told me he has more business than he can handle. Maybe he could hire me. I could chip into the kitty a bit more that way."

I furrow my brow at him, discomfort rising in my belly. "Wait. You want to use my boat for your friend's charter business?" I ask him.

"Well, why not? It's hardly a massive enterprise, just spending a season living aboard, days on the beach or at sea, nights with the locals, football, dancing, hiring kayaks or going on dives . . . we could go full beach bum for a while, and fly you home a few times so you could see Olivia. Or we could have her come out to see us."

"Slow down, Grant," I say, because something about this is making my head spin. "You seriously want me to keep this boat?"

"I . . . ," he says. He does slow down and looks over my face carefully. "I mean, it's a brilliant sailboat, don't you think?"

"This boat is the only thing of value I have in the world," I tell him.

"Well, but you just said you were going to miss it, only ten minutes ago."

"It's my ex-husband's boat," I go on, ignoring him. "You want me to give you my ex-husband's forty-foot yacht so you can use it to bum around in the Bahamas?" I say, not sure I even heard right.

If I did . . . have I been a fool?

There it is: that shame I thought I was done with. Hot and fast, it climbs up through my skin, insisting that *of course* the only way a man like Grant would ever be interested in someone like me has to be a con. A long con for a free sailboat. What would Alistair say if he could see me right now? He'd laugh and say, "I told you you'd never be able to take care of yourself."

"I don't want you to give it to me—"

I refuse to let him finish. "Grant, I'm going to wake up tomorrow and sell *Becky Ann* for hundreds of thousands of dollars. I'm forty-two damn years old, and that money is the only money I have to live on. My second act is dependent on that money."

"Unless you start a second act with me," he says, and now I can tell his confidence is faltering. "Then we live on my savings, at least at first. We can see what comes up."

"I don't want to risk my life on 'what comes up,'" I say. "I want . . ." I hesitate as I try to figure out why such a plan feels so unappealing— and then, unbidden, I think of my daughter, Alistair, all of the Larkins. "I want to be in control of my own future," I try to explain. "I don't want to be at the mercy of some charming guy and his whims. I've tried that. It ruined my life."

Grant looks injured. "You're not risking your life," he says. "Or your boat. If we try it, and we don't like it, you can come back. You—well, I—sold *Becky Ann* in a week. I can sell her again."

"Are you sure about that?" I ask him.

"Very sure," he says. But it's too late. The old fears are rising up, higher and higher. Have I been taken in, played for a fool, when I thought I was finally finding my footing?

"I was going to use the money from the sale to try to buy back my old house," I tell him.

He frowns at me and tilts his head. "You were?"

I wasn't, not really, but now I'm wondering if I should, just to protect myself from making a mistake. "Well, I was going to use it to buy some house. I need somewhere to live."

"It seems like you like living here," he says.

"With a two-foot-square kitchen and a toilet that runs on a hand pump?" I ask him.

"Yes," he says back, dead serious. "And with constant rocking, and the pinging of the rigging on the mast all night long, and occasional seasickness, and a lukewarm shower. It seems like you don't truly mind any of those things, at least not in the short term."

He might be right about that. He might be right that I don't miss vacuuming 2,600 square feet or hosting eight-couple dinner parties, at least not yet. Or that I have no one to host dinner parties for anymore, or that a winter in the Exumas is probably heaven on earth compared to the dark, slippery, icy mess that is January in New England. But he said it himself. This is all very short-term thinking. This is the difference, perhaps, the real, important difference, between twenty-six and forty-two.

"I need to be thinking about the long term," I tell him, somberly. "I still owe you money for selling this boat, and more for sailing here with me."

"Becca, I don't want your money."

Something in me goes cold. "But you do want my boat," I say. "Is that what you're really doing with me? Is this an elaborate seduction to get a free yacht?"

Grant sits up, climbs to the edge of the berth. "That's laughable. No! How could you ask that?"

"Because I'm afraid," I tell him honestly. "What is going on here? Why would you want to be with someone so much older than you? Have you given this even a moment's thought? And if you have, why don't you have the same concerns as me?"

His posture shifts. Grows still more distant. "I have concerns, sure. But that's not the same as fear. But you . . . I haven't seen you so fearful since . . . since the first day's lesson, really. In fact, you've always seemed so brave, I couldn't understand how you managed to stay with your ex for years and years after your marriage died. I thought it was devotion to Olivia, misguided loyalty maybe. But I can see now that you are *driven* by fear. A week of bravery, sure, but a lifetime of cowardice," he says.

I clamp my mouth shut, afraid if I try to argue with him, I'll cry. I've thought the same things about myself. Hundreds of times. But now I'm different. Now I'm ready to be bold. Aren't I?

"You don't want to be even a little brave with me, Becca?" he asks me. "Not even just a winter-on-the-beach worth of brave? Not even when it's me asking you, and not Alistair or Olivia? A decent bloke who just wants a chance to try and make you happy?"

I don't know what to say to him. It's too much. It is too scary. I am too much of a coward. I do settle for the crumbs.

I shake my head, not trusting what I might say if I open my mouth. "I'm sorry," I finally manage to creak out. "I'm sorry, Grant, but I can't do that."

"Then you're right," he tells me as he pulls on his deck shoes and heads for the companionway. "We really shouldn't be together."

33

I hardly sleep, and when the morning finally breaks into the fore hatch, when the light comes streaming in over my exhausted mind, I put my pillow over my head and beg night to come back around. The trip is over today, but I'm not the same woman I was when it started. I'm changed inside.

The thing is, my circumstances, once we land in Miami and do what we came here to do, will be exactly the same. The only thing different is me. All that's left to do now is pack up the boat and head back to Maine to try and pick up the pieces.

I let myself sink into a deep puddle of self-pity, so there are tears staining my bedding when Grant knocks on my door.

"Becca?" he calls. "Are you awake?"

I want to tell him to go away, but the thing about the boat is that there's work to be done on it every day, and today is no different.

"I'm awake. I'm coming." I sound as reticent as Liv on the morning of her SAT.

"No, don't. Stay there. I have to tell you something before you open the door. I don't want to have to see you. I don't want you to try to talk me out of it. I just want you to listen."

Curiously, I sit up and put my legs over the end of the berth so I'm as close to the door as I can be. Can I somehow feel Grant on the other side? His warmth, his spirit? No, this boat is too well built, my berth too well sealed up, to get any more than the dampened sound of his voice. "Ok, I'm listening," I say.

"I want to let you know that I don't think you're a coward," he says. "Not really. That was my bruised ego talking. I wanted an excuse that goes beyond your just not being that into me."

I am that into you, *I want to shout.* I'm crazy about you, and I'm a coward. You had it all right before.

"I've had an amazing time with you," he goes on. "But I'm only twenty-six, and my amazing time is probably your palate cleanser," he says. "That's the real way our ages are different. The sixteen years between us, you're right, they're not nothing. You've spent those sixteen years growing up, muscling through hard times, and raising a child—not just taking care of a baby, but taking your daughter through every stage of her childhood. And you've had experiences I will probably never have—a great big house, status, sophistication. I have no idea of knowing what those things were worth to you."

I shake my head, even though he can't see me.

"Yet I still think I have something real to offer you. I think I've brought joy into your life. I think I could bring more of that, if you'll just take a chance. But I should never have made it sound, even for a second, like I was here for the boat, the money, any of that. I just . . . I didn't think about what it would feel like for you. I forgot that, to you, *Becky Ann* is so much more than a boat. It's not just where you learned to sail or where you conquered the Eastern Seaboard—it's also where you were betrayed. And now, it's your nest egg. Your entire future."

My chest feels tight.

"So just in case there's the tiniest chance you're willing to consider something . . . something more after today, let me be clear. I like this boat, sure I do. But I don't need it to be happy with you. There are as many scenarios where we are good together as there are boats in the ocean. Scenarios in Maine, in Ireland, in Timbuktu. So I am going to ask you to forget everything I said about keeping the boat, and instead only focus on one question. The same question I've asked you every time you've tried something new. Is it your gut, or your fear, that's telling you no right now? Because if your gut says we should go our separate ways, fine. If it's fear, I don't think I can accept that. And the Becca Ann I've gotten to know wouldn't accept it either."

There's a silence, and I wonder if I should be responding to him. I wonder if I *can* respond to him. His words have brought a fresh torrent of emotion to my throat, blocking the path for anything I might hope to say.

"Ok, don't answer. Not yet. I'm all packed, and I've moved everything left in the galley to the cooler. I'm going to go above and tidy things up a bit. Take all the time you need," he says.

I bite my lip and listen. I hear him going up above. I hear his footsteps on the coach roof. I want to throw my door open, run up the companionway, wrap my arms around him, and pull him down to the deck. I want to show him with my body what I can't seem to explain with my words. How much I want him, how much I want things to be different.

But my fear is just too strong. Strong enough that I can no longer hear what my gut instincts might have to say.

No, I tell myself. No. That's not true anymore. I know exactly what I want. I want to eat the cake.

Old baggage, worries about my child, fears of starting over, or getting old, or losing love, these are genuinely hard things to push past. But guess what, Becca Ann?

You can do hard things.

I pull on the last semiclean shirt and pants in my provisions, and then cram everything left in my berth into the oversized duffel I'd planned to check on my flight home. Then, after a stern pep talk, I go above, and with tears in my eyes, I take Grant by both hands and put the most gentle kiss I can muster on his soft lips.

"I'm freaked out, Grant," I tell him. "I don't honestly know which part of it is fear and which part of it is common sense. But what you just told me . . . and what we've had on this trip—I'm never going to forget it. Not for the rest of my life."

He doesn't answer. He just pulls me in tight, and puts his arm on my back, and presses his lips to mine with a heat that burns me down to my core.

And there is so much passion between us in that moment, it's entirely possible that this kiss could become so much more than just a kiss. Is it a promise? Is it a goodbye? I would ask him, but our phones chime, almost exactly in unison.

We pull back and look at each other. "What's that?" I ask him.

"Hold on," he says and takes his phone out of his pocket. "Oh! I wasn't expecting that," he says, vaguely enough that I dig in my own pocket and unlock my own phone.

And then I say "Oh!" too. "A text from Olivia," I exclaim.

"She says she's here, in Miami," says Grant, sounding mystified.

"And she's waiting for us now, on the dock," I read aloud in startled surprise.

34

With that, we put our energy into bringing in the boat, leaving the murky conversations between us for later, and, though Liv and I have been on rocky footing for a while, and though I am on rocky footing with myself about my decisions for my future, my heart does a happy dance at the thought of seeing my daughter, just like it always has, since the day she left for college. As we motor closer and closer to our designated berth, I see several people I think might be her, until finally I realize one of them IS actually Olivia. Olivia, as in my daughter, Olivia, standing there on the dock, watching as I jump from the rail to the dock and immediately set about tying the bowline. As I am setting the springs, I see Grant toss out the line from the far side of the boat, and Livvie catches it, a slow smile creeping across her face. She loops it over the brad expertly. I hear Grant cut the engine, and I toss the stern line to him and jog up to the main dock to see my daughter. And though we did not last part ways on the best of terms, it seems like time has softened our conflicts. Or maybe, my letting her start to grow up a little has been the thing that will heal us after all.

"I wasn't sure you'd come in the end," I exclaim, even while wrapping her up in a giant hug. "But I'm so glad you did!"

"Oh Mom!" she says. "You're crushing my ribs."

"Oops, sorry. I think I'm stronger than I was when we left Maine. Look at this." I show her my newly formed biceps in a series of silly bodybuilder imitations.

"Whoa, Mom!" she says. "Look at you."

"Sailing is a great workout. Everything in a boat is either heavy or slippery," I tell her.

"Everything?" she asks. I follow her meaningful gaze to Grant.

"Really?" I ask her, cringing. "Are we there already?"

She looks down and shakes her head. "I think? I mean, I saw him first, but then I said it would be ok." *And it's not really her decision to make,* I silently argue. "But then after I said that, I was like, *is* it okay with me? I wasn't sure. And is it any of my business anyway?" she adds, as though she can read my mind. "So anyway, yeah, no. Let's not talk about it."

Ok. Look at me respecting her adult boundaries. No problemo. "It's a deal," I say. "So, after our disagreement in Philly, I didn't think you'd be meeting me today. What made you decide to fly all the way down here?"

She stammers for a moment. "Ah . . . well, you see, I don't want to upset you," she begins, and I notice she's leading me somewhere, so I start to follow.

My stomach tightens. "I don't want to upset you" is adult-child code for "I'm definitely about to upset you."

As we walk, she turns to me and takes me by the hand. "It's kind of about the boat, actually."

"The infidelity, you mean?" I ask. "I know you're upset about it. But you have to understand, things like that are rarely just one sided, in a marriage. It's a lot more complicated than that . . ."

Liv stops walking and turns to face me down. "So you're saying it's your fault he used his sailboat as a fuckpad?"

"Oof, that word," I say. "I know I sound old fashioned, but do you have to swear like a sailor all the time?"

"I am a sailor," she says, resuming her aimless stroll. "And so are you. You can say fuckpad all day long now."

"Enough. Your dad's . . . extracurriculars were not my fault, but honestly, it's not my business anymore. And that's a really good thing. I don't think you should let it bother you."

"It does bother me. But I'm talking to him about it. He says he knows he was in the wrong."

"Well, I hope you guys can get back on even footing," I say. "Even if it takes time."

"Mom, the thing is, Dad also said—"

"Oh! This is exactly where I was supposed to be headed," I realize aloud. We're standing outside the marina's private clubhouse. Through those doors, I'm supposed to find an office, and in that office, the new title holder of my boat.

"I know," she says. "Mom, that's what I'm trying to tell you."

I open the door. A cool blast of AC hits me, frigid. I've gotten more comfortable with wild swings in temperature over the last three weeks and less accustomed to climate control. I wonder what the Bahamas would feel like. Maybe not as hot as Miami in July, as they're a bit more northerly than the rest of the Caribbean. But hardly chilly.

A man stands up from the front office. "You must be Ms. Larkin," he says. Then he looks back and forth between Olivia and me. "You two could be sisters."

I smile awkwardly. This sort of thing used to flatter me so much, but now I feel . . . somehow different about my age. Less interested in being anything but myself, I guess. My forty-two-year-old, fierce, naked-on-a-sailboat self. "This is my daughter, Olivia," I say.

"Oh yes. I've got all her paperwork here too," he says.

"No, she doesn't have any paperwork," I correct. "I'm the seller. Rebecca Larkin. She's just here for moral support." I laugh.

"Mom," she says. There's a warning in her voice. I turn to her.

"What is it, Liv?"

But before she can answer, the notary gestures to an interior office. "If you'll both take your seats, and make sure you have a driver's license, proof of ownership, deed, and title, registration," he says. "Olivia, you'll just need two forms of ID and the paperwork from your dad's office."

I blink. "Your dad's office?" Somewhere, in the farthest reaches of my mind, I start to understand.

"Mom, I'm trying to tell you," she says. "Dad is the one buying your boat."

"No," I protest like an idiot. "I'm selling this boat to some holding company."

The notary keeps trying to herd us into the office. "Is this Alistair Larkin a brother of yours?" he asks.

My head spins to look at him. "Sorry, what? Alistair is buying my boat?"

"Well, it's his boat," says my daughter.

"No," I tell her, with a conviction that comes from cutting through waves and harnessing the wind. "It's my boat. I have the title, right here, Olivia, if you have any doubt."

"Sorry, I just mean . . . it *was* his. And now he's paying you for it. Isn't that good news?"

"Good news?" The bottom of my stomach seems to drop out. "Good news?! Why would he make me sail all the way to Miami just so he could buy back his own boat?" I say, my anger whipping up wild, fierce, and strong.

"He, ah . . ." She trails off. "I don't think he knew you'd be the one to deliver it. I think he figured you'd never really find out he was the buyer."

242

"But he did know I was delivering it!" I shout. "I talked to him just before we left. And you talked to him while we were sailing. He knew exactly what was going on the entire time." The question is, did Liv?

"He just . . ."

"He just what, Olivia. What exactly did your father just do to me?"

"He wanted you and me to have the time together," she says.

I inhale sharply, begging myself, pleading, to keep my temper.

But my temper has been in check for far, far too long.

"How long did you know about this?"

"Know about what?" she asks.

"Don't do that," I say to Olivia. "Don't play dumb. Have some freaking integrity, Olivia Maeve Larkin. How long did you know it was Dad buying the boat out from under me? Did you know in Philly? Is that why you left? Did he tell you while we were still sailing?"

She looks down. "He told me before we left," she says softly.

My heart seems to want to fall out the front of my chest, it hurts so badly. "You knew? You knew I was sailing my ex-husband's boat to Miami just so he could have it back?"

She cringes. "He loves this boat."

"Then why didn't he try to buy it from me back in Maine?" I demand. "Where I could have told him to go to hell?"

She sighs. "He wanted it repositioned," she says. "And as you know, that's a lot of work."

The very last drops of my decorum evaporate. "He wanted it repositioned?" I shout. "Why? Was he out of women in Maine to take to his FUCKPAD?"

"Mom, calm down," Olivia tries.

"I don't want to calm down," I shout. "I am angrier than I have ever been. Ever been in my entire life. I am so angry at Alistair, and I am so angry at you for being his henchman. What happened to you to make you think acting like this was ok? Is it just in your genes? Is everything Alistair touches just one massive lie deep down?"

Tears rise up in my daughter's eyes. "No, no, Mom," she says. "I really wanted to hang out with you. I wanted to try offshoring, see if I could handle her on my own."

"Well, you couldn't," I say meanly. And truthfully.

"I know," she says. "I fucked it all up. That's why I called Grant. Do you think I *wanted* to talk to him, much less ever see him again? I was mortified to have to reach out."

"That's because you sent your teacher a picture of your breasts," I remind her coldly.

She sets her chin. And when she does, she looks just like her father. "The point is, I got Grant to come and sail you the rest of the way. And I did it so you could have your money."

"You did it so your dad could have his fuckpad," I say bitterly. "Without the inconvenience of a repositioning trip, or craning her out of the water, or, I don't know, just looking me in the eyes."

"Dad's not buying the boat for . . . you know . . . ," she says to me carefully, like I might hit her. Like I might douse us both in gasoline and set the entire marina on fire.

"I'm sure that's what he told you, Liv," I begin, but she's shaking her head adamantly. "Then for what?"

"I swear I didn't know. He didn't tell me this until a couple of days ago."

"Tell you what."

"It's for me. He bought the boat to give to me."

The words sink in. My whole body goes slack. Even my jaw falls open, like I'm a cartoon. I am a cartoon. In Alistair's mind, I'm the caricature of the ex-wife, the miserable old harpy, traded in for a series of younger models. The best years of my life behind me and only a life-time of bitterness ahead. And the daughter I spent so long protecting?

Now she's the poor little rich girl. The daddy's girl who had to get stuck in the middle of her parents' divorce, and all she got was a forty-foot yacht.

"Congratulations."

"Mom, I don't have to take it," she tries.

"Oh, you have to take it, all right. I want my money," I say. "I don't want anything from you but the amount that the holding company agreed to pay me. Sign the paperwork, Olivia, and I'll hand over the keys." I turn to the notary. "Get out the papers. Tell me where I need to sign."

The poor notary is gaping at us like he just saw a high-speed car wreck. He kind of did. But when I shoo him along, he reaches into his attaché and provides everything we need. "Pen?" I ask him. He hands one over. I clutch it like a knife, signing over the title, the insurance guarantee, the contract in three places. Knowing as I do, it's not just *Becky Ann* I'm parting with today. It's the relationship I had with my daughter. After all these years, after all that sacrifice, I've lost her to the Larkins once and for all. And there's nothing left to do but sign.

"There," I say, when I've inked the last set of initials. I drop the keys that open the companionway door and start the engine. I don't drop them on the table. I drop them on the floor.

"Mom, please. I want you to listen to me."

"No, thank you," I say to her, as calmly as I can muster. "I will talk to you later. When I am not so hurt. When I don't feel so betrayed."

"When will that be?" she asks, and she sounds so very young when she asks that for one fleeting second I almost want to fold her into my arms.

But it's long past time for this kid to grow up. "I don't know, Olivia. It might be a long time." *It might not be ever,* I can't help but think.

Tears are running down her face. My daughter, crying. In the past it's been a sight I can hardly bear. I don't like it now either. But I can't be the one to dry her tears tonight. For twenty-one years I've been her person. I've been loyal and devoted and true. Every decision I've made, every path I've taken, has been with her best interests at heart. But today, that bond has been broken.

"Good luck with the boat," I tell Olivia, my voice cold and quiet. "She's nimble and fast, if you know what you're doing."

And then, in some kind of stunned, angry daze, I leave the office, the clubhouse, even the marina. Thinking only that I have to get away. Away from *Becky Ann*, from my daughter, from the woman I used to be. If I somehow could run away from my entire past life on my own two feet, that's exactly what I'd be doing now.

35

I am in Miami, at the harbor, with no plane ticket home, no hotel, no car, no place to go. And, because I am a sailor now, albeit one with no boat, I can see a tiny row of dark-black clouds on the water's horizon: a storm rolling in.

My heart hurts. My soul hurts. And underneath my feet, I can't shake the sensation that I'm still rocking around on the water.

"WAKE UP," I shout at my eustachian tubes, like a weirdo. "YOU'RE ON LAND NOW."

But the eerie feeling of endless rolling waves refuses to go away.

There's a cab out in front of me now. The shouting—the driver must have thought I was hailing him. Ok, fine. I'll take a cab somewhere. I have sixty bucks in cash in my wallet.

And significantly more being wired into my bank account right now. As the cabbie loads my bags into his trunk, I look at my bank statement.

Wow.

I am homeless, boatless, and daughterless. But I do have a lot of money.

I get in the back of the cab. I know I need to talk to Grant, owe him some kind of explanation about why I've disappeared, but I can't face him yet. I can't face myself. For a few awful hours last night, I thought

Grant had been using me for my boat, and I was humiliated. Now I realize that it's been my own daughter hustling me all this time. That what I thought was meant to be a sweet, if misguided, mother-daughter sailing adventure was actually the intricate machinations of the man I once loved more than life. The man I gave twenty-odd years to.

Let's just say I'm seriously questioning my own judgment right now. "Where to?" the cabbie asks. I see from his ID that his first name is Monty. He has a big warm smile, and his car is a tidy Tesla sedan with a vast stretch of leather in the back seat. At once I remember that I hardly slept last night, that I haven't had a hot shower in weeks.

I look left and right out the cab windows. Across South Pointe Drive, the towers of a Marriott and a Hilton stick out in bright South Beach colors. "Which is cheaper?" I ask, gesturing to the chains. I have no desire to blow my new nest egg on some ritzy hotel I'll only be crying and sleeping in.

He looks at me for a second. "Neither," he tells me. "This is one of the most expensive spots in the city. And both are happy party places. You want to go to a happy place?"

My face is a muddle of tears and salt. My nose is stuffed up. I look like a woman who has been crying. I look like a woman who is *currently* crying.

"Take me someplace close, sad, and affordable," I tell him. I have no idea what's next for me, but now there is absolutely nothing holding me back. I am utterly and completely untethered.

And it's not as scary as I thought it would be. It's just sad.

I wipe away an errant tear and try to compose myself. I can call Grant when I'm ready. Tell him what just went down. Tell him it's time to say goodbye.

He nods. "I can do that. But lady, whoever he is, he's a fool. Will he be looking for you?"

"No. I don't think so. I think he knows to give me space."

"Did he cheat?"

"No."

"Steal?"

"No."

"Run over your dog?"

I look up in surprise and see the cabbie smiling gently back at me.

"He didn't do anything wrong," I admit.

The driver frowns at me. "Well, someone did something to make you so unhappy."

I nod. "That would be my ex-husband. He did something, and then something else, and then yet even more somethings. And now that I've tried to leave him, he's made messing with me into an Olympic sport. In fact, he just used our daughter against me to win the gold."

"And now you are going to go cry in a cheap hotel?"

"And drink. I have half a bottle of good gin in my bag."

"It's not the worst plan I've ever heard."

I smile at him weakly. "I'm just very tired," I admit. "I sailed all the way here from Maine to sell my only possession left after the divorce—a boat. A big, expensive boat. But when I got here, I found out the shell company who was buying it belonged to my ex. And he bought the boat as a gift to buy my daughter's affection. And, worst of all, she fell for it. And after I found all this out, I did a runner on my much younger lover who wanted me to keep the boat so we could sail around the world like high-class hobos."

"Ah. The same old story, then."

Despite my clogged nose and weepy face, I can't help but let a little laugh out.

"I would have kept the jailbait and the boat," he tells me.

"I was trying to be sensible," I explain.

"Always a mistake," he says.

This time I laugh in earnest. Oh Monty. If he only knew how many times I made the safe, rational choice, out of responsibility, or fear, or whatever. That this escapade was actually me trying something new.

Only for it to end every bit as badly as everything else.

My ironic laugh sort of dissolves back into noisy tears. I dig around in my bags for a tissue, and Monty falls into the kind of awkward silence that must be a normal occurrence in a cab driver's life. After I've blown my nose loudly a few times, I stare out the window, trying to see glimpses of the water between buildings.

Somehow, after weeks of sailing, I still just want to look out over the water.

That feels like very important information.

"Hey," I call out to the front seat. "Monty? I've changed my mind," I tell him. "Can you take me to a hotel with a view of the ocean?"

As soon as the words are out of my mouth, I feel how right they are.

"Sure thing, lady," he replies. He makes the next right turn, and I see the blue expanse start to come into view. And I realize, that's where I want to be now. I'm not a landlubber anymore. I'm not a little bungalow with a steady job and a pretty garden kind of woman anymore.

I belong out *there*.

And absolutely nothing is stopping me. My daughter, well, she's screwing up big time. She should never have taken that boat from her dad. She won't be able to afford the berth, make the insurance payments, or take care of the maintenance. She can't even buy her own plane tickets to get down here to sail it. Alistair knows all that. He knows he'll be running the show, paying the bills. That she can't manage such a large endeavor on her own.

He knows that as long as she's got the boat, he's got her.

He thinks he's the puppet master of some great plot. He thinks he can control her—and me, probably—for the rest of our lives. But I know myself better than that. I know how I raised my daughter. And I know, no matter how awful I feel right now, that I did right by her.

I taught her how to persevere when times were hard. I showed her what it meant to be brave and strong when life seemed scary and uncertain. And I have proven, in the last month, that there is life, wonderful, exciting, challenging, exhausting life, after the Larkins.

And I suddenly know, with absolutely no doubt whatsoever, that Liv'll figure this out in her own time too.

So it's time to dry my tears.

It's time for me to start my second act.

And I suddenly know exactly what it will be. I take a huge breath. At last, my tears have stopped. So has the cab. Monty is parked in the porte cochere of a beautiful independent art deco hotel that backs right up to a sandy stretch of South Beach, maybe a half mile from where we started driving twenty minutes ago.

"This is it," Monty tells me. "Better get inside. There's weather in the forecast."

I nod gratefully and swipe my debit card in his reader, adding a hefty tip, because, after all, I can afford it. "Thank you, Monty. You've been a huge help."

"Good luck figuring it all out, ma'am," he says to me.

"I think," I tell him, and myself at the same time, "it's all going to work out exactly right."

36

My hotel room is small and a little shabby and has a stunning view of the water as the clouds roll in one after another and then puff away before they can amount to much. It's perfect. I haul all my stuff into a corner, roll my shoulders in exhaustion, and beeline for the real, hot, spacious shower.

Everything seems possible after that.

I flop down on the bed and flail for my phone. When I grab it, I send just a short text to Grant. I'm sorry I vanished. I needed some time.

I expect to hear nothing back. After all, I kind of abandoned him in the marina without so much as a word.

Instead, my phone buzzes almost immediately.

You're all right, he writes back. Take the time you need.

I can pay you now, for everything you've done for me, I tell him.

This isn't about money, Becca. It has never really been about money.

I just hold the phone close to my heart. Because what can I say?

Thank you. That's what I can say. Grant, I have to tell you something. Alistair was the buyer we rushed all that way to meet. He's the whole reason we did this trip. And Liv knew all along.

I know. I saw her at the marina. She was upset. I might have yelled at her a little.

Me too, I say. More than a little, I admit.

She's in way over her head with this mess, he tells me. She doesn't even know what she doesn't know.

I think she'll find out in due time, I tell him. Sometimes . . . I try to think of the right way to say this. Sometimes Larkin girls need extra time to figure even the most obvious things out, I say at last.

There's a long pause, and I feel like a character in a young adult novel, watching the three dots come up, disappear, come up again. But it's not a feeling I mind when it comes to Grant Murphy. Not even a little.

Take the time you need, he eventually writes back. I've come across a little project at the docks to keep me busy. Just don't leave Miami without telling me, ok?

I have to laugh. A project. At the docks. After we've been on land for, what? Four hours? Grant is addicted to boats. And . . . I am starting to get hooked myself.

Same goes for you, I write back. I send him my hotel information, just in case, and then add, We'll talk soon. Xx.

I drop my phone somewhere to my left. My back sinks gratefully into the mattress, and I know sleep isn't far off. My heart still aches from Liv's betrayal, and my throat is tight with the gratitude I have for Grant. But in the place where there was so much anger toward Alistair, I feel something new.

Apathy.

Where there was anger, and hurt, and disappointment, I feel . . . apathy.

At long last, I am completely free.

I close my eyes and let tears of relief leak out the cracks of my eyelids. It feels so, so good. I haven't cried myself to sleep in a very long time. I haven't let myself feel things this deeply for years. At some point, some years ago, all the shock, and sorrow, and pain gave way to a kind of numbness. It was a numbness that protected me. Let me stay in a bad situation for far too long, put far too much of my emotional energy on my daughter. Made me believe my own life had come and gone.

And now, the haze is clearing. My energy is restored. I've woken up to my senses, my desires, my capabilities.

My last thought, as I give in to the pull of exhausted sleep, is this: I know who I am now, independent of my husband, and his family, and his nonsense. And I know what I want. Or rather, who I want to become.

———

When I wake up next, I am coming out of a dream of the sea.

It's the Irish sea. It's the water up by one of the lighthouses. Grant and I are sailing something small and fast, and I'm at the helm and the wind is with us, and the lighthouse, for some reason, is ringing.

Nope, that's my phone.

My phone is ringing.

I pick it up sleepily.

Then sit straight up in bed when I see the missed calls.

Alistair

Alistair

Alistair

Alistair

He's called me four times. And texted me more. His texts start out inquiring after Liv, have I seen her, did she say where she was going? Why isn't she returning his calls? Why aren't I returning his calls? And so on and so forth.

Well, I think, *this is going to be fun.* I hit return call on his number, punch speaker, and wait for it to ring through.

"Hello?"

"You need to stop calling me," I tell him, calmly but firmly. "Our connection has ended. You've manipulated me, and Liv, and successfully driven a wedge between us that it could take years to repair. But that's it. You are done hurting me. If you want your daughter to turn out like just another Larkin, amoral, apathetic, and humiliating to be associated with, keep doing exactly what you're doing. If it turns out she really can be bought for the cost of a Black Watch 4100, then your work here is done. It's sad to consider, and for a second there I worried that maybe somehow I failed her, but you know what? I did my best. And I think I raised a fundamentally decent person who has a lot more to learn about her life. After all, I was a decent person twenty-two years ago, and I survived the Larkin family just fine."

"Becca—wait. It's Livvie. I can't get ahold of her. Is she with you?"

"Wait, what?" When I thought over this scenario, I sort of imagined Alistair was waiting in the wings somewhere in Miami, twisting his mustache and getting ready to rechristen *Becky Ann* with a thousand-dollar bottle of champers.

"I've been trying her since the sale. I . . . the notary said it was a bit contentious."

"A bit," I say. "But I haven't spoken to her since."

"Can you send her a text or something? Maybe she's just not speaking to me."

I can't help it; I feel myself gloat a little into the phone. "Now, why would she be upset with you? Didn't you just buy her a mid-six-figure sailboat for no reason at all? And all it cost her was her freedom and her relationship with her mother?"

"I know you're upset, but don't take it out on her," Alistair tells me.

"Actually, Alistair, I'm pretty ok, now that I've had some time to adjust. I'm going to take your big fat check, and my hot new guy, and go live my life a little. See where the wind takes us."

Alistair coughs. "Ok, sure, Becky. Whatever. Before you go back to Oz, though, could you text our daughter and make sure she's still alive?"

"It would be my pleasure," I tell him. And then I just hang up. I'm about to text Liv when there's a knock at the door of my hotel room. Before I can even get to the peephole, I hear a familiar voice. A voice I love.

"Mom?"

I throw open the door. My daughter, soaked to the bone, eye makeup running down her face, tear tracks and raindrops mingling over her cheeks.

"Olivia," I say, carefully.

"Mom, I've been looking all over Miami for you," she tells me. "I called every hotel I could google and checked with Natasha and Richard to see if you'd flown home. I combed every inch of the marina. I was thinking of calling the hospitals."

"Oh sheesh, Liv. Why would I be in the hospital?"

"I don't know, I was in freak-out mode," she replies. "I just felt like, maybe what I did was so stupid and selfish I actually killed you."

I tilt my head at her. "What you did was stupid and selfish, but it would take a lot more than that to do me in."

"I'm so sorry, Mom. I am so, so sorry."

"You'd better come on in," I say. "And get specific."

"I know you must think I'm an idiot. I think I'm an idiot. But I want you to know, I just didn't understand what was going on. I thought, when we started out, that it would be fun for us to sail together. I thought it would be good for us. For both of us, not just me."

I look into her eyes, considering. "It was good for me," I tell her honestly. "But not in the ways I was thinking. I thought it would bring us closer together, but in the end, it made me see that you still have a lot of growing up to do. And I hope, I really hope, that you're going to grow into someone I can be proud of, in time. But today, at the marina, I doubted that more than I've ever doubted you before."

Liv looks down, ashamed. "I think Dad's been kind of . . . manipulating me, I guess. Using me to get to you. But that's no excuse. I made it easy on him. I was embarrassed when I got back from Philly. I felt like a failure. I had taken on way too much. And Dad told me not to feel bad, that it wasn't my fault, that I just needed more experience. And then, when you called me asking about those, those condoms, I just . . . I didn't know whose side to be on. Dad cheated, but you were sleeping with my TA . . ."

I arch my eyebrow at her. I won't apologize for that. I haven't done anything wrong.

"I know," she says. "And Dad pays my bills, and he was giving me that internship, and then he offered me the entire boat . . ."

I nod. "It's heady stuff, at twenty-one. I remember it too. I remember what it's like when someone you love offers you what feels like the world. It's hard to say no to that."

She presses her lips together and looks up at me, right in the eyes. "I took her out, Mom," she tells me. "I tried to single-hand her. I wanted to prove to you, well, to me, too, that I could handle her. But she's too much boat for me. I couldn't manage. I couldn't even get the jib unfurled before I gave up and headed back in. And then, I finally saw the situation for what it was." Liv's voice changes, gets quieter. "All the situations."

I nod her onward. I know what she is telling me.

"I'm not taking that job, Mom. I'm going to try something different. I'm going to try to live on my own for a bit. If it's possible, I want to keep Dad in my life, but I need to learn to function without his money. It messes with you," she tells me. "It makes you feel trapped, stuck doing things you don't want to do."

I nod again. "I know, honey," I tell her. "Believe me, I know. And for what it's worth, I think you're doing the right thing. The hard thing, and the right thing."

"We can do hard things, right?"

I shrug. "I know I can. I just sailed fifteen hundred nautical miles from Maine to Miami to prove to myself that I could. I think you'll find you're every bit as tough as I am."

"I'm scared," she admits to me.

I smile gently at her. "Now you know how I felt," I tell her.

"And now I know why you said you were going to be ok," she replies.

I tuck her into my arms.

"I think you're going to be better than ever," I tell her. "And I'll always be there to cheer you on. But I won't actually *be* there, at least not for the near term."

Liv looks at me, surprised. "Where are you going?" she asks me.

"I'm going to start my second act," I tell her. "And it's going to be a lot better than I ever dreamed of."

"Really? Is there anything I can do to help?" she asks me.

"As a matter of fact, there is," I tell her. "Grab a fresh shirt from my bag over there, and my oilies if you want to stay dry. We're heading back to the marina. I'll explain it all to you on the walk over there."

"Wait, you're going back to the marina? After god knows how long on a boat, in every kind of weather, and all that canned food and shelf-stable milk, you want to go back?"

"Yeah," I tell her easily. "That's the only place I really want to be."

37

It takes Grant and me about four weeks to sail from South Beach to Bimini, an out island in the Bahamas, and then on to Freeport. Most of that time is spent getting the right visa and then waiting for a weather window so we don't have any unexpected hurricanes to manage on the way over. The trip itself is easy—even a little boring—and Grant warns me that the weather is so lovely in the Caribbean that I will have to get used to calm seas for now.

I think I'm ready for that.

The visa, when it finally comes, allows me, just me, to own and operate a seasonal cruise charter business that will anchor off of Great Abaco when not zipping around the barrier islands with tourists in tow.

It's a small, nimble operation that offers as much business as we care to take on. I'm in a slightly unprofessional relationship with my only employee, but so far, we're making it work.

There are few scenarios I could imagine where I was still living aboard *Becky Ann* six months after my divorce, but here we are, paying my daughter a monthly rent on her / formerly my / formerly Alistair's sailboat, because life is crazy sometimes. The rent we pay just covers Liv's rooming with her two best friends back at college. Everything else she needs is coming from her part-time job cashiering at the school cafeteria, where her touchiness about shelf-stable foods has been softened somewhat, I have to hope.

Her grades sank a little the first few weeks that she was working a lot. But now she's getting the hang of it. And Alistair is, according to reports, getting the hang of his daughter's new boundaries. Even just going by our daily video calls, I can see how Liv's coming into her own independence a little more every day, and she relates how nobly Alistair is handling such a drastic change. It may be a few years before we're all easy pals, but this, really, is good. Weird, but good.

I take to salt life almost the moment we get to the islands. Grant teaches me the basics of boat maintenance, and I teach him the basics of baking in the tiny galley, but we both agree our tenure on *Becky Ann* has a time limit. Grant has sunk his savings into a lovely, if more modest, thirty-footer that needs work. He spends a lot of his off days in the boatyard with a belt sander, and, maybe because of his irresistible singsong accent, or maybe because he's just ridiculously friendly, odds are fair on any given night that we'll have guests aboard for dinner.

The best part about cruising life is all the amazing people you meet. They come from all over the world, with amazing stories of how they chucked it all and went to live their wildest adventures. And I have a story of my own I don't ever get tired of telling.

I'll be honest; at this point, I have no idea how my adventure story ends. Grant is still way younger than me—although no one who comes to this anchorage would so much as bat an eye, so laissez-faire are sailors—and I'm still hoping the day will come when Liv's grown, married, and ready to welcome a new generation of baby Larkins. If that day comes, I will make sure it's a generation who will learn from their favorite grandma how to tell right from wrong, how to honor their commitments. I will teach them how to survive things, hard or otherwise, with grace and integrity, and when the time comes, I will teach them to sail.

But I'm hoping that that time is at least a few more years away.

The ocean is big, my nest egg remains safely untouched back on the mainland, and Grant will need crew on his new boat, when it is ready to launch.

My adventure has only just begun.

ACKNOWLEDGMENTS

I would like to thank my agent, Holly Root, and editor, Chris Werner, for seeing this novel through several Greek letters' worth of pandemic. Someday we will look back on these years and think, *Well, that was weird, but I can hardly remember it.* And it will be wonderful.

Thanks also to Tiffany Yates Martin and Alex Levenberg and the entire team at Lake Union, and Barbara Kingsolver, Glennon Doyle, and the countless other parents teaching children (and adults) that we can do hard things. Darby Sugar, without you, certain nautical logistics would forever be a mystery to me.

I am so grateful to count on the friendship and support of Abbie Chaffee, Jennifer Sabet, Kris Adams, Sara Naatz, Mandy McGowan, Kelly McNees, Barbara Poelle, Ellen Schumacher, Tania Nayak, Camille Pagán, Leah Sugar, Katie Rose Guest Pryal, Sandi Shelton, Sonja Yoerg, Erin Celello, Orly Konig-Lopez, the Ferreter Family, and Tina Juntunen, as well as all the well-wishers on the internet, many of whom might be real. Thank you for cheering me on.

Thanks to my family, especially Sally, Douglas, Roger, and Kristine Harms, and to my adored son, Griffin. And thank you, Chris. Sometimes I wonder how I got so lucky.

ABOUT THE AUTHOR

Photo © 2020 Lea Wolf

Kelly Harms is the *Washington Post, USA Today*, and Amazon Charts bestselling author of seven novels, including Audie nominee *The Seven Day Switch* and *The Overdue Life of Amy Byler*, a Goodreads Choice Award and WFWA Star Award finalist. Her work has been translated into a dozen languages. A former literary agent, Kelly traded the New York hustle and bustle for the dream of being an author in a quieter life in Madison, Wisconsin, with her sparkling son, Griffin; her fluffy dog, Scout; and her beloved Irishman. When she's not getting lost reading a book, she's either writing or on the water, in the water, or near the water. For more information visit www.kellyharms.com.